THE LAST SUMMER

Mary Jane Staples

CORGI BOOKS

THE LAST SUMMER
A CORGI BOOK: 9780552145138

First publication in Great Britain

PRINTING HISTORY
Corgi edition published 1997

3 5 7 9 10 8 6 4 2

Set in 11/12½pt Linotype New Baskerville by
Phoenix Typesetting, Ilkley, West Yorkshire.

Corgi Books are published by Transworld Publishers,
61–63 Uxbridge Road, London W5 5SA,
A Random House Group Company.

Addresses for Random House Group Ltd companies outside
the UK can be found at: www.randomhouse.co.uk
The Random House Group Ltd Reg. No. 954009

The Random House Group Limited supports The Forest Stewardship
Council (FSC), the leading international forest certification organisation.
All our titles that are printed on Greenpeace approved FSC certified paper
carry the FSC logo. Our paper procurement policy can be found at:
www.rbooks.co.uk/environment.

Printed and bound by CPI Cox & Wyman, Reading, RG1 8EX.

Jonathan Hardy went into Lyon's teashop and saw there was a pretty girl sitting alone at a table for two.

'Mind if I join you?' he asked.

'Pardon?'

'D'you mind if I have this seat?'

'Well, I don't see that I can say no', she said.

So Jonathan sat down and smiled at here. 'You don't mind me talking to you, do you?' he asked.

'Well, yes, I do.'

'Oh, sorry,' said Jonathan. 'Is it because you're shy?'

She had nice chestnut hair and looked about seventeen. The nippy arrived and Jonathan ordered baked beans on toast and college pudding with custard. The pretty girl was eating expensive chicken salad.

'Excuse me asking,' said Jonathan, 'but are you rich?'

'I think you're trying to pick me up,' said Emma Somers.

'Oh, no,' replied Jonathan. 'I'm up from the country I am, don't know any better. I've got straw in my hair, see?'

She took a look. 'You're a chump,' she said. Of course she shouldn't really allow him to pick her up like this – but he really was rather nice, in spite of his sauce. And by the time they'd finished their lunch, Emma had told him quite a lot about herself – including letting him think her name was Trudy. Well . . . it didn't do to tell cheeky chaps everything.

Also by Mary Jane Staples

The Adams Books
DOWN LAMBETH WAY
OUR EMILY
KING OF CAMBERWELL
ON MOTHER BROWN'S DOORSTEP
A FAMILY AFFAIR
MISSING PERSON
PRIDE OF WALWORTH
ECHOES OF YESTERDAY
THE YOUNG ONES
THE CAMBERWELL RAID
THE FAMILY AT WAR
FIRE OVER LONDON
CHURCHILL'S PEOPLE
BRIGHT DAY, DARK NIGHT
TOMORROW IS ANOTHER DAY
THE WAY AHEAD
YEAR OF VICTORY

Other titles in order of publication
TWO FOR THREE FARTHINGS
THE LODGER
RISING SUMMER
THE PEARLY QUEEN
SERGEANT JOE
THE TRAP
THE GHOST OF WHITECHAPEL

and published by Corgi Books

To Shelley, Wendy and Julie

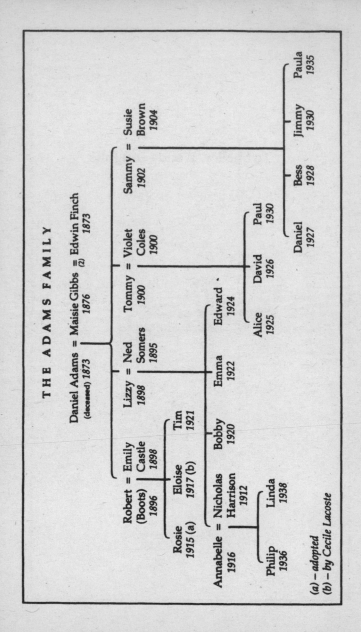

THE ADAMS FAMILY

Daniel Adams = Maisie Gibbs = Edwin Finch
(deceased) 1873   1876   (2)   1873

Robert = Emily Castle (1896 = 1898)
- Rosie 1915 (a)
- Eloise 1917 (b)
- Bobby 1920
- Tim 1921

Lizzy = Ned Somers (1898 = 1895)
- Emma 1922
- Edward 1924

Tommy = Violet Coles (1900 = 1900)
- Alice 1925
- David 1926
- Paul 1930

Sammy = Susie Brown (1902 = 1904)
- Daniel 1927
- Bess 1928
- Jimmy 1930
- Paula 1935

Annabelle = Nicholas Harrison (1916 = 1912)
- Philip 1936
- Linda 1938

(a) – adopted
(b) – by Cecile Lacoste

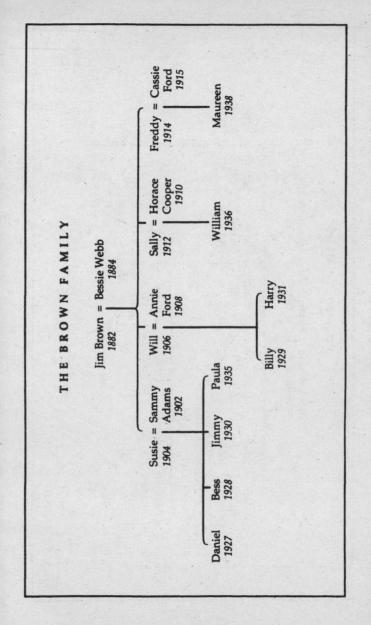

THE BROWN FAMILY

Jim Brown = Bessie Webb
1882   1884

Susie = Sammy Adams   Will = Annie Ford   Sally = Horace Cooper   Freddy = Cassie Ford
1904   1902   1906   1908   1912   1910   1914   1915

Daniel   Bess   Jimmy   Paula   Billy   Harry   William   Maureen
1927   1928   1930   1935   1929   1931   1936   1938

Chapter One

The Hardy family's house in Stead Street, Walworth, had a mind of its own. That is, it didn't behave. At least, not as it should have done, and as the rest of the houses did. It was built, as they were, of Victorian weather-resistant bricks and mortar, and looked, as they did, firm and solid. But it didn't behave in a firm and solid way. It moved about. At least, its floors did, and now and again a mantelpiece would quiver and things fall off it. Or a door would rattle. On the consoling side, whenever a floor did move it wasn't as if an earthquake was about to bring the whole house down. The movement was just a little series of tremors accompanied sometimes by cheerful creaks, as if the floor in question was having a giggle.

Elder son Jonathan would say, 'Floor's moving, Mum.'

'Blessed thing,' his mother, Jemima Hardy, would say, 'can't keep still today, I suppose.'

Or elder daughter Jane would say, 'Your pipe's going to fall off the mantelpiece again, Dad.'

'Time I gave that little old mantelpiece-devil a belting,' her father, Job Hardy, would say.

9

And it was quite common for someone to say, 'Kitchen door did some rattling in the night, Mum.'

'If that there blessed door finishes up falling off its hinges, I'll know who to blame,' Jemima would say.

The family wouldn't have been living there if life in a Sussex village hadn't begun to threaten dire poverty and homelessness. Mrs Jemima Hardy, formerly Jemima Tristle, was the daughter of a Sussex farmer. She'd upset her parents by making it plain she wanted to marry the local village handyman, Job Hardy. Job was handsome, outgoing, good-natured and given to laughter, even when he dropped his sledgehammer on his foot and broke his big toe.

'Painful?' said the village doctor.

'Aye,' said Job.

'So what's making you laugh?'

'Well, I did my schooling,' said Job, 'and my reading, writing and arithmetic, and came out educated. So it be a damn old fool thing to do, an educated chap dropping a sledgehammer on his foot. That be enough to make anyone laugh, I reckon.'

Jemima could have married the son of another farmer, but wanted Job. Job said no, he couldn't provide decent for a girl like her. All right, you'll be sorry when I drown myself in the village pond, said Jemima, twenty at the time. Now don't you talk like that, Jemima Tristle, said Job, upstanding at twenty-three. Well, marry me, then, said Jemima. Can't afford to, said Job.

A week later little Lucy Atkins came rushing into the cottage in which Job lived with his widowed aunt, his parents being dead, and his aunt being the tenant.

'Job, Job, come quick,' gasped Lucy, 'Miss Jemima Tristle be in the pond, and keeps sinking, she do.'

Job ran to the pond, and there was Jemima, splashing and kicking amid the scattering ducks. As soon as she saw Job, she sank. Job went in after her and hauled her out.

'You be a holy terror, Jemima Tristle, doing a thing like that,' he said.

'Don't care,' said Jemima.

'You'll care all right if I throw 'ee back,' said Job.

'No, I won't, so throw me back,' said Jemima.

Job laughed.

'Best I take you to the cottage and get you dried off,' he said.

'Well, go on, do that,' said Jemima, sopping wet as he carried her, 'but it won't do any good. I'll jump straight back into the pond, that I will.'

'Next time I have to fish 'ee out,' said Job, 'I'll smack your bottom.'

'Mercy me, would you do that, Job Hardy?' said Jemima, arms around his neck, clothes dripping water.

'That I would,' said Job.

'That be a sign of a man in terrible love,' said Jemima, as he carried her into the cottage.

'Can't help my feelings,' said Job, 'but can't marry you, wouldn't be fair to you.'

But Jemima persisted, and one day Job called at

her father's farm and spoke to her parents about the matter. Mr Tristle, bow-legged, hard-faced and bristling, told him he'd horsewhip him if he didn't get out of the farmhouse in ten seconds, while Mrs Tristle, thin and tight-lipped, stared coldly at him. Jemima, defiant, stood beside him, and after attempting to reason with the hostile pair, Job decided it would be a Christian act to bring Jemima under his own roof, where his aunt would give her kindness and affection. Girl like her, he thought, shouldn't have to put up with parents like these. Always been a law unto themselves, always been a harsh couple. The wonder of it was that they had a daughter as pretty and smiling as Jemima. As for looking down their noses at him, it wasn't as if they owned their land. They were only tenant farmers, and didn't spend much on keeping Jemima in too many new Sunday frocks or bonnets. Still, she wasn't kept in downright hardship, and never went hungry. All the same, Job thought it might be a kindness to get her away from them.

So he married her as soon as she was twenty-one. Her parents didn't even attend the wedding. Jemima didn't care, she had Job, her handsome, laughing handyman. They lived in the cottage, along with his kind and elderly Aunt Matty, and in turn Jonathan, Jane, Jennifer and Jonas were born. But they became poorer and poorer, Job's work earning him less than enough to provide for his family as a man should. Jemima felt a little sad, because his ready laugh gradually became more forced. A man who couldn't keep his family decently dressed and fully fed didn't find a lot to laugh about. Her parents never visited. They had cut her off, and if ever they saw her they cut her dead.

Worse was to come. In 1930, Job's elderly aunt died, the aunt who'd been such a help and a comfort. She hadn't much to leave, just some bits and pieces of furniture, although there was an old and handsome grandfather clock and a well-preserved tea service. She left the clock to Job and Jemima, and the tea service to her other nephew, George Hardy, and his wife, who also carted off the bits and pieces, George being the elder nephew. A week after Aunt Matty's death, when Job was hoping to take over the tenancy of the cottage, he received a month's notice to quit from the owner, who required it for his spinster sister. What with that and their impoverished state, he and Jemima didn't know where to turn. However, fortune at last favoured the brave, and Jemima and Job had been the bravest of couples in the way they had endured poverty and cared for their children. Job received a letter from a cousin who'd gone up to London to better himself many years ago. There was work available for Job, he said. The Southwark Borough Council were looking for a replacement driver for one of their watercarts, and he'd spoken to someone he knew in the town hall. Accordingly, Job could fill the vacancy, providing he was in sound health and applied within three days.

Job went up to London and applied, successfully. The watercarts were now motorized, but that was no problem to Job, who could and had turned his hand to anything. He'd driven tractors for farmers

13

when they required a stand-in for an absent farm-hand. While in Walworth, he found a house available for rent in Stead Street. A three-up, three-down house, plus a scullery and a large backyard, at a rent of only eight shillings a week. Eight bob. Since he'd be earning two pounds two shillings a week driving a watercart, Job had a sudden feeling the family was going to enjoy comparative affluence.

Jemima, happy for him, happy for her whole family, gladly moved to Walworth and found herself in the heart of cockney South London. That had been nine years ago, when Jonathan was eleven, Jane seven, Jennifer five and Jonas two. Walworth was bustling, humming and alive with people, people boisterous, extrovert, neighbourly and helpful. There were drunks, mind, and saucy street kids. Jemima had never heard such sauce in the way they called out to her daughters.

'Oi, watcher, Jennifer, watcher, Jane, 'ow's yer Sunday drawers?'

Or in the way they addressed her.

"Ere, missus, wha'dyer talk all funny for?"

And one boy said to Jonathan, her eldest, 'Crikey, yer all bleedin' country bumpkins.'

They all retained a Sussex burr.

But cheeky street kids and their like didn't matter. Job's laughter came readily again, and the women of Walworth looked at him, smiled at him, and said things to Jemima like, 'My, that's a fine man you got as yer 'usband, Mrs 'Ardy.' Jemima thanked the Lord for interceding on their behalf and for making it possible for Job to provide well

14

for his family. A man who couldn't was only half a man, and most men knew it. It was a great terrible blow to a man's pride to see his wife and children in want, and during their years together in Sussex, Jemima had suffered guilty moments for forcing him into marriage. Once they began a new life in smoky old Walworth, all guilt vanished and there were smiles on every face. They were country folk, yes, but very adaptable, and they liked the warm-hearted cockneys and the welcoming atmosphere of the East Street market, which particularly appealed to Jemima.

She and Job sent their three younger children to the local church school, while Jonathan qualified for a place at West Square School, as did Jane and Jennifer when they reached the age of eleven. This provided them with a higher education. The handsome old grandfather clock ticked away in the parlour, recording the hours they spent at school, and the hours they spent at home.

In winter, the family put up with the fogs, and Job and the children all came home to a warm kitchen, a red-hot range fire and a hot supper. Jemima shopped in the market, which she found a housewife's paradise, almost. And Job, early on in their occupation of the house, took up all the paving stones in the backyard and turned it into a vegetable plot, with space for some spring and summer flowers, much to Jemima's delight. Despite Walworth's soot, the vegetables thrived and so did the flowers. Well, said a neighbour, the driver of a coal-cart, soot's good for ground that's asked to grow things, did yer know that, Job?

'You should,' he added, 'you bein' a country bloke.'

'Aye, I know, Herbert,' said Job. 'Like some sticks of rhubarb?'

'Not 'alf, mate, and I'll get me old lady to provide the 'ot custard.'

Naturally, when the family first discovered the house was beset by little movements, it worried them. Job talked about polka geese.

'Polka geese?' said Jemima, educated up to the age of fourteen at her village school.

'Aye,' said Job, 'you can't see 'em, but the little devils throw things about if they get cross.'

'Job, that dursen't account no way for floors dancing up and down, and mantelpieces doing the same,' said Jemima.

'Doing the polka, I reckon,' said Job. 'I've heard about polka geese.'

Jemima found out he meant poltergeists. Whatever the cause, it made the family nervous, and when Jemima spoke to a neighbour about it, the good lady said, 'Ah, well, thought yer might mention it one day, Mrs 'Ardy, thought yer might.'

'Do 'ee mean the house has always been like it?' asked Jemima.

'Far back as I can remember, but it never did no real 'arm, just put tenants off, and none ever stayed longer than a few months, as I recall.'

Jemima knew then why the rent was only eight shillings a week. The landlord obviously reckoned that even the most nervous tenants would put up with trembling floors for an outlay as small as that. So she and Job went round to see him. He wasn't a bad old buffer with his white hair and his white mutton chops, even if his optics did look like boiled bull's-eyes. They asked if he knew exactly what was wrong with the house.

He assured them nothing was wrong with it, it had stood the test of time and would stand a lot more.

'Well, we be certain sure ourselves the ceilings won't fall in,' said Job, 'but doors rattling, mantel-pieces jumping and floors dancing, that be a mite disturbing, Mr Renshaw.'

'Specially for the children,' said Jemima.

'Well, I'll tell you,' said the old buffer of a land-lord, and explained that during the construction of that particular row of terraced houses in the old Queen's time, an Irish gang of building workers had been part of the labour force, and it was this gang that had been primarily responsible for putting up the house now being rented by the Hardy family. They were a singing lot, those Irish, and full of blarney, and not always sober. They were always telling tales about the leprechauns that had come over from Ireland with them. When the house was finished and inspected, a member of the gang told the foreman they were short of one leprechaun. The foreman said think I'm as barmy as you are, do you, Patrick Cooney? And the Irishman, Patrick Cooney, said that on the soul of his dear old mother, he could swear that one leprechaun had got lost somewhere in the house. But not to worry, he was a merry little spalpeen, so he was, and wouldn't harm a fly.

'Mr Renshaw,' said Job, 'do you be telling us it's

a leprechaun that's making floors dance and doors rattle?'

'That's the story,' said Mr Renshaw, 'and the fact is, no one's ever come to any harm. You learn to live with it, and I'll keep the rent firm at eight shillings a week. The usual rent is fourteen shillings.'

Since the outlay of only eight shillings meant Job was able to provide so well, Jemima said they would learn to live with it.

'I'm not unfond of Irish leprechauns,' she said.

'Notable for bringing people luck,' said Mr Renshaw.

'Well, durned if we won't stay,' said Job, 'for I've a notion the children might have soft spots for them little creatures.'

So the family learned to live with the mis-behaving house and what they came to regard as its chuckling leprechaun, although Jemima had moments when she threatened to drown it if she ever found it. Jonas, the youngest of her children, said she mustn't, that she'd drown their luck if she did.

In 1936, when Jonathan left school at seventeen, he obtained a job as a junior with a firm of account-ants at Camberwell Green. They paid him fifteen shillings a week, which Job thought pretty miserly, but which Jemima thought at least made a start for him. Jonathan gave her five bob out of his weekly earnings, and saved what he could out of the rest for shoes and clothes. When in 1939 he was awarded a rise of two-and-six, from which he gave his mum an extra bob, Jemima was fair tickled.

Later on that year she said blessed if what Jonathan was giving her each week wasn't making her feel rich.

'Might us think about moving?' asked Job.

'Ur?' said young Jonas. Eleven, he was inclined to look a bit scruffy because his hair never stayed properly brushed and his socks always seemed to wander slyly down to his ankles. 'Ur?' he said again, slightly shocked.

'Moving?' said sixteen-year-old Jane, brown-haired and pretty like her mother, and still attending school.

'What for?' asked fourteen-year-old Jennifer, round-faced, snub-nosed and slightly podgy.

'Considerations, might I suggest?' said Job.

'Blow them,' said Jennifer.

'Parlour door's rattling,' said Jonathan.

'Ah, there's the considerations,' said Job, still a fine-looking man at forty-five.

'Blessed old door,' said Jemima, now forty-two and a trifle buxom, but still with a rosy country tint to her complexion.

'That's little Patrick you're talking about,' said young Jonas. The family had given the unseen leprechaun a name.

'I'll give him little Patrick,' said Jemima. 'More like noisy Patrick, that he is, with his rattling and chuckling. Still, I don't know we want serious to move, Job.'

They'd all come to like the house, and the garden created and nurtured by Job. And they liked their neighbours, and their proximity to the market.

19

'Little Patrick wouldn't like us leaving,' said young Jonas.

'Might be a nice change, though, to move into a house that stays still,' said Jonathan, personable, lanky, and with the same kind of firm shoulders as his father. 'Bedroom floor moved a bit in the night, as if it was having a last waltz with the bed.'

'No, it didn't,' said young Jonas. He shared a bedroom with his brother. The girls had a bedroom each, and Jemima and Job used the downstairs back room, as was customary in Walworth. Well, no-one thought of using the downstairs back as a dining-room, not when it was cosier to eat all meals in the kitchen. Young Jonas frequently complained it wasn't fair for his sisters to have a room each. Jemima asked why it wasn't fair. Well, they're only girls, said young Jonas. Job said that were an unkind thing to say, that some girls were a sight more valuable than some boys, and that if young Jonas didn't come round to fair-mindedness he'd have to have a tanning maybe. Jonas said he wasn't keen on having a tanning. Downright sensible of you, Jonas, said Jemima, and everyone laughed, including young Jonas. He said now, 'Bedroom floor didn't have any waltz with the bed.'

'Foxtrot?' said Jennifer.

'Foxtrot's more like it with that lively old leprechaun,' said Jane.

Job's deep-throated laugh arrived, and the rest of the family smiled at him.

The street door resounded to a knock before someone pulled the latchcord, opened the door and called.

'You in, Jane?' It was Alfie Hardcastle from next door. Seventeen, smitten with Jane and trying to make her his first girlfriend, Alfie, unfortunately, had ears that stuck out and caught the wind like sails, and had been getting nowhere at a galloping speed.

'Tell him I'm out,' whispered Jane to Jonathan. Jonathan called.

'My understanding is that she's out, Alfie.'

'Bless me,' said Jennifer, 'listen to old Jonathan.'

'What's Jonathan's understanding?' asked young Jonas, a boy who imbibed knowledge.

'A fib,' said Jemima.

'Is that right, Jane's out?' called Alfie.

'That's my understanding,' called Jonathan, and Jane giggled.

'Well, me sister 'Melia's 'ere, lookin' for you, Jonathan,' called Alfie.

Amelia Hardcastle – sixteen and frisky, and flirtatious as well, to be truthful – had Jonathan in her cupidinous sights. It was Saturday afternoon, the month the summery one of June, the year 1939, and like many other Walworth girls, Amelia was determined not to let the dark clouds fostered by Adolf Hitler rain on her. A good time was there for the taking if only she could entice Jonathan into her mum's parlour.

'I'll come in and get yer, shall I, Jonathan?' she called.

Jonathan and Jane both made fast exits. Out they went through the scullery door into the backyard, now a flourishing little garden, and put themselves out of sight of the kitchen window. Into the kitchen

21

came Alfie and Amelia Hardcastle, to be greeted with typically friendly smiles from Jemima, Job, Jennifer and young Jonas. Amelia was pert and plumpish, Alfie loud and thin.

'Oh, beg yer pardon, Mrs 'Ardy,' said Amelia, 'I thought Jonathan was 'ere.'

'So did I,' said Alfie, 'wasn't it 'im that told me Jane was out?'

'Was it?' said Jennifer.

'Well, he did come home from his work a while ago,' said Jemima, willing to fight a battle to prevent her elder son being eaten alive while he was still a young man. 'I'm sure I can't think where he be now.'

'Somewheres about, I reckon,' said Job.

'Maybe up the market,' said Jennifer.

'Nor I shouldn't wonder that he's not,' said young Jonas, muddling things up with his negatives. Well, it perplexed Alfie no end.

'Wherever and all, he'll be with Jane,' said Jemima.

'Never 'eard the like,' said Amelia, 'a bloke like Jonathan goin' out with 'is sister. It don't 'ardly bear thinkin' about, specially when he could've took me.'

'My, it's terrible hard luck on our Jonathan,' said Jennifer.

'Crikey, don't all of you still talk funny?' said Amelia.

'No, not much,' said young Jonas. 'You do, though.'

'Me?' said Amelia, sulking a bit because Jonathan wasn't around.

'And Alfie,' said young Jonas.

'Yer barmy,' said Alfie. ''Ere, me dad says Adolf Hitler ain't 'alf muckin' up people's goodwill.' Hitler, despite all he had promised Neville Chamberlain, the British Prime Minister, had marched into Czechoslovakia in March, and a merciless carve-up of that nation had taken place. 'Did yer know there's goin' to be conscription in this country for blokes that's only as old as twenty?'

'Oh, Lordy,' said Jemima, 'we hoped we wouldn't have to talk about such things this weekend. Job did three years in the Army in the Great War, that he did. Blessed if we want any more wars, nor conscription.'

'We be certain sure we don't,' said Job.

'You goin' to put the kettle on in a bit, Mrs 'Ardy?' said Amelia.

'Well,' said Jemima, 'I—'

'Floor's moving, Mum,' said Jennifer.

'Oh, 'elp, I can't stay for no cup of tea, after all,' said Amelia, and fled.

'I best go after 'er,' said Alfie, and he scarpered too. Everyone in Stead Street knew about the Hardy house, and some of the young people like Alfie and Amelia were put off by the possible advent of the legendary leprechaun.

'Floor's not moving,' said young Jonas.

'Oh, well, it sent those two home,' said Jennifer, 'and Jane and Jonathan can come in from the garden now.'

Job shouted with laughter. They were all laughing a second later.

In the parlour, the grandfather clock ticked on, while in Czechoslovakia, Himmler's Gestapo units were rounding up communists, dissidents, intellectuals and Jews.

Chapter Two

The afternoon was warm and sunny, London bathed in bright light. Summer had decided to begin its reign in royal style, as if to compensate for spring's sulks, and in London's parks young men were strolling in shirt sleeves and young ladies in light dresses, without, it seemed, letting the aggressive ambitions of Hitler bother them at all.

In Ruskin Park, the playground of the lower middle classes of Denmark Hill and the working classes of Camberwell and Walworth, people were enjoying an atmosphere entirely peaceful. The grass was a perfect green, the flower-beds colourful. The public tennis courts were all being used. On one of them, Robert Adams, known as Boots, was playing a mixed doubles, partnering Polly Simms against his niece Annabelle and her husband Nick Harrison. Nearly four years married, Annabelle and Nick were the parents of a three-year-old boy and a one-year-old girl, both children in the care of Annabelle's mother for the afternoon. Boots felt it was safe to say that Annabelle, after the impulsive and erratic enthusiasms of her earlier years, was now in a state of level-headed content, and given to congratulating herself. Well, since she wasn't yet twenty-three, she was entitled to award herself the occasional prize for being a wife, a mother and a typical worker of the world in all she did in the way of domestic chores.

In view of what was happening in Europe, Boots had frequent worries about the younger generation, particularly about couples like Annabelle and Nick, Cassie and Freddy Brown, and Sally and Horace Cooper. Cassie and Freddy were also parents, and so were Sally and Horace. The possibility of another war involving the United Kingdom was a very real one. If it happened, Nick, Freddy and Horace were all of an age to be conscripted. For that matter, Boots himself would have to go, since he was on the Officers' Reserve list. Then there was his son Tim, eighteen in a few months time, and Annabelle's brother Bobby, nearly nineteen. Bobby, in fact, was in the Territorials, having joined over a year ago. As a Territorial, he'd be called up immediately.

Damn that.

'Boots, wake up!' yelled Polly.

A ball, struck by Nick, was looping gently over his head. It landed behind him.

'Has something happened?' he asked.

'Yes, you boobed, and it's thirty-love to me and Nick,' called Annabelle.

'Buck up, Boots old soldier,' said Polly, as elegant in her white tennis dress as in any of her Mayfair creations. She was forty-two and hated it. But there she was, still slender and without any real indication that maturity was about to overtake her. Her Colleen Moore hairstyle still kept faith with her, giving her the perennial look of a Twenties flapper refusing to grow old. And she was still in love with Boots. It was the most cursed thing ever, this absurdly prolonged attachment to a man who had never made the slightest attempt to take advantage of it. Paradoxically, however, she didn't want to be cured. She was sure that if she stopped loving him, all her most sensitive emotions would dry up and leave her feeling like a brittle husk of a woman. If the fieriest nuances of her longings had calmed down, there were still moments when she fantasized imaginatively and uninhibitedly about the two of them. She sometimes felt the reason why she still wanted him was simply because she had never had him.

She glanced at him as she prepared to receive service from Annabelle. A long-limbed and distinctive man, a few months older than herself, in his cream flannels and white shirt he had the same appeal for her as when she first met him. He looked amused with himself, but she was sure that his little lapse of concentration hadn't related to something droll.

Annabelle served, Polly returned, and Nick countered with a mishit that turned into a drop shot. Polly and Boots dashed for it together. They collided, not drastically, but in warm buffeting fashion.

Heedless of their having muffed the return, Polly murmured, 'I liked that, sweetie, do it again.'

'Forty-love,' called Annabelle, wondering if her

Aunt Emily was altogether in favour of Polly partnering Boots.

Boots had phoned around for a partner, but no one was available, not even Annabelle's sister Emma, a girl who usually jumped at a chance to play. And Eloise, Boots's French daughter, was a duffer at games. So Boots, with Emily's permission, phoned Polly. The permission, of course, was only given after Boots assured Emily he had no devious designs on Polly, now or ever, and that even if he had they wouldn't surface on a tennis court without the risk of some spectators running to fetch a policeman. It's an arrestable offence, implementing devious designs on a woman on a public tennis court, he said.

'I suppose you think that's funny,' said Emily.

'Well, some spectators might laugh at it,' said Boots, 'but I'm convinced any church-going ladies there would hurry off to find a bobby.'

That kind of absurdity always weakened Emily. It made her laugh when she didn't want to.

'I ought to give up listening to you,' she said, 'you could charm the horns off Old Nick 'imself, you could. Well, all right, ask that woman, then, but only for tennis, d'you hear me, Boots?'

'Loud and clear, Em,' said Boots.

'That's a lie,' said Emily, 'I've never been a loud woman in all my life. Well, perhaps I yelled a bit up to the age of sixteen, but Walworth girls had to yell to make themselves 'eard. After I was sixteen, my old dad used to tell me I was music to his ears.'

'Your old dad was a good old dad, Em,' said Boots.

'Yes, he was, wasn't he?' said the disarmed Emily.

Polly was delighted to be asked. During the times when she was out of contact with Boots and his family, she could suffer debilitating boredom. When Rosie had been around, Polly would ring her and they'd arrange to go out together. Rosie, however, having acquired a degree in English Literature at Somerville College, was now attending a teachers' training college near Bath.

The game went on in the sunshine, Polly a dashing and extrovert player, Annabelle quick and enthusiastic, Nick very good and Boots full of expertise.

'You could come back to tea with me after the game,' said Polly to Boots during a change-over.

'I could, but I'll have to say no,' said Boots.

'Thought you would, you stinker,' said Polly.

'Well, you know I need to steer a careful course,' said Boots.

'Hope you lose the rudder, hit the rocks and sink,' said Polly. 'It's your service.'

Boots smiled as he walked to the perimeter wire to pick up balls. On the path beyond, a couple were strolling, the young man showing his young lady the afternoon edition of an evening paper.

'Look at that, Hetty, you could join the Army if you want, they're recruiting volunteers for a women's lot called the ATS, just in case.'

'They're not recruiting me,' said the young lady. 'Me do soldiering? Not likely, and not in any case.'

Boots grimaced to himself as he advanced to the baseline to serve.

'What's the score, Polly?' he asked.

'No idea, but let's make this a love game, shall we, old sport?' murmured Polly, always irrepressible whenever she was in company with him.

At home, Mrs Maisie Finch, known to her daughter and sons as Chinese Lady, turned off the wireless and went into the garden. There she found her husband, Edwin Finch, relaxing with a book.

'Edwin?'

'Yes, Maisie?' Mr Finch glanced up at her. Sixty-four, and due to retire in September, when he would be sixty-five, the grey in his hair added its own touch to his distinguished looks without making him seem his age. He was a healthy man, mind and body. Chinese Lady, thinking how kind and helpful he had been as a lodger many years ago, and how affectionate and supportive he had been as a husband, patted his arm.

'Edwin, I don't want to interrupt your reading, but something ought to be done about the wireless,' she said.

'Isn't it working, then?' asked Mr Finch.

'I mean there's always too much about that Hitler comin' out of it,' said Chinese Lady. 'I never did like him, not his looks, nor his loud mouth, and it's a downright disgrace that the wireless can't stop talkin' about what him and his Germans are up to. The other day I even had to listen to someone talkin' about what he likes for tea. Cream buns, would you believe. Young Alice, Tommy's first-born, likes cream buns, but I should hope no-one would ever talk about it on the wireless.'

'I think we'll escape that, Maisie,' said Mr Finch.

'I want you to ask the Government to do something with the wireless people,' said Chinese Lady.

Mr Finch coughed.

'Ah, the Government,' he said.

'Yes, you work for the Government, Edwin, so I expect they'd listen to you. Ask them to tell the wireless people not to keep talkin' about Hitler and his Nazi Germans. I'm at the end of my patience, and Em'ly said only yesterday that if she has to listen to much more, she'll have to be taken into a home.'

'A home, Maisie?' said Mr Finch.

'Yes, you know, one of those Bedlam places where they look after people that's been driven mad,' said Chinese Lady. She frowned. 'I might have to join her there myself just to get away from our wireless.'

'Wouldn't it be a better solution if we took a hammer to it?' said Mr Finch.

'Not when it's nearly new, bought only at Easter,' said Chinese Lady.

'Shall we buy one of these new television sets, then, and let the wireless remain silent?' suggested Mr Finch, always careful to give the impression that he took Chinese Lady seriously whenever she was a little over the top.

'I hope you're jokin', Edwin,' she said. 'From what I've heard, we'd have to look at Hitler as well as listen to him. Besides, television's not natural, and whoever invented it couldn't of known what he was doin'. No, best for you to get the Government to do something about the wireless people, Edwin.'

'Well, Maisie—'

'I know I can leave it to you,' said Chinese Lady. 'Now, would you like a nice cup of tea?'

'I would, Maisie, and thanks.'

'I'll have one out here with you, while there's just the two of us,' said Chinese Lady. Emily and Eloise were shopping in Brixton, and Tim was playing for his cricket team.

While waiting for the kettle to boil, Chinese Lady thought about Germany and about her proliferating family, her children, her grandchildren, and her great-grandchildren.

If a war came, what would happen to all of them? Several of her friends and neighbours said there'd be so many bombs that only a few hundred people would survive.

Chinese Lady decided to blame the wireless for everything that was currently upsetting.

In the Hardy house in Walworth, Job was in fine form over a pot of afternoon tea, and the kitchen was vibrating to gusts of laughter.

'Door's rattling,' said Jane.

'No, that's me,' said Jonathan, 'blessed if my spine isn't doing it from laughing so much.'

'I knowed a young chap once that didn't have a spine,' said Job. 'Reg'lar queer on the eyes, it were, to see him quivering like vanilla jelly.'

Jemima shrieked, so did her daughters, and the kitchen vibrated again.

'Vanilla, Dad?' said young Jonas.

'Aye,' said Job. 'Well, he were a bit yellow to look at, don't you see.'

'Oh, did he have yellow jaundice?' asked Jane.

'No, too much custard,' said Job.

In a house in Wansey Street, close to the town hall, a singing voice floated from the landing down to the open front door.

'I'm ready, Freddy.'

'Good lassie, Cassie,' called Freddy Brown. 'Not before time,' he added.

Down the stairs came his wife Cassie, generally acknowledged to be scatty and delectable at one and the same time.

'I heard that,' she said.

'Well,' said Freddy, whose good-looking physiognomy as a husband was generally admired by Cassie, 'when a poet meets a poet—'

'I didn't mean that,' said Cassie, 'I meant that bit about not before time. You don't want me lookin' any old how when we go out together, do you?'

They were going to do some shopping in the Walworth Road.

'On me honour, you look a treat,' said Freddy.

Cassie was wearing a bright summer dress and a light brown hat with a round curved brim. Her dark hair was styled in curling waves. Up to the time of her marriage she'd always worn it long and ribboned, but had had it styled on the morning of her wedding, which she thought befitted a young lady about to become a wife.

'Where's Muffin?' asked Cassie.

'In her pram on the doorstep,' said Freddy. Their infant daughter of ten months had been baptized Maureen Ruth, Ruth after Cassie's late mother, but Cassie had quickly come to call the baby Muffin. Neighbours asked Freddy where that came from, and Freddy said from Cassie's liking for the Walworth muffin man's muffins.

He conceded now that she did look an exceptional charmer in her bright summer dress and halo hat. He knew Cassie loved dressing well. Before her marriage she'd never had much to spend on clothes, but she always managed to look nicely turned out because of the generosity of her dad, who forked out happily on her account every so often. Freddy forked out these days, since he believed, as a husband, that what was his was also Cassie's and Cassie, of course, believed in that even more than he did. Cassie was very fond of his wages, which were a handsome three pounds a week. He was assistant to Tommy Adams, manager of an Adams garment factory in Shoreditch.

That job had come about through the intercession of Polly Simms. Polly liked Freddy and Cassie, and after their marriage she phoned Sammy to suggest he could find a better job for Freddy than his present one in the Southwark brewery. Sammy said he had Freddy's prospects eternally in mind. Well, do something about them, said Polly, so that he can keep Cassie in the style she deserves. Polly, I think you're coming it a bit, said Sammy. Get on with it, Sammy, said Polly, or I'll let Susie know you're seeing too much of your old flame, Rachel Goodman. Sammy nearly collapsed. Don't talk like that, Polly, he said, it's not even true. Susie won't know that, said Polly. Some women ought never to have been invented, said Sammy. Well, please this one, said Polly, and do something for Freddy.

That left Sammy scratching his head a bit. He had a word with Boots, and Boots pointed him at the obvious. Tommy, manager of the Shoreditch factory, also kept an eye on progress at a second factory, and could do with an assistant. Freddy was a sharp young bloke, and Tommy took him on with pleasure at three pounds a week. That wage, together with the money Freddy and Cassie had in the bank, enabled them to take out a mortgage on their Wansey Street house.

Cassie considered she had made a very good marriage. At twenty-three, she had a providing husband, a house that would eventually be their own, a treasure of an infant daughter, and the pleasure of having her good old dad living with them. If there were some ups and downs, the downs hardly dented the surface of the togetherness she enjoyed with Freddy. She liked togetherness, and could be exceptionally nice to Freddy on certain occasions, usually at night, when she would ask him if he fancied a little bit of extra togetherness. On one such occasion, Freddy pointed out it was Sunday. Cassie had a thing about being respectful on the Sabbath. Oh, I forgot it was a holy day, said Cassie. Still, she said, the Ten Commandments didn't actually forbid it every Sunday.

This afternoon, they were set for their outing. Cassie's dad was busy in the backyard, chopping up a couple of wooden crates for firewood. Cassie emerged from the house, and Freddy took a look at what she was carrying.

'What's that?' he asked.

'Just my new umberella,' said Cassie.

'It's not goin' to rain,' said Freddy. 'Besides which, it's not an umberella.' In cockney fashion, he and Cassie both added an extra 'e' to the word. 'Cassie, that's a parasol.'

'Yes, it's a lovely day for a parasol,' said Cassie.

'Cassie, if you 'appened to be drowning,' said Freddy, 'I'd jump in and save yer life with pleasure, but I'm not goin' along the Walworth Road pushin' this pram if you're wearin' a parasol. In the Walworth Road, kids chuck banana-skins at parasols, and I've got a feelin' they'll all land on me. At Ascot, well, that's different, but not the Walworth Road.'

'Freddy, don't fuss,' said Cassie, bending over the pram.

'Cassie, me mind's made up,' said Freddy.

Cassie regarded her sleeping infant.

'Who's my little cherub, then, who's my little Muffin? Freddy, I'm ever so proud of you for bein' her father.'

'Well, I'm proud meself,' said Freddy, 'but I'm not changing me mind. Put the parasol in the pram and we'll take it back to the shop and change it for a lampshade.'

'All right, we'll see, Freddy love,' said Cassie.

Which meant, of course, that ten minutes later, Freddy was pushing the pram along the Walworth Road and Cassie, beside him, had her pink parasol up. The sun shone, trams clanged, kids stared, women cast glances and men grinned. A woman stopped to admire the babe.

'My, ain't she an angel?'

'Yes, and she's all ours,' said Cassie.

'And I like yer parasol.'

'So does my husband,' said Cassie. 'This is him.'

'My, ain't yer proud, young man?'

'I'm not talkin' much at the moment,' said Freddy, 'I'm lookin' out for banana-skins.'

Cassie giggled as they went on their way. Two uniformed Territorial men passed by. Cassie affected not to notice them. Military things were a sort of blot on the landscape these days, and Cassie, like many other people, felt that if you ignored them and didn't talk about them, the blot would go away.

Chapter Three

Noon on Sunday morning saw Jemima and her family coming out of St John's Church along with the rest of the congregation. It was a fact that many Walworth people went regularly to church, the women in the hope that faith in the Lord's goodness might result in their husbands bringing home better wages. Their hope sprang from the Lord's word.

'To him that hath not shall be given all that he hath not, and from him that hath shall be taken away all that he hath.'

That seemed like a genuine Robin Hood act on the part of the Lord, with which the Walworth hath-nots agreed. So did the Labour Party, the champions of the poor, although the Conservative Party pointed out that if the rich were deprived of all they had, then all that they consequently had not would have to be taken care of by dipping into the pockets of the newly rich.

The poor people of Walworth couldn't see any sense in that, so mostly they voted for the Labour Party, whose members weren't going to worry about the deprived rich.

'Well, I'm hurrying home with your dad to put the roast on,' said Jemima to her offspring.

'We're all going down the market to see Jennifer earn two bob,' said Jonathan.

'Ah, going to do her little act, is she?' grinned Job.

'I don't know I hold with that,' said Jemima, but off her sons and daughters went.

The East Street market had a difference on Sundays. There were fewer fruit and veg stalls, and an increased number of stalls selling clothes, new and second-hand, or boots and shoes, also new or second-hand. There were tipsters offering racing certainties for sixpence, among them the well-known Prince Monolulu, a jovial coloured gentleman of large proportions and a famously large smile. And there were quacks selling medicinal wares. Jonathan, Jane, Jennifer and young Jonas attached themselves to a crowd listening to one quack who styled himself Dr Juniper. At the moment, he was doing fairly good business selling Dr Juniper's Miracle Ointment, guaranteed to soothe rheumatism, lumbago, arthritis, varicose veins and chilblains.

'In fact, ladies and gentlemen, I tell no lie when I inform you it can even cure said complaints. Unfortunately, and it grieves me to say so, for a cure you'll need two tins. I could tell you one tin would be enough, but that wouldn't be honest. One tin for soothing, two tins for a cure, and if me honesty comes as a bit of a shock to you – ah, two tins sold to you, sir, that's a bob – no, I'll cut me price for two tins, call it tenpence. One tin for you, lady? Well, it'll make a new woman of you. It's a pure herbal liniment, my friends, and my own professional recipe. I've had competitors trying to break down my lab door to get at it.'

'Cor, why'd yer keep it in yer lav?' asked a curious kid.

'Laboratory, my boy, laboratory.'

'Never 'eard of it,' said the kid.

'You will in time. Now, ladies and gents – ah, two tins for you, missus? Here we are, just a single bob for the pair.'

''Ere, you just said you'd cut the price to tenpence for two,' protested the female customer.

'So I did, and so I will. Tenpence, then, sweetheart. Is it for your rheumatics, say?'

'No, it's for me old man's lumbago, which is chronic.'

'I'd feel for him, lady, if I didn't know his sufferings will be over in a month. That's how long two tins will last at two applications a day as per instructions on the label. Look at me, ladies and gents, I don't have an ache anywhere, nor a single varicose vein. Well, I wouldn't have the face to come among you with this miracle ointment if I was chronic with rheumatics, would I? Any more takers? I've only got a few tins left – there we are, sir, one for you, then. All done? Right, now let me introduce you to the Juniper Miracle Cure for Headaches, as is printed on the label of each bottle. Not a powder, nor a pill, nor an Aspro, but a genuine herbal medicine guaranteed to cure a blinder in five minutes dead.'

'Bleedin' queer cure, that is, if it turns yer into a

corpse,' said a middle-aged man.

'Don't joke, sir, it pains my professional pride. I always come among you seriously on the grounds that chronic ailments don't happen to be a laughing matter. You see this bottle that holds a full quarter-pint of the medicine? You'll note it's a pure gold colour. That's the ambrosia herb, known as ambercitus, which is Latin. It was first used in Egypt, and I daresay some of you that read books know that Queen Cleopatra never had a headache all her life, which fact was recorded by Julius Caesar before sundry daggers done him in. Sad day for him, that was, and might have given Cleopatra her first headache if she hadn't had a flagon of this ambercitus handy on her mantelpiece. It's all recorded posthumous, as some of you might know. Now I might be grieving you again by telling you a bottle will set any customer back a bob – don't faint, lady, just be forgiving. It'll be the best bob anyone who suffers horrible headaches has ever forked out – no, all right, say tenpence, and I'll starve for the good of the cause.'

'I never 'eard of no 'eadache bein' cured in five minutes,' said a woman.

'Yes, you have, missus, I've just notified you. All right, you don't believe me. Fair enough, I'm septic myself on occasions. But I'm willing to demonstrate. Anyone here got a blinding headache, anyone at all?'

The crowd shifted about and everyone looked at everyone else. Jonathan, Jane and young Jonas all looked at Jennifer, and Jennifer uttered a pitiful groan.

''Ere, what's up with 'er?' asked a young woman.

'Oh, I got a terrible old headache,' moaned Jennifer.

'There y'ar, Dr Juniper,' said the young woman, 'what about this girl, then?'

'Would she come forward?' invited Dr Juniper.

'No, I couldn't, not in front of everybody,' said Jennifer, trying to blush and suffer at the same time.

'Please, young lady, do step forward,' said Dr Juniper.

'Well, all right, but it won't hurt, will it?' said Jennifer, and came forward, a hand to her head, her Sunday frock colourful.

'Oh, the poor thing,' said an elderly woman, 'fancy an 'orrible 'eadache at her age.'

Dr Juniper invited Jennifer to sit on an upturned crate. She seated herself and moaned faintly.

'Believe me, this won't upset you or pain you,' said Dr Juniper, and poured a dose of his miracle medicine into a large spoon. Jennifer lifted her head bravely and drank bravely. 'Excellent, splendid, what a courageous patient,' said Dr Juniper. The crowd was larger, all eyes on Jennifer. Jonathan, Jane and young Jonas were a trio of bland innocents.

'Oh, my poor head be fair buzzing,' sighed Jennifer.

'Relax, just for a few minutes,' said Dr Juniper.

'Yes, all right, doctor,' said Jennifer, and closed her eyes.

'Poor young girl,' said the elderly woman.

'I shan't ask for any of you to buy a single bottle

if it fails to relieve this young lady's unfortunate suffering,' said Dr Juniper.

'I wouldn't buy, anyway, until I'm sure it's at least done 'er a bit of good,' said another woman.

Amid the buzz of the market and the silence of the audience, Jennifer sighed and sighed until suddenly her eyes opened. She put a hand to her head again and looked up at Dr Juniper in worshipping fashion.

'Oh, doctor, it's gone,' she breathed. 'I be a new girl with no blessed headache. Oh, me gratitude knows no bounds.'

'Bless you, my child,' said Dr Juniper with a touch of Sunday morning reverence.

'Well, I be blowed,' said Jane, 'he's cured our sister.'

People surged forward, and Dr Juniper drew bottle after bottle out of a large box in his willingness to part with his miracle fluid at a bob a time with tuppence discount to advertise his compassion. When all customers had been served, he turned to Jennifer and handed her a bottle.

'There, young lady, for you at no charge.'

'Oh, thank you, doctor, how kind,' said Jennifer, receiving a concealed silver florin with the bottle.

Home she went then, with her brothers and her sister, a smile on her face. Jane was giggling.

'You Jennifer, you ought to go on the stage,' she said.

'Yes, I'm good, that I am,' said Jennifer.

'What a performance,' said Jonathan. 'Dr Collins next week, say?'

'I might,' said Jennifer. She performed in this

way most Sunday mornings, acting as a sufferer for the benefit of different market quacks, since she had a standing arrangement with them.

On arriving home, she was questioned by Jemima.

'Jennifer, did you get up to your tricks again?'

'That she did, Mum,' said Jane, 'we all watched her.'

'So did I,' said young Jonas.

'I don't hold with it,' said Jemima, 'especially on a Sunday.'

'Still, two bob's two bob,' said Job.

'Job Hardy, don't you go encouraging her,' said Jemima, 'and nor don't you lot encourage her likewise.'

'Believe me, we were all mesmerized,' said Jonathan.

'Me too,' said young Jonas.

'Jonathan said all of us, didn't he?' remarked Jane.

'Yes, it was me as well,' said young Jonas.

'That boy,' said Jennifer, 'can't someone bash his head in?'

'Your mum did that to me once with a saucepan,' said Job.

'Oh, Lordy, was it painful, Dad?' asked Jane.

'It would have been, if she hadn't missed,' said Job.

The Hardy family talked, joked and laughed about many things, but seldom about what was now an everyday subject, the menace of Hitler's Germany. Hitler, in Jemima's opinion, was a man who'd come to a bad end and was best not mentioned. In any case, she and her family had too much faith in people's liking for laughter to believe any of them would prefer the miseries of another war.

That afternoon, a little bit of bedlam was going on in the garden of a house on Denmark Hill. It was the house owned by Sammy and Susie Adams, and the bedlam was entirely due to the noisy antics of their four children, Daniel, Bess, Jimmy and Paula, twelve, ten, nine and four in that order. It has to be said that Bess was the ringleader. It could hardly be otherwise, considering she was sitting on Daniel, and he by no means a weedy boy. Bess's plumpness, however, outweighed him, and she was encouraging Jimmy and Paula to pull his shoes off and tickle his feet.

Sammy, taking note of the yelling horseplay through the kitchen window, said, 'Who's goin' out to quieten them down?'

'You are,' said Susie, who had the kettle on for the mid-afternoon pot of tea. Susie was in her thirty-fifth year, Sammy was now thirty-seven, and if he still had an electric vitality in his business life, it was Susie who still had the measure of him at home. 'But not just yet, Sammy.'

'Could be risky, leavin' them to it,' said Sammy. 'In another minute or so, I'll lay odds on Bess tryin' to run Daniel over with the lawnmower while Jimmy and Paula hold him down.'

'Well, don't let's panic yet,' said Susie. 'First tell me if you think Hitler's goin' to do something that'll start a war.'

'Eh?' said Sammy, taken aback.

'I'll get upset if there's a war, Sammy.'

'What brought this on?' asked Sammy.

'Our Sunday paper and the wireless,' said Susie. 'Can't you do something?'

'Me?' said Sammy, who had his own good reasons, including business reasons, for being dead set against any war. 'Now, Susie, what can I do?'

'Well, not much by yourself,' said Susie, 'but there's Boots. He's the thinking one. And you and Tommy are both grown men now. The two of you could get together with Boots and work something out with him, couldn't you?'

'Susie, might I ask if you're sayin' that seriously?'

'Well, I think it is serious, Sammy. Everyone's lettin' Hitler have his own way. Someone's got to think up some way of stopping him.'

'Right this minute, Susie,' said Sammy, 'someone's got to stop Daniel from being buried in the lawn. Bess, Paula and Jimmy are all sittin' on him now.'

'He'll survive,' said Susie. 'Sammy, why don't you and Tommy and Boots go and see Winston Churchill? He's the only one in Parliament who's takin' Hitler seriously.'

'Pardon?' said Sammy.

'Well,' said Susie, 'you and Tommy could be sort of steadfast and determined, Boots could put his thinking cap on, and Winston Churchill could supply experience, as well as breathing fire and flame. That ought to amount to a lot of something.'

46

'A lot of serious something?' said Sammy, as the garden echoed to yells and shrieks.

'Well, of course,' said Susie, 'nobody else is doin' anything at all.'

'Come to that,' said Sammy, 'what could even Winston Churchill do?'

'He's against Hitler, and so am I,' said Susie.

'I can't think you're makin' a serious suggestion,' said Sammy. 'Still, after I've sorted the kids out and had a cup of tea, I'll phone Boots.'

Which he did. He then reported to Susie that Boots had just died laughing. Susie, who never took setbacks lying down, rang Boots herself and told him Hitler was no laughing matter.

'I agree, Susie.'

'Well, do something.'

'We're all playing garden cricket at the moment,' said Boots.

'That's what they call fiddling while Rome is burnin',' said Susie. 'Go and see Winston Churchill, and take Sammy and Tommy with you.'

'I can't right now, Susie, I'm batting and I'm ten not out. Lizzy's bowling—'

'Never mind that,' said Susie, 'there could be a war if someone doesn't blow Hitler up.'

'We need a bomb, Susie.'

'There, I knew you'd think of something if you gave your mind to it,' said Susie. 'I'll see if Sammy knows anyone who could supply the bomb.'

'Well, do that, Susie,' said Boots, 'and while you're in this serious frame of mind, write to Mr Churchill at the House of Commons.'

'Write to him?' said Susie.

47

'That's it,' said Boots, 'strike while your iron is still hot, and let him know we all support him in his opposition to Hitler. Yes, very good idea, Susie.'

'D'you know, I think I'll do that,' said Susie.

'And I'll get back to the cricket,' said Boots.

Susie wrote the letter that evening.

> *Dear Mr Churchill,*
>
> *I'm writing to tell you that my family and me, and all my nearest and dearest relatives support you in what you're trying to do, wake our country up to the wickedness of Hitler and his Nazis. It's our belief something ought to be done about him before he starts another war, and if anyone can think of something it's you as everyone else in our Parliament seems soft in the head. Well, it's either that or they've got the wind up so badly that they're frightened of upsetting him. We all admire you for your beliefs and not being afraid to upset him yourself, and we'd like you for our Prime Minister as we think Mr Chamberlain is one of those who's gone soft in the head, poor man. I don't wish to be disrespectful, as he's obviously a very nice person, but waving his umbrella about isn't doing much good at all. I'd rather see pictures of him carrying a rifle, although I'm really not an aggressive woman, just a worried one.*
>
> *I am Yours Sincerely,*
> *Susie Adams, Mrs.*

Sammy blinked when she let him read it.

'Well, what d'you think?' demanded Susie.

'Ah, yes,' said Sammy.

'What d'you mean?' asked Susie.

'He'll like it,' said Sammy.

'You've got a funny look on your face,' said Susie.

'Yes, I like it as well,' said Sammy valiantly.

'I'll send it, then,' said Susie, and let him post it for her the next day.

Chapter Four

Jonathan had a punishing Monday morning at work. His immediate superior was Mr Harold Spinks, fussy, crabby and nit-picking. He also sniffed a lot. His every criticism was delivered to an accompaniment of sniffs, which played the very devil with Jonathan's ears. Blow me, he thought, if I don't wipe his nose with my blotter one day. That, and the fact that there was an atmosphere of ponderous professional seriousness throughout the offices, made him think he wouldn't want to stay there for the rest of his working life. Occasionally, he put a question to one of the partners. When am I going to start climbing the accountancy ladder? When you're qualified was the unvarying answer. When will that be? We'll let you know when we think you'll be ready to take the exam. A chap he'd recently met during one of his lunchtime breaks told him it was cheaper for his firm to employ him as he was, that they'd have to at least double his wages when he was qualified. So they wouldn't be in any hurry to recommend him for the exam. Jonathan sort of growled a bit at that.

However, being the cheerful son of a laughing

dad, he was his usual happy-go-lucky self as soon as he reached Lyons teashop at lunchtime. He normally had something to eat there when he had a decent amount of money in his pocket. Otherwise, Jemima supplied him with sandwiches, which he ate while sitting on a bench in the little oasis of Camberwell Green. One met other workers there, including girl clerks. Jonathan liked meeting people, and now that he was nineteen he naturally liked meeting girls. He admitted, however, that Amelia Hardcastle, the girl next door, was one he preferred to dodge. He had an idea she could prove a bit dangerous.

The teashop was crowded, mostly with office workers looking for a tasty but cheap lunch, and there wasn't a single vacant table. That didn't worry him, he was always willing to share. He saw a girl sitting at a table for two, a table against the far wall. He went across.

'Mind if I join you?' he said.

The girl looked up.

'Pardon?' she said.

'I mean, if this vacant seat's not taken, d'you mind if I have it?' said Jonathan.

'Well, I don't see that I can say no,' she said, so Jonathan sat down. Nippies bustled about. Cups rattled, cutlery tinkled, and the teashop smelt of coffee, tea, baked beans on toast, poached eggs on toast, and other snacks. Jonathan, not a reserved chap, smiled at the girl.

'D'you come here a lot?' he asked.

'Pardon?' she said again, and in a cool fashion.

Jonathan, who liked to get acquainted with the

people he came across during his lunch breaks, said, 'You don't mind me talking?'

'Well, yes, I do,' said the girl.

'Oh, sorry,' said Jonathan. 'Excuse me, but it's not because you're shy, is it?'

Cheeky devil, thought the girl, and said, 'Yes, that's it, I'm dreadfully shy.'

'Well, I'm blowed,' said Jonathan. He hadn't expected that answer. Bless my dad's boots, he thought, it's hard to believe of a modern girl. There weren't many like her in Camberwell and Walworth. He couldn't think why she was different. If she'd been plain and lumpy-looking, that could easily have made her shy and awkward, but she was all of attractive in her snowy white summer blouse. She had very nice features, as well as big brown eyes and rich chestnut hair. And her decorative blouse was not only fetching, it looked of very good quality. So it couldn't be that poverty was her problem. He thought she was about seventeen, a nice age for a girl. He regarded her with interest. She obviously didn't think much of being looked at, because she said pointedly, 'And no, I don't come here a lot.'

'I'm like that myself, a sometimes customer,' said Jonathan. 'I don't always have enough money to eat out. I'm a bit flush today. Well, it's Monday. By Wednesday, I'll be back to sandwiches. I work round the corner at Atwell and Parsons, accountants, and they don't pay juniors much.'

'Oh, really?' said the girl.

'No, not much, blow 'em,' said Jonathan. 'D'you work here in Camberwell, if I might ask?'

'Do you have to talk to shy girls? Don't you—'
The girl checked as a Nippy arrived with her lunch,
a cold chicken salad plus a roll and butter.

'There we are, miss,' said the Nippy, and then
addressed Jonathan, whom she'd served on other
occasions. 'And what can I get you, young sir?'

'Well, I'm splashing out today,' said Jonathan.

'My, my, reckless, are we?' said the Nippy,
notepad at the ready, pencil poised.

'Yes, as well as baked beans on toast, I'll have
college pudding with custard,' said Jonathan. 'I
make that sixpence. Well, thruppence for the
baked beans on toast, tuppence for the college
pudding, and a penny for the custard.'

'You sure you want to be as reckless as that?' said
the Nippy.

'More,' said Jonathan, 'I'll have a cup of coffee
to follow, blow me if I won't.'

'I don't know I'll get over the shock of all that,'
said the Nippy, and went off with a smile. Jonathan
looked at the girl's expensive chicken salad. That,
with the roll and butter, would cost her near to
one-and-six.

'Excuse me asking,' he said, 'but are you rich?'

'I beg your pardon?'

'Sorry, I'm being nosy,' said Jonathan.

'I think you're trying to pick me up,' said the girl.

'Might I correct that impression?' said Jonathan.
'I be an honest, straightforward chap, and simple.'

'You're what?'

'I be an honest, straightforward—'

'Yes, I did hear,' said the girl. 'Why'd you talk like
that?'

'I'm up from the country,' said Jonathan. 'I be Sussex-born, that I be, and got straw in my hair, see?'

She took a look.

'You're off your chump,' she said, and began to eat her lunch.

'No, I am Sussex-born,' said Jonathan, 'like all my family, but we came up to London nine years ago so's my father could earn his fortune. He hasn't earned it yet, he drives a corporation watercart.'

'How interesting.'

'Have you always been shy?' asked Jonathan.

'Always.'

'That's sad,' said Jonathan. 'No wonder you find it difficult to talk to people.'

'It's even more difficult with someone who's trying to pick me up.'

'But I'm not,' said Jonathan, 'I just like meeting people.'

Up came his baked beans on toast then. The hot beans in tomato sauce lay liberally over the toast, shining moistly.

'Thanks, Trixie,' said Jonathan.

'Talk about reckless, college pudding and custard as well,' said Trixie the Nippy, and looked at the girl. 'Havin' you on, is he, miss?'

'He's trying,' said the girl.

'Well, call me if you need 'elp,' said Trixie, and departed again with another smile, and the girl got on with her lunch.

'D'you work here in Camberwell?' asked Jonathan.

54

'Have I asked if you do?'

'Well, I told you I do,' said Jonathan, tackling his simple snack with relish.

'But I didn't ask, did I?'

'No, I suppose shy girls don't ask,' said Jonathan. 'If you must know, I work for a firm a little way up Denmark Hill.'

'What firm is that?' asked Jonathan. 'Would I know it?'

'It's Adams Enterprises.'

'I've heard of them in our office,' said Jonathan. 'My firm would like to have them as clients.'

'How interesting.'

'I think people are interesting. I'm Jonathan, by the way, Jonathan Hardy. What's your name?'

'Help, is there no escape?' asked the girl of her food.

'Oh, sorry,' said Jonathan, 'I keep forgetting you're shy.' He gave her a smile across his baked beans and her chicken salad. 'Still, I'd like to say I don't think being shy is dreadful, not in a girl. I think it's nice in a girl.'

'Do you?'

'Yes, I do. I said so. My parents don't like me saying anything I don't mean. Did you say what your name was?'

'Gertrude,' said Emma Somers, the younger daughter of Lizzy and Ned Somers.

'Gertrude?' said Jonathan, who was a natural at striking up lunchtime acquaintances. 'Gertrude Smith?'

'Gertrude Potter.'

Blow me, thought Jonathan, that explains some

of it, I'd be sensitive myself if I had a name like that.

'Well, I like the short version of Gertrude,' he said.

'Short version?' said Emma, trying to discourage him by concentrating on her food.

'Trudy,' said Jonathan. 'You don't have to be shy about that.'

'Well, I am.'

'That's a shame,' said Jonathan. 'I mean, shyness can be burdensome, I suppose.'

'Burdensome?'

'Like a heavy cross,' said Jonathan. 'My dad met a chap down in Sussex once. He was carrying a sheep on his back. Great big thing it was, and dead as mutton, and it was bowing him down. My dad asked him why he was carrying it, and he said he had to because his wife wouldn't. She told him a dead sheep was his cross, not hers. I suppose that's what you meant by burdensome.'

'I didn't mention burdensome. You did. But why was the man carrying the dead sheep?'

'Bless my mum's bedsocks, that's an interesting question,' said Jonathan, having polished off a good portion of his baked beans and toast while noting that this girl Trudy wasn't quite halfway on with her chicken salad. 'Only I don't know the answer, because Dad didn't ask him.'

'Was he too shy to?'

'My dad? Not much,' said Jonathan, and laughed.

'I did say I didn't want to be talked to,' said Emma.

'Yes, I know,' said Jonathan, 'but sometimes it's

good for shy people to have a chat. D'you read books? That helps, it gives you something to talk about.'

'I can read,' said Emma, 'and do joined-up writing as well. And being dreadfully shy, I like reading more than talking.' That, of course, was a fib. Emma Somers was as articulate as any of the younger generation of the Somers and Adams families.

'Well, that's a fair knockout, that is,' said Jonathan. 'You must be the only girl alive who likes reading more than talking. My sisters talk all the time. Excuse me, but you're not eating your lunch.'

'Could it be all this talking?' said Emma.

Trixie reappeared with her tray.

'Here's your reckless afters, young sir,' she said, and placed the college pudding with hot custard in front of Jonathan.

'I don't know how to thank you,' said Jonathan.

'My pleasure, I'm sure,' said Trixie. 'Your salad all right, miss?'

'Yes, thanks,' said Emma.

'Well, you don't have to hurry,' said Trixie, 'specially now you've got company.'

That left Emma making a face.

'What book you reading at the moment?' asked Jonathan, tucking into his pudding and custard.

'If you must know, it's *Gone With The Wind*,' said Emma.

'What, the one they're turning into a film?' said Jonathan.

'Yes, that one,' said Emma.

'I be fair amazed,' said Jonathan, 'It's as big as three books in one, and I don't know how expensive.'

'I had it for a birthday present,' said Emma, resigning herself to the obvious fact that he wasn't going to be deterred from chatting her up. She could believe he was a Sussex character, because of the burr in his voice and the way he lapsed into country dialect at times.

'I get socks for my birthdays,' said Jonathan.

'I don't know what to say to that,' said Emma.

'I get flummoxed myself sometimes,' said Jonathan.

'Flummoxed?' said Emma.

'That's a Sussex word,' said Jonathan. 'My mother once said she was fair flummoxed. She wasn't, of course, she always knows exactly what she's doing. Well, she's had to know in bringing up four of us. How many of you in your family?'

'I can't believe this,' said Emma, 'you're now asking for the story of my life, I suppose.'

'I'm a good listener,' said Jonathan blithely.

'Can't you take pity on my dreadful shyness?' asked Emma.

'I think you're doing fine,' said Jonathan. 'It's hardly shown so far. I be certain sure that talking helps. Did you say if you've got brothers and sisters?'

'No,' said Emma, 'I didn't.'

'Well, Trudy, if you're an only child—'

'I'm not, and who said you can call me Trudy?'

'To be honest,' said Jonathan, 'I think it suits you much better than Gertrude. Some names don't always suit. My mother had a friend in Sussex whose name was Honolulu—'

'Honolulu?'

'Fact. Her dad had been a sailor who went to Honolulu and was always talking about it. Of course, everyone called her Lulu, which Mum said suited her much better. Well, I mean, imagine meeting her and having to say "Good morning, Honolulu". You don't mind me calling you Trudy, do you?'

'Yes,' said Emma.

'Yes, you don't mind?' said Jonathan.

'No, I do mind,' said Emma.

'I thought if we ran into each other again some lunchtime—'

'We won't,' said Emma.

Trixie brought Jonathan's coffee then, together with his bill.

'It's a lot today, eightpence,' she said. 'It's what comes of bein' reckless.'

'I'll probably just have a poached egg on toast tomorrow,' said Jonathan.

'You're a one, you are,' said Trixie, departing again.

'Will you be in here tomorrow?' asked Jonathan, sugaring his coffee.

'No, I'll be in hiding,' said Emma.

'Why, is someone after you for a bad debt?' asked Jonathan. 'One of our neighbours, Mrs Stokes, goes into frequent hiding on the days when the rent collector calls. It's sad, that, when a family doesn't have enough to pay the rent, so Mum lets Mrs Stokes hide in our kitchen.'

'I'm fascinated,' said Emma, seventeen and developing admirably.

'Better than being shy,' said Jonathan, drinking his coffee. 'Anyway, if you do happen to be in here tomorrow, I'll look out for you.'

'You don't have to,' said Emma.

'I've enjoyed talking to you,' said Jonathan, 'I like company at lunchtime. Eating by yourself, well, it don't be very exciting, I reckon, nor sociable.'

'Do you mind if I say you sound daft when you talk like that?' said Emma.

'Well, I were a village boy once,' said Jonathan. He gulped coffee. 'I need to get back to my work now, I've got some adding up to do, and if I don't get it finished quickly, I'll get done to a turn by the bloke in charge of me.'

'Good grief,' said Emma, 'you don't get ground down at your office, do you?'

'Well, I'm going to look for another job some-time, and that's a fact,' said Jonathan. He finished his coffee, put tuppence on the table for a tip and picked up his bill. 'Don't mind if I push off now, do you, Trudy?'

'Not a bit,' said Emma.

'It's been a pleasure talking to you. Hope we meet again. So long.' Off he went, leaving Emma to herself at last.

Everything went quiet at her table, which was a welcome relief.

That afternoon, Emma, the junior shorthand-typist, was taking some extra dictation from her

Uncle Boots, the general manager of Adams Enterprises.

At one point, she asked, 'Oh, could you repeat that, sir?' She alternated 'sir' with 'Uncle Boots' depending on her mood, or who else might be present.

'Discount on this particular order will be five per cent,' said Boots.

'Oh, thanks,' said Emma, 'only I think I'm a bit deaf from having been talked to all through my lunch.'

'Who was responsible?' asked Boots.

'Some very peculiar young bloke from Sussex,' said Emma. 'He was trying to pick me up, of course.'

'Who won?' asked Boots.

'I did, naturally,' said Emma, 'and next time I see him I'll disappear fast before he sees me. I don't want to become a deaf shorthand-typist, do I?'

'You're a promising asset at the moment,' said Boots, 'so ask your Uncle Sammy for a rise.'

'He'll collapse,' said Emma.

'Do him good,' said Boots, 'a collapse six times a year makes your Uncle Sammy realize life is something to hang on to.'

'But what makes him collapse six times a year, Uncle Boots?'

'Your Aunt Susie,' said Boots.

'Uncle Boots, you are funny.'

'Funny peculiar, I daresay,' said Boots, 'but we're all a bit barmy.'

'Oh, if everyone is,' said Emma, 'that's ever so comforting.'

'Let's get on,' said Boots.

'Yes, sir,' said Emma, thinking that if anyone was extra barmy, Jonathan Hardy was.

Chapter Five

Reaching the end of Browning Street on his way
home from work that evening, Jonathan saw his
dad's watercart on its way through Brandon Street
to the market. It was spouting cleansing water into
the gutter.

'Hi, Dad!'

Job saw him through his cabin window. He
grinned and waved.

'Be home myself in a tidy little while, son,' he
called.

Good old Dad, thought Jonathan. He'd put up
well with the kicks of life and with not having
helpful in-laws. Mum's parents were durned old
miseries, they'd never written her a single letter,
nor ever sent her any kind of card. Better off
without parents like that, she was, he thought. Nor
did she ever cry about it. She was always quick to
laugh, to follow his dad's laugh with her own kind.
His dad meant the world to his mum, you could tell
that, and what his mum was worth to his dad
couldn't have been counted in gold bars. They
even laughed about the winter fogs that came
down and put a yellow blanket over Walworth.

'Lost my durned way home tonight, Jemima.'

'Lost my blessed way round my kitchen, Job.'

'Hope I don't lose my way to bed later.'

'Hope we can find where the bed is, Job.'

'Where be our children?'

'Looking for each other up and down the stairs.'

'That old durned fog gets everywhere, Jemima.'

'So it do, Job, so blow some holes in it.'

Jonathan, approaching his house, made a quick dash as Amelia Hardcastle, home from her factory job, leapt out of her open door. She beat him to his own door, her vivid tangerine Hollywood sweater placing itself boldly in his way.

''Ello, Jonathan, ain't you a love?' she said.

'Am I?' said Jonathan cautiously. 'Why?'

'I like yer talkin' voice,' said Amelia, 'and you got a nice mouth. D'you do lots of kissin'?'

'Only at Christmas,' said Jonathan. 'For the rest of the time, my dear blessed mother—'

'Yer what?' said Amelia.

'Well, you know my mum, don't you?'

'Ain't you a scream, callin' 'er yer dear blessed mother?'

'Well, she's very blessed,' said Jonathan, 'and dear to all of us.'

'Oh, yer soppy date,' said Amelia, 'you don't 'ave to talk like Tod Slaughter comin' the old acid, do yer?'

'Sometimes I do,' said Jonathan, 'I could go for being an actor at the Elephant and Castle Theatre.'

'You can take me to the pantomime there at Christmas,' said Amelia.

'I was saying about my dear blessed mother not

64

minding about Christmas kissing, but making me polish my shoes and help old ladies across roads for the rest of the time,' said Jonathan. 'And go to Sunday church.'

'I ain't ever been to no church,' said Amelia, expression and sweater both defiant.

'Tck, tck,' said Jonathan, wondering if there was a way of escape around the sweater.

'Tck, tck?' said Amelia. 'What d'yer mean, tck, tck?'

'Jesus won't want you for a sunbeam.'

'Oh, ain't you really a scream, Jonathan?' said Amelia. ''Ere, you've got a visitor, did yer know?'

'No, I didn't know. Who is it, the Lord Mayor?'

'Your aunt,' said Amelia. 'Well, that's what Jane said before she stopped me goin' in to say 'ello.'

'Some dear old aunt she be, do she?' said Jonathan, and Amelia giggled.

'I never 'eard no-one talk funnier,' she said. 'Can't yer talk proper, like me and Alfie?'

'I've tried,' said Jonathan, 'but my mouth seems to sort of fall to pieces. Excuse me, I'd better go and see this aunt.' He did a quick shuffle and entered the house. Hearing voices in the parlour, he went in. His mum, his sisters and his brother were all there, seated, and so was a portly lady in a blouse and skirt, and a hat with cherries. A Sussex village hat. On the parlour table were cups and saucers, a teapot and what was left of a homemade coconut cake.

'Oh, there you be, Jonathan,' said Jemima, a picture in a blue dress that softly flowed over her healthy figure. 'Here's your Aunt Belle come to see us. She's cousin George Hardy's wife, and met all of you lots of times when you were little.'

'Hello, Aunt Belle,' said Jonathan.

'Well, give us a kiss,' said portly Aunt Belle.

'We've all given her one,' said Jane.

'Me too,' said Jennifer.

'And me,' said young Jonas.

'Well, I said so, didn't I?' complained Jane.

'You didn't say I did,' protested young Jonas.

'I said all of us,' remarked Jane.

Jonathan planted a friendly kiss on Aunt Belle's cheek.

'What brought you?' he asked.

'Family feelings,' she said, 'and I'm downright sad me and your Uncle George haven't been able to call once or twice, nor seen any of you since the funeral of Aunt Matty. And it were unkind of your mum's parents to treat her like she didn't belong when she married your dad.'

'We've never known grandparents,' said Jane.

'Nor I haven't, either,' said young Jonas.

'Didn't I mean you, then?' said Jane.

'Yes, and so do I,' said young Jonas.

'Yes, one and all, I reckon,' said Jonathan.

'Still, your Aunt Matty were kind,' said Aunt Belle, roundly stout while Jemima was nicely buxom. 'Gave your mum and dad some tidy help in their suffering years.'

'More sociable than suffering,' said Jemima, 'Job not being given to glooming. But I won't say it wasn't a struggle.'

'I think the larder door's rattling, Mum,' said Jennifer.

'Wind getting up, I daresay,' said Jemima.

'Getting up in the house of all things?' said Aunt Belle, cherries bumping on her hat as she turned her head.

'Comes in through the kitchen window,' said Jonathan.

'Goodness, is it under this floor?' asked Aunt Belle, looking askance at the lino.

'Floor's moving, Mum,' said young Jonas.

'That old devil's got into the wind, looks like,' said Jemima.

'What old devil?' asked Aunt Belle.

'Well,' said Jonathan, 'you've heard of a devil of a wind, haven't you, Aunt Belle? Tidy old one we get in Walworth sometimes.'

'So we do down by Beachy Head way and all,' said Aunt Belle. 'Goodness, it's got under your floor, that it has, Jemima.'

'Oh, we're all used to it, Belle,' said Jemima.

'Nor don't I not notice,' said young Jonas.

'That boy'll be a regular daft loon in a year or so,' said Jane.

'Jonathan,' said Jemima, 'your Aunt Belle's been saying what a great shame poor Aunt Matty didn't have anything much to leave except her tea service and grandfather clock.'

It was ticking away, the clock, its shining brass pendulum, with its round disc, moving gently.

'Well, it were a great shame your mum and dad only getting that old clock,' said Aunt Belle. 'Mind, as I mentioned to your mum, Jonathan, your Uncle George, finding himself now kindly able to be a help, is willing to take it off your dad's hands for five pounds.'

'Five pounds?' said Jonathan.

'Your Uncle George not only being financially able nowadays, but kind and willing as well, he thought he'd make the offer,' said Aunt Belle. 'That'll be a nice help, five pounds?'

'Buy a new suit for Dad, a new outfit for Mum, and a new shirt for me,' said Jonathan. 'Bless financial ability, Aunt Belle, but I don't reckon Dad'll part with the clock like he would a pair of boots.'

'I told your Aunt Belle that,' said Jemima.

'We all did,' said Jennifer, and she and Jane looked at young Jonas, daring him.

'Not me,' he protested, 'I said could Uncle George make it ten pounds, that's what I said.'

'Oh, I don't know he could do that, Jonas, that's a tidy lot of money,' said Aunt Belle. 'Still, I'll wait to see your dad before I go for the train home, and ask him if he'd like us to take the clock off his hands.'

Job arrived just a few minutes later. He showed surprise and pleasure to see cousin George's wife, gave her a smacker on her rosy chops, told her she was a fine figure of a woman, durned it she wasn't, and laughed. After asking how cousin George was, and being told he was making his way nicely repairing tractors, Job said that were a pleasure to hear and was there anything more of a like happy kind? Jemima then mentioned cousin George's willing offer for the grandfather clock.

'Well now,' said Job, and thought about it.

'Aunt Belle mentioned Uncle George might make it ten pounds,' said young Jonas.

'Now, Jonas,' smiled Aunt Belle, 'that I never did. Perhaps six, maybe, seeing your Uncle George is very kindly disposed now he's so able.'

'Well,' said Job, 'Jemima and me being fond of that old clock, which has come to us from Aunt Matty, I don't reckon it be right to part with it.'

'It be a country cottage clock, Job,' said Aunt Belle, 'which don't look suitable here. That don't give you offence, I hope, being said with thoughts of what Aunt Matty might think about it ending up in a London house. Aunt Matty weren't fond of London, nor any city. Spent her young days out there under the sun in Africa, doing missionary work with her brother, George's dad, who prayed she wouldn't get ate up by lions. Mind, it wouldn't surprise me if George did offer just a bit more, on account of thinking Aunt Matty might like the clock finishing up back in the country. That don't give you offence, Job?'

'No offence, Belle,' said Job, 'it's a kind thought right enough. A country grandfather clock ought to tick away in the country, and maybe, later on, when Jemima and me go back to Sussex, you can be certain sure we'll take that old grandfather tick-tocker with us.'

'Yes, Job and me, we be wishful to spend our retirement back in Sussex,' said Jemima.

'We all be that wishful,' said Jane, 'except I'd best not mention young Jonas.'

'I don't mind mentioning myself,' said young Jonas.

'I don't mind not leaving me out,' said Jonathan.

'Those boys are both plain daft,' said Jennifer.

'Remember, Job, how kindly willing me and George are to give the clock its proper home now, and say for a little bit more than five pounds,' said Aunt Belle. She jumped a little in her chair. 'What's that?'

'Oh, this old parlour door's rattling a bit,' said Job.

'Wind's getting up again,' said Jonathan.

'Some little old devil's gone jumpy,' said Jemima.

'Wind devil, that's what,' said Jonathan.

'I think I'd best be on my way now,' said Aunt Belle.

'Reckon I'll see you to the tram stop,' said Job.

'Ah, still a kind gentleman, that you are, Job,' said Aunt Belle. She said goodbye to the rest of the family, told them she'd been downright pleasured at seeing them again, and on her way out of the house with Job, said she weren't terrible keen on him having a latch-cord to his front door. Anyone might get in and make off with Aunt Matty's grandfather clock, she said.

'Not that old timepiece, I reckon,' said Job, 'nor anything else. In Walworth, this here door could be left open night and day and we could still have no worries.'

'Temptation, though,' said Aunt Belle.

'I'll have a look at that clock, maybe,' said Job in bed that night.

'Worth more than five pounds, you think?' said Jemima.

'Well, Aunt Matty, as I recall, spent a few years and more in Africa when she were young,' said Job.

'Belle mentioned that,' said Jemima.

'Might be a fair old idea to examine that clock's innards,' said Job.

'What's put that into your mind?' asked Jemima.

'Well, cousin George has always had his own grandfather clock,' said Job, and chuckled. 'Don't see why he wants Aunt Matty's unless summat's suddenly made him think there's more to its innards than works.'

'More to this house than rattling doors too,' said Jemima.

'Aye, little Patrick,' said Job, and chuckled again.

Emma went out for a walk with her boyfriend, Donald Ashley, that evening. Donald Ashley, nineteen, was a stockbroker's clerk with a bright future. And he was bright himself. Emma would have simply passed him on to some other girl if he'd been dull, never mind that he was good-looking. In telling him about some barmy bloke who'd been born in Sussex, she had him laughing.

'I couldn't stop him talking,' she said, 'it went on for hours.'

'Hours?' said Donald.

'It seemed like it,' said Emma. 'I told him I didn't want to be talked to, that I was shy.'

'Shy?' said Donald and laughed.

'Yes, but he still kept trying to pick me up.'

'He wants sorting out,' said Donald.

'No, I just think he needs a doctor to examine his head,' said Emma. 'I tried to put him off by telling him my name was Gertrude Potter.'

'You're joking,' said Donald.

'So he said that as Gertrude didn't suit me, he'd call me Trudy.'

'What a character,' said Donald. 'Does his mother know he's out?'

'Well, if he's out tomorrow,' said Emma, 'I'll be in hiding.'

'Shout if he finds you, and I'll come running,' said Donald. 'I'll make sure he keeps off the grass. By the way, I suppose we both realize that as I'm nearly twenty, I might be conscripted any moment into what they're calling the militia.'

'Oh, blow that,' said Emma, and made a face, not so much at the possibility of Donald being conscripted as the possibility of war.

Anyone who'd taken history at school knew that wars didn't solve anything because the losers always wanted to take revenge. One war begat another. And they caused slaughter and misery. All that slaughter in the last war, for instance. And her dad had lost a leg, and Uncle Boots had suffered blindness for four long years.

There just couldn't be another one.

'There you are,' said Mrs Lizzy Somers when her daughter Emma and her younger son Edward appeared for breakfast the following morning. Her elder son Bobby was already on his way to work, as was husband Ned. 'My, Emma, you hair does look nice today.'

'Oh, does it, Mum?' said Emma. Her hair, a deep chestnut springy with tight curls, was bouffant from a sustained brushing.

'She's given her hairbrush a hard time this morning,' said Edward as they sat down to their breakfast of eggs and bacon. Lizzy always liked to put a good breakfast into her children. 'Still, it does look nice, your hair, sis.'

'Well, thanks,' said Emma.

'Are you still doin' well at the office?' asked Lizzy, who knew Emma liked working for the family firm.

'Oh, I'd be doing even better if I weren't so shy,' said Emma.

'Eh?' said Edward, looking astonished.

'Shy?' said Lizzy, looking amazed.

'Oh, did I say I was?' asked Emma.

'Emma, you've never been shy,' said Lizzy.

'I think I meant modest,' said Emma.

'Never heard of it in this house,' said Edward, fourteen and at grammar school.

'Will you be comin' home to lunch today, Emma?' asked Lizzy. Emma often came home for lunch, being only a short bus ride from the offices. Yesterday, she'd gone to crowded Lyons. She liked eating out sometimes.

'Yes, I think so,' said Emma. She mused for a moment, then said, 'No, p'raps not, though. We're very busy at the office, and I might only have a short break, so I'll have a quick lunch at Lyons.'

'Well, all right, love,' said Lizzy, mature at forty, but not matronly. She still had an Edwardian figure. If it had looked out of date during the mid-Twenties, when the flappers went in for flat chests

73

and high hemlines, the longer skirts and complimentary bodices of the Thirties turned the tables again for Lizzy.

'I don't mind only a short break,' said Emma, 'I'm a devoted shorthand-typist.'

Lizzy smiled. There was nothing shy about Emma. She had her fair share of self-confidence. And she was beginning to go quite steady with Donald Ashley from farther down the road. Donald, with his very promising job in the City, was just right for Emma as her first real boyfriend. Unlike Annabelle, she'd never collected boyfriends by the dozen. Mind, once Annabelle had met Nick, it was as if she'd been struck by lightning, and she'd simply been unable to look at anyone else. Emma was sort of cooler and more controlled in the way she regarded boys. While she might not have decided that Donald was going to be her one and only, she liked him right enough, Lizzy was sure. He was quite the young gent and could be very amusing. Emma liked being amused. And she really did enjoy her job with the family firm, especially as she had a soft spot for Boots and Sammy. Her sister Annabelle had preceded her there, although as an assistant bookkeeper, not a shorthand-typist.

They left the house together, Emma and Edward, and Lizzy saw them off. Emma turned and waved when they reached the gate of their house in Sunrise Avenue, off Denmark Hill.

''Bye, Mum, don't let the window-cleaner fall off his ladder.'

Lizzy smiled. Emma could be a bit of a joker, like her Uncle Sammy.

Away to the south-east, towards Kent, the sky rumbled. It wasn't the rumble of thunder, it was man-made not God-sent, and the sound was becoming familiar. Airplanes again, thought Lizzy, without having the slightest idea that RAF flight formations were testing new deliveries of Hawker Hurricane fighters. In the event of war, the RAF meant to be ready to meet the threat of Germany's powerful *Luftwaffe*.

The rumbling died away, but Lizzy was frowning as she closed the door.

Chapter Six

Emma managed to get the same table at lunchtime, and the same Nippy.

''Ello again,' said Trixie.

'Hello,' said Emma.

'Will the young sir be joining you?'

'Only if my luck's out,' said Emma.

'He's a caution, that one,' said Trixie. 'Finish up in Parliament, I shouldn't wonder.'

'We'll all have to call for help, if he does,' said Emma, and ordered a slice of veal and ham pie with salad.

'My pleasure, miss,' said Trixie, noting it down and hurrying away.

By the time Emma's lunch arrived, she was still alone and thinking she was going to be spared more unwanted talk, some of it downright potty if yesterday's was any guide. She got on enjoyably with her lunch, and let the minutes go by.

'Hello, Trudy, you're here again, then. Sorry I'm a bit late.'

Emma jumped as Jonathan sat down in the vacant chair. It took her a second or so to recover, when she said, 'What are you doing here?'

'I said I'd be coming in, but only for a poached egg on toast. You said—'

'Who are you?' asked Emma.

'Jonathan Hardy. We met yesterday.'

'Go away,' said Emma.

'Meeting you again isn't embarrassing you, is it?' said Jonathan.

'Yes, it is.'

'Believe me, I won't take any notice,' said Jonathan. 'As it happens, I'm a bit bitter myself.'

'Bitter?' said Emma, already beginning to feel helpless.

'Yes, old Spinks kept me at it till I'd finished an addition of a thousand different entries in a cash book,' said Jonathan. 'I reckon he's after wearing me down till there's nothing left of me except bones. You're looking nice again today, Trudy.'

'What I look like is nothing to do with you,' said Emma, 'and you're trying to pick me up again.' And she thought of her Aunt Susie's sister Sally, who had regaled a family gathering of how her husband, Horace Cooper, had spent weeks trying to get off with her when she was working in an Adams shop in Kennington, and how she'd given in at last in order to stop him driving her to drink.

'No, I'm not trying to pick you up, blowed if I am,' said Jonathan. 'I just like making friends with girls, that's all. I don't be a winking and grinning chap.'

Help, what a giggle, thought Emma.

'You don't have to talk like a country yokel, do you?' she said.

'Born like it, I were,' said Jonathan. 'You look as

if you're having another nice lunch. Carry on, I won't interrupt.'

Emma, thinking she must have been out of her mind to come into Lyons today, said, 'Is that a promise I can rely on?'

'Yes, carry on,' said Jonathan, and up came busy Trixie.

'Well, young sir?' she said.

'Hello,' said Jonathan, 'just a poached egg on toast today, if that's all right with you.'

'Gone off bein' reckless, have we?' said Trixie.

'It's my finances,' said Jonathan.

'I've got the same problems,' said Trixie, and away she went.

'I hope you don't get paid starvation wages in your job like I do in mine,' said Jonathan to Emma, who looked up from her food.

'You promised not to interrupt me,' she said.

'Oh, sorry,' said Jonathan, 'but I can't help thinking I'm stuck with a firm of skinflints. You even have to pay a penny for your afternoon tea. Still, a job's a job. Listen, Trudy, d'you know anything about grandfather clocks?'

Emma couldn't help a pitying look. He really was potty, poor bloke.

'I'm weak in the head,' she said.

'Are you?' said Jonathan. 'I thought you only had to worry about being shy.'

'I mean I'm weak in the head to have come in here today,' said Emma. 'And why should I know anything about grandfather clocks at my age?'

'How old are you, then?'

'I was only seventeen when I came in,' said

Emma, 'but I'll feel like a hundred by the time I leave if you don't stop asking me daft questions.'

'It's just that we've got an old grandfather clock left to my parents by my dad's aunt,' said Jonathan. 'What d'you think an old one is worth? Only our Aunt Belle is offering a fiver for it. Well, her husband is.'

'Do you mind if I just eat my lunch?' said Emma.

'Go ahead,' said Jonathan. 'I won't ask any more questions. But I must say it's pleasing to see you again, and seventeen's a nice age for girls.'

'Oh, really?' said Emma.

'Yes, I think it's their best growing-up age,' said Jonathan.

'I'm thrilled,' said Emma.

'I only mentioned our grandfather clock in case you were interested.'

'Why should I be?' said Emma. 'I told you, I don't know anything about grandfather clocks.'

'I don't know much myself,' said Jonathan. 'It looks like we're both fairly ignorant. That's sad, that is.' He laughed.

'If it's sad, why are you laughing?' asked Emma.

'Well, laughing's always better for you than crying,' said Jonathan.

'Even at a funeral?' said Emma.

'That reminds me, my dad went to a funeral once,' said Jonathan. 'They were burying an old chap who'd been the village joker all his life. His headstone had already been done, and it said, "Here at last lies Ebeneezer Cook, wrapped tidy in his coffin, who split his sides in merriment, and died of too much laughing".'

Emma nearly choked on a piece of veal and ham pie.

'You're potty, you made that up,' she said when she was over her fit.

'No, I didn't, it's true,' said Jonathan, 'and if you're ever down in Sussex and near the church-yard in Little Ditchling, you'll find it on one of the headstones.'

'I can hardly wait to get there,' said Emma.

'Your poached egg on toast, young sir,' said Trixie, arriving with it.

'Thanks,' said Jonathan.

'You kept the young lady waitin' today,' said Trixie artfully.

'It wasn't my blame,' said Jonathan, 'I was kept in the cage until I'd finished a certain job.'

'Problems, problems,' said Trixie, and bustled away.

'Could you pass the salt, Trudy?' asked Jonathan.

Pushing the cruet forward, Emma said, 'I still haven't given you permission to call me Trudy.'

'But didn't we sort that out yesterday?' said Jonathan, sprinkling a little salt over his poached egg. 'When you mentioned your name was Gertrude, didn't we agree Trudy suited you better?'

'You said it did, I didn't.'

'I thought that if we were friendly, it would help you along a bit,' said Jonathan.

'Oh, I'm crying for help, I don't think,' said Emma, 'but I do have a feeling that in another five minutes, you'll tell me you're my best friend.'

'No, I just be a straightforward country chap that

likes talking to you,' said Jonathan.

'Straightforward? Barmy, more like,' said Emma.

'Sometimes,' said Jonathan, 'you strike me as not being a bit shy.'

'Well, I am,' said Emma, 'especially when strangers keep talking to me.'

'Me?' said Jonathan, enjoying his egg on toast. 'I'm a stranger?'

'Yes, of course you are,' said Emma, 'I don't know you.'

'That's not much of a joke, Trudy,' said Jonathan.

'It wasn't a joke,' said Emma.

'It's all right, no hard feelings,' said Jonathan. Emma wrinkled her nose. It seemed impossible to discourage him. 'By the way,' he said, 'I went to the library by the Walworth Road town hall last evening to see if I could get a copy of *Gone With The Wind*. No luck.'

'You can ask them to reserve you a copy,' said Emma.

'I did,' said Jonathan, 'and I'm about two-hundredth on the list. The library lady said I could look forward to borrowing it sometime in 1941.'

'Oh, dear, that's mournful, that is,' said Emma, with just the hint of a smile.

'Well, I'd certainly like to get my turn with it,' said Jonathan. Everybody who enjoyed a good book had either read *Gone With The Wind* or wanted to. It was the biggest-selling novel of all time, even if its size also made it one of the most expensive. Waiting lists of borrowers at public libraries were a mile long, and had been ever since the first publication of the book in the UK two years ago. And now that it was being turned into a film, featuring Clark Gable and Vivien Leigh, the demand for the novel was greater than ever. 'I'll look forward to sometime in 1941,' he said.

'You mentioned the library in the Walworth Road,' said Emma. 'Does that mean you live in Walworth?'

'Yes,' said Jonathan, 'ever since we came up from the wilds of Sussex nine years ago.'

Emma could have told him her mother and uncles came from Walworth, but decided not to. It would only encourage him into trying to make a lifelong friend of her.

'Carry on eating your lunch,' she said.

'It's all I can afford,' said Jonathan. 'You can tell me about yourself, if you like, Trudy.'

'Why should I like?' said Emma. 'I told you, you're a stranger to me, good as, and I didn't ask you to come and sit here.'

'I just thought that if you told me about yourself, you'd forget your shyness,' said Jonathan. 'Talking to people does that, I think, and I'd be interested to hear about where you live, what your family's like, and if you're being courted.'

'If I'm being what?' said Emma.

'Courted,' said Jonathan.

'Courted? Don't make me giggle,' said Emma. 'Have you been living in the Ark? No one says courted any more. You mean dated.'

'Dated, right,' said Jonathan. 'What was I saying?'

'Eat your boiled egg,' said Emma.

'It's poached,' said Jonathan. He cut a corner off what was left of the slice of toast, dipped it into the yolk to coat it with gold and ate it. 'Let's see, weren't you going to tell me about your family, where you live and so on?'

'No,' said Emma.

'I'd be interested,' said Jonathan.

'Look,' said Emma, 'you're still trying it on, aren't you?'

'I'm not trying anything, believe me.' Jonathan ate another piece of golden-coated toast. 'Don't you like company at lunch?'

'Do I look as if I need it?' asked Emma.

'Well, no, I can't say you do,' said Jonathan, 'you've got a nice way of hiding it.'

'I'll scream in a minute,' said Emma.

'Be ructions all over Lyons, if you do,' said Jonathan. 'Would you like to tell me about yourself?'

'I'd mostly like some peace and quiet,' said Emma.

'It's always a bit noisy in here at lunchtimes,' said Jonathan.

'Yes, I've been listening to it,' said Emma, but again was unable to discourage him. He carried on in his blithe way, drawing her into the conversation. He asked her if she was enjoying *Gone With The Wind*. She found herself telling him it was riveting, that Scarlett O'Hara was a real madam, but that one couldn't help liking her and cheering for her. 'But actually,' she said, 'I haven't known who to cheer more, her or Rhett Butler, who's utterly wicked and dashing.'

'Ah, that be worrying,' said Jonathan.

'What d'you mean?' asked Emma.

'According to such things as I've learned, heard and read about,' said Jonathan, 'girls live in mortal danger from having a weakness for the wicked. That's sad, Trudy, that is. Give a girl the choice between two men, one honest and clean-living, the other a tidy old villain with white teeth and a black moustache, and ten to one she'll pick the villain. It's the excitement of his villainy, you see. What's sadder, of course, is that after a year of wicked excitement and hurtful beatings, she'll be down on her knees asking the Lord what she's done to deserve her bitter lot.'

'Wait a minute,' said Emma, 'where'd you get all that from?'

'Reading, learning and observing,' said Jonathan. 'I'm naturally fond of learning and observing.'

'You'll end up in a museum, you will,' said Emma.

'Makes no difference how I'll end up,' said Jonathan, 'girls will always go daft over wicked and dashing blokes.'

'Only girls who are already daft,' said Emma.

'Being a chap kindly disposed towards girls, I'd like to believe that,' said Jonathan, 'but, unfortunately, I can't. My dad, one of the honest kind, told me he was durned lucky having my mother wishful to marry him. There was a farmer's son keen on her, a chap who was wicked and dashing as soon as he could walk and talk, but my mother, being a woman of sense, chose Dad. Dad said most other girls in the village would have preferred the farmer's son.'

'How did he know that?' asked Emma.

'Dad's very observing of the ways of females,' said Jonathan.

Emma blinked and said, 'Do you and your dad talk to each other like you're talking to me?'

'Well, we talk,' said Jonathan.

I'll get as potty as he is if I don't escape him, thought Emma.

'I've got to get back to work now,' she said.

'Well, it's been pleasing having your company again,' said Jonathan. 'I won't be in here tomorrow, I'll be bringing sandwiches and eating them on a bench in the Green. I don't suppose you'll be bringing sandwiches yourself.'

'No, nor eating them on a bench in the Green,' said Emma.

'Still, if you change your mind,' said Jonathan, 'perhaps you could bring *Gone With The Wind* with you, and read bits to me?'

'Perhaps I could do what?' said Emma.

'If it's another nice day—'

'I'm going,' said Emma, getting up, 'I'm going while I've still got the strength. Goodbye.'

'Goodbye, Trudy,' said Jonathan, and watched her as she paid her bill and departed. He noticed she'd left a silver threepenny-bit for a tip. What a nice generous girl.

Sammy Adams had some frowning moments during the afternoon. Uneasy rumblings in Europe weren't going down well as far as industry and commerce were concerned, except for firms engaged in the armaments trade. I ought to have bought a factory making tanks, thought Sammy. You get paid very profitably for making tanks to order, even if they don't get used, which we all hope they won't. What went wrong with Boots's thinking apparatus that he didn't see a tank factory would be a good acquisition after we sold off our scrap metal business? I can't think of everything myself. On the other hand, he did try to stop the sale of our scrap metal business. Ruddy headaches, the price of scrap metal's rocketing. Still, our new factory's meant we've been able to tender for some WD contracts covering the supply of uniforms for these militia lads who are going to be called up. Look on the bright side, Sammy Adams. Bright side my flaming eye, what's Chinese Lady going to say if she suspects the Adams outfit might be on the way to being classed as war profiteers? She'll set light to both factories, and my trousers as well. Blow any war. Who's our Prime Minister? That bloke with a brolly, Neville Chamberlain. Pity he didn't use it to poke Hitler in both eyes, and let him see stars before he went blind. And that Susie, writing to Winston Churchill and now talking about divorcing me if I let a war happen. What can I do?

Someone entered his office then, someone humming a song.

'I'm available now, Uncle Sammy,' said Emma, sitting down with her shorthand notebook open.

'Was that you humming a song?' asked Sammy.

'Oh, was I?' said Emma.

'Sounded like it,' said Sammy.

'Sorry, Uncle Sammy.'

'Sounded like "Happy Days Are Here Again",' said Sammy.

'Oh, did it?' said Emma.

'Happy days might soon be gone with the wind unless Hitler and Goering don't get dropped into a redhot volcano,' said Sammy. Emma laughed. 'Did I say something funny?' asked Sammy.

'It's only that I'm reading *Gone With The Wind*,' said Emma.

'Read it myself a few months ago,' said Sammy, 'but it didn't strike me as bein' a comic book.'

'Sorry, Uncle Sammy. D'you want to dictate now? Oh, first, you don't believe most girls prefer to marry wicked men, do you?'

'Only after they've married hopeless ones,' said Sammy, 'and it's too late then. Right, letter to that bloke in the Ministry of Defence – what's his name now?'

'Mr G C Jonathan,' said Emma.

'Eh?' said Sammy.

'I mean Mr G C Saunders,' said Emma.

'Saunders, that's the bloke,' said Sammy, 'and I don't know where you got Jonathan from.'

'Oh, silly me,' said Emma.

I knew it, she thought, just two lunches in his company and he's sent me potty. Well, that's the end of him.

Over supper, Jonathan said, 'I'm going to get the pleasure of reading *Gone With The Wind*.'

'I reckon I've heard of that,' said Job.

87

'Dad, everyone has,' said Jane. 'I'm saving up to see the film up West when it comes to this country.'

'I'm going with you,' said Jennifer.

'Have you saved up enough already, then?' asked Jane.

'No, you're older,' said Jennifer, 'you're saving up for me as well.'

'I be doing what?' said Jane.

'Saving up for both of us,' said Jennifer.

'Not likely I'm not,' said Jane.

'Who's saving up for me?' asked young Jonas.

'Jonathan,' said Jennifer, 'he's oldest and biggest, and in a job.'

'I've got working expenses,' said Jonathan.

'Jonathan,' said Jemima, 'are you getting the book from the library, then?'

'Yes,' said Jonathan, 'sometime in 1941.'

'Sometime when?' asked Jane.

'1941,' said Jonathan.

'Jonathan, that's two years,' said Jemima.

'Lord knows if you'll still want to read it by then,' said Jane.

'Specially if he's in the Army,' said Jennifer, and Jemima gave her a look. They all knew the Government might soon be after Jonathan for the newly formed militia. Jemima, however, discouraged any talk about it, and Job, who'd served during the Great War, was like others of his kind in believing no-one would be mad _nough to start another.

'By the way,' said Jonathan, 'I met a girl who's reading the book. She's got her own copy.'

'Bless me, you've met a girl, Jonathan?' said Jemima.

'He's met lots,' said Jane.

'I haven't,' said young Jonas.

'Well, you're not old enough,' said Jennifer.

'Yes, I been lucky so far,' said young Jonas.

'I met this girl at lunchtime yesterday,' said Jonathan.

Since everyone knew he was always meeting some young people during his lunch breaks, the only surprise was that he was giving this one a particular mention.

'Crikey, is she gone on you, Jonathan?' asked Jane.

'Wants her head looked into if she is,' said Jennifer.

'Now how can any girl be gone on a chap she's only seen twice, yesterday and today?' asked Jonathan.

'Oh, it sometimes be possible, Jonathan,' said Jemima.

'Old Farmer Simpson's prize heifer fell in love with Farmer Boddy's prize bull the minute she saw what he'd got,' said Job.

Jemima shrieked.

'Job, don't you say such things at supper, you hear me?' she said.

'Keep 'em till after, shall I, Jemima?' said Job.

'No, keep them unspoke,' said Jemima. 'Jonathan, who be this girl you've met twice?'

'I told you, Mum, a girl I met in my lunch hour,' said Jonathan.

'But what's she like?' asked Jane.

89

'A lot different from Amelia next door,' said Jonathan.

'Ah, that Amelia next door,' said Jemima warningly.

'What's different about this other girl?' asked Jane.

'Well, there's not as much of her as there is of Amelia,' said Jonathan, 'and she's terrible shy.'

'Sounds a nice girl, then, don't she?' said Job.

'Does she blush?' asked Jennifer.

'I don't recollect I've seen any blush so far,' said Jonathan, 'but she says she's always been shy. Not that she sounds like it, she can hold her own, that she can.'

'Your mum used to blush when she were fourteen,' said Job.

'I never did,' said Jemima.

'Only when you were fourteen,' said Job. 'Blush like a June rose you used to then, specially that time I helped you over a stile.'

'Job Hardy, you be trying to make me blush now,' said Jemima.

'Showed Dad her Monday washing, I expect,' said Jane.

'Never you mind,' said Jemima. 'What's this girl's name, Jonathan?'

'Gertrude Potter,' said Jonathan.

The female members of the family all shrieked. Job grinned, and young Jonas blinked.

'Gertrude Potter? I don't believe it,' said Jane.

'Fancy meeting a girl with a name like that,' said Jennifer.

'You're fair amazed, I suppose,' said Jonathan.

'Flabbergasted,' said Jennifer.

'So be I,' said young Jonas.

'No wonder she's shy, poor girl,' said Jane.

'I call her Trudy,' said Jonathan, 'she can't be shy about that.'

'Jonathan, that's nice and thoughtful of you,' said Jemima. 'Trudy's a kindness to a girl. Instead of waiting till 1941 before you get the book from the library, why don't you ask her if she'll lend you her copy?'

'She'd only lend a book like that to her best friend, I reckon,' said Jonathan. 'In any case, I don't know if I'll be seeing her again.'

'Why not?' asked Jennifer.

'She's shy about meeting a country chap any more,' said Jonathan.

'Jonathan, have you been making fun of her?' asked Jane. 'You're a one for doing that.'

'It don't do to make fun of girls,' said Job.

'I've only talked to her,' said Jonathan.

A slight disturbance made itself felt.

'Dad, front door's shaking,' said young Jonas.

'So's a few windows,' said Job, 'but nothing to do with that little old devil of ours. More like the Goddards and the Tuckers are at it again.'

Everyone scrambled up from the kitchen table except Jemima, who said, 'Wait, no one's had their afters yet.'

'Later, Mum,' said Jonathan, and then they were all streaming from the kitchen in their hurry not to miss what the Goddard and Tucker families were doing to each other. Out of the house they surged to join people already in the street. The

Goddards and Tuckers lived close to the Hardy house, and were immediate neighbours to each other. One moment they were living chattily on each other's doorstep, the next they were fighting like cats and dogs.

There they were, out of their houses, the mums and dads and their kids. Both mums were beefy women, and both dads were brawny. Both families were going at it hammer and tongs, spare boots, bits of wood and saucepan lids flying about. Mrs Goddard was yanking at Mrs Tucker's hair, and Mrs Tucker was doing her best to make a dishcloth out of Mrs Goddard's blouse. Mr Goddard and Mr Tucker were exchanging blows, and it was their kids who were chucking things.

Crash, bang, wallop.

'Oh, yer bitch, let go me 'air!' yelled Mrs Tucker.

'I'll scalp yer!' screamed Mrs Goddard, blouse already ninety per cent wrecked and a corset showing.

'Gotcher!' yelled a Tucker kid, banging a Goddard kid's head with an old boot.

'I'll learn yer, yer bleeder!' roared Mr Goddard, aiming a York ham of a fist at Mr Tucker. He missed, and Mr Tucker hit him in his breadbasket.

''Ow'd yer like yer eggs done?' bawled Mr Tucker.

Mrs Goddard's shredded blouse fell to her waist, and a watchful street kid let out an exultant yell.

'Crikey, ain't she got some dumplings?'

Mrs Tucker herself fell then, to the ground, and Mrs Goddard picked up a pail of potato peelings that she'd brought as ammunition, and dropped the lot on her outraged neighbour.

Job, a grin on his face, made himself heard.

'Coppers be coming, missus!'

'Oh, me gawd,' breathed Mrs Goddard, 'I already done seven days.'

The fighting families separated and did a lightning bunk back into their homes.

'Dad, it were just getting interesting,' said Jennifer.

'Not neighbourly, though,' said Job. 'More like a war, don't you see. Best everyone saves themselves for a real one.'

'Won't be a real one,' said Jane.

'No, I don't reckon there can be,' said Job reassuringly.

Amelia appeared and pushed herself close to Jonathan.

'I 'ate fightin',' she said. 'Kissing's better. Come for a walk, Jonathan?'

'Well, I'd like to, Amelia, that I would,' said Jonathan, 'but our mum's waiting to serve our afters.'

'We've 'ad ours,' said Amelia.

'None of us have had ours,' said Jennifer.

'Nor I haven't, neither,' said young Jonas.

'Excuse us while we go and have ours,' said Jonathan, and escaped Amelia not for the first time.

'I'll come in and see yer later, Jonathan!' yelled the frustrated Amelia.

'I'll be out later,' called Jonathan, disappearing.

Chapter Seven

'Is Donald comin' round this evening, Emma?' asked Lizzy after supper.

'Yes, Mum, and I'll be in the garden reading my book,' said Emma.

'Well, it's nice out in the garden these light evenings,' said Lizzy. 'You'll enjoy your book out there.'

'Point is, will Donald enjoy it?' said Ned.

'Enjoy what?' asked Lizzy.

'Sitting in the garden watching Emma reading her book,' said Ned.

'Dad, I'll stop reading when he arrives,' said Emma.

Donald was there twenty minutes later, looking very personable in a navy blue suit. He and Emma shared a companiable get-together in deckchairs that were close to each other, Emma with her book on her lap.

'Still not finished it?' said Donald.

'I've just started the last chapter,' said Emma.

'That's the dramatic one,' said Donald, who'd read the book himself.

'Yes, it begins with Scarlett realizing she actually

loves Rhett Butler,' said Emma.

'And it finishes with—'

'Oh, don't tell me, you booby, it'll spoil it for me,' said Emma. 'Listen, d'you think girls fall more for devilish men than upright ones?'

'I think you've got Rhett Butler on your mind,' said Donald.

'Well, he really is devilish,' said Emma. 'And exciting too.'

'I'll try his style one day if it's going to make me exciting,' said Donald.

'That's no good,' said Emma, 'you have to be born that way.'

'Well, I was born the other way, and that's why I'm a decent, well-behaved character,' said Donald. 'Incidentally, the Stock Exchange is all over the place, some shares hitting rock-bottom and a few rocketing. It's the European situation. No-one knows what's going to happen, and the only big concerns doing really well are those in armaments. Our firm is—'

'Who wants to know about the rubbishy old Stock Exchange?' asked Emma.

'It's a kind of pointer to—'

'It's boring,' said Emma.

'Not to everyone,' said Donald.

'I'm not everyone, I'm me,' said Emma, 'and the Stock Exchange is boring, so there.'

'What d'you want me to do, chase you round the garden?' asked Donald.

'That sounds even more boring,' said Emma.

'Sorry I spoke,' said Donald.

'Oh, that's all right,' said Emma, 'you're quite a

nice straightforward chap on the whole.'

'Chap?' said Donald.

'Bloke,' said Emma, wondering how 'chap' slipped out, considering it wasn't in general use except in books about country folk.

Donald didn't stay long, he'd got some shares listing to do and after he'd gone, Emma asked her mum if Uncle Boots and Uncle Sammy had been a bit devilish when they were young. Lizzy said no-one had thought Boots was until that business with a French war widow in France, and that Sammy had only been devilish over money, especially when he charged their mum interest on his little loans to her.

'Still,' said Emma, 'all that money he saved helped him to start his business, didn't it?'

'Granted,' said Ned.

'Yes, I've got to admit it did,' said Lizzy, 'and I've got to further admit he turned it into a goin' concern for the whole family.'

'Well,' said Emma, 'both Uncle Boots and Uncle Sammy being a bit devilish has worked out happily for their families, hasn't it? I mean, Aunt Emily and Aunt Susie haven't ever bemoaned their bitter lot, have they?'

'Aunt Emily and Aunt Susie haven't ever done what?' said Lizzy.

'I think she said bemoaned their bitter lot,' smiled Ned.

'Emma, are you all right, love?' asked Lizzy.

'No, I've gone a bit potty,' said Emma.

'Well, try to get over it, there's a good girl,' said Lizzy, 'I still have a bit of trouble with your father sometimes, specially when he and Boots get together.'

'Yes, well, Dad's a bit devilish too,' said Emma.

The following morning, she advised her mum she'd be having a Lyons lunch again. Unlike Jonathan, Emma was fairly flush throughout the week, earning five pounds a month at her job, with a promise of a rise on her eighteenth birthday. Moreover, her mum only took five shillings a week from her for her keep. And that was taken because Lizzy believed a son or daughter should contribute something, as a matter of principle, and Ned agreed.

Out Jonathan came at lunchtime, having endured a morning of carping from sniffy old Spinks. The sunshine was welcome after the stuffiness of the offices, where all windows were kept shut on the Victorian principle that air from the outside did malodorous things to the air inside. Jonathan entered the little oasis of Camberwell Green, where people such as other office workers were either strolling around or sitting on benches. Two girls and a bloke on one bench waved to him.

'Come and sit with us, Jonathan,' one girl called.

Jonathan's attention, however, was already engaged, on a girl sitting by herself and reading a book. She didn't look up, she remained engrossed. Jonathan advanced. He noted a Lyons white cardboard lunch box on her lap.

'Well, I'm blessed,' he said, 'I didn't expect to see you here, Trudy.'

Emma looked up.

'Oh, it's not you, is it?' she said, placing *Gone With The Wind* aside.

'Is it even more embarrassing for me to meet you out here instead of in Lyons?' asked Jonathan.

'Yes, even more,' said Emma. 'I thought you'd be in Lyons again.'

'No, I did say I was bringing sandwiches and eating them here.'

'You sure you did?' said Emma.

'I be certain sure,' said Jonathan.

'Don't start that country talk again,' said Emma. 'Look, I think some friends of yours are calling you.'

'Oh, just some acquaintances I've met here a few times,' said Jonathan. 'I'll sit with you, shall I?' He seated himself beside her.

'Don't you have any consideration for how shy I am?' asked Emma, playing that fib up for all she was worth. 'You could sit with your acquaintances.'

'Yes, I could,' said Jonathan, unwrapping his sandwiches, 'but I think you need me more than they do.'

'I what?' Emma could hardly believe her ears. 'Did you say I need you?'

'I mean you need having someone to talk to more than they do,' said Jonathan. 'You'll never get over your shyness if you avoid people, and it's no bother to me to be a help.'

'It's another blessed liberty when you haven't been asked to,' said Emma.

'Now I don't want you to worry or feel too embarrassed,' said Jonathan. 'If you don't want to talk a lot to start with, I'll just keep you quiet company, and you'll hardly know I'm here.'

'Be a blessed miracle, that will, I reckon,' said Emma, and having delivered herself of that, her mouth dropped open. Jonathan was grinning. 'That wasn't me said that, was it?' she breathed.

'Well, Trudy, yes, it was,' said Jonathan. 'A little bit of country talk. Came right out with it, that you did. Little devil you are, Trudy, taking me off like that.'

'I've heard about people being driven to drink, like the sister-in-law of an uncle of mine once was,' said Emma, thinking of Sally again. 'Now I know what it feels like. Jonathan Hardy, if you get me into the habit of talking like you do, my parents will think I've gone daft.'

'I don't think you'll ever go daft, Trudy,' said Jonathan. 'I mean, you don't twitch or make funny faces.' He glanced at the large volume beside her. 'That couldn't be *Gone With The Wind*, could it?'

'If you must know, yes, and I've just finished it,' said Emma. She had actually finished it last night, after Donald had gone, but she'd wanted to read the last chapter again because it was so dramatic.

'Well, now you can tell me all about it,' said Jonathan. 'Would you like a cucumber and lettuce sandwich, made by my mother?'

'Thanks, but I went into Lyons and bought one of their lunch boxes,' said Emma. She opened it, revealing a crisp buttered roll, a piece of Cheddar cheese, a red tomato and a Granny Smith apple, the latter all the way from New Zealand.

Jonathan got on with his sandwiches, and Emma bit into her roll and cheese.

'Speaking of embarrassment, Trudy—'

'You don't have to,' said Emma.

'Well, while I'm waiting for you to tell me something about the book,' said Jonathan, 'it won't hurt to let you know I gave a tram conductor a dud penny once. I didn't know it was dud, but he knew straightaway. He said he could have me arrested. I was so embarrassed I near fainted in a lady's lap. Still, I managed to say to the conductor that as I had starving parents and four ragged sisters, could he let me off this time. So he did, and I gave him a good penny, and he wished my ragged sisters luck. Some tram conductors are decent chaps, Trudy.'

'Some other kind of chaps ought to stay down in Sussex,' said Emma.

A tram clanged past the Green, and a bus lumbered. Emma's snowy white blouse was brilliant in the sunshine, while Jonathan's grey clerical tie sat in casual fashion on his striped office shirt. He'd left his jacket and waistcoat on his desk chair. The little Green, set though it was in the heart of busy Camberwell, actually had an atmosphere of peace and calm. Emma decided it was quite a nice place in which to eat a simple lunch. She regarded her tomato, ripe and rosy, and she thought about her clean blouse.

'You're doing some thinking,' said Jonathan.

'Yes. Would you like my tomato?'

'It's yours,' said Jonathan, 'you've only got the one.'

'You can have it, if you like,' said Emma, and offered it.

'That's kind of you,' said Jonathan, and took it. Emma watched as he bit into it, and she waited for juice to splash his shirt and tie. But he bit cleanly all the way through it, and not a drop of juice fell.

'You've bitten it right in half,' she said, her mouth watering. She loved tomatoes.

'Best way with whole tomatoes,' said Jonathan. 'Little devils they can be if you don't show 'em you mean business. My sister Jennifer had one shower itself all over her best frock on a picnic once. Well, now that there's only half left of this little devil, would you like it, Trudy?'

'No, thanks. Well, all right.' Emma couldn't resist. Jonathan gave it to her, and she enjoyed it in between mouthfuls of bread and cheese. A half was easier to eat than a whole one.

'Fine tomato, that was,' smiled Jonathan.

'Yes, I liked my half,' said Emma.

'Not much went on your blouse, either,' said Jonathan.

Emma cast a dismayed glance at her blouse, but saw only spotless white.

'That's not funny,' she said.

'Has anyone told you, you wear very nice blouses?' asked Jonathan.

'Yes, everyone, including tram conductors,' said Emma, who bought most of her outfits from Adams Fashions at a family discount.

'I expect you enjoyed the last chapters of *Gone With The Wind*,' said Jonathan.

'Yes, I read the last chapter twice because it was so dramatic,' said Emma.

'Will you be going to see the film when it opens in the West End?' asked Jonathan.

'Yes, but it'll be ages, they haven't finished making it yet,' said Emma. 'Not that I mind, I wanted to read the book first.'

'Have Mr and Mrs Potter read it?' asked Jonathan.

'Who?' said Emma.

'Your mum and dad,' said Jonathan. 'Are there any others?'

'Any other what?'

'Potters,' said Jonathan. 'Brothers and sisters.'

'Excuse me,' said Emma, 'but I don't talk to strange chaps about my family, I've already told you so.'

'I meant to ask you yesterday, does your family call you Trudy?'

'Will you stop asking questions?'

'Well, could I just ask you one more?' said Jonathan.

'What's one more?' Emma eyed him suspiciously.

'Why did the cannibal want to be a detective?'

'All right,' sighed Emma, 'why?'

'So's he could grill his suspects,' said Jonathan.

'Oh, someone help me,' gasped Emma.

'What d'you want help for?' asked Jonathan.

'Terrible jokes like that kill me,' said Emma.

'They're supposed to make you laugh,' said Jonathan. 'Laughing's good for people. Could I just have a quick look at the book?' Silently, Emma handed the novel to him, and because it was so thick he opened it at the last page. He whistled. 'Bless my mum's Monday washing,' he said, 'a thousand and forty-seven pages. Trudy, have you read right through it?'

'Yes, I started at the beginning and went right through to the end,' said Emma, watching him as he turned pages. She decided he actually did have a country look with his healthy complexion, firm features and strong-looking shoulders. He made her think of breeches, leggings, haystacks and stiles. And straw.

'That be downright sensible, starting at the beginning,' he said. 'Shows you're all there, that does, Trudy.'

'Oh, you chump,' said Emma, 'you don't suppose anyone starts at the middle of a book, do you?'

'My dad read an old picture book once,' said Jonathan, still leafing through Emma's novel, 'and he started at the middle. Mind, it was when he was young.'

'But wasn't he taught at school to start at the beginning?' asked Emma.

'Oh, he was taught that all right,' said Jonathan, 'but with this old book, he couldn't. All the front pages were torn out up to the middle.'

'I'm going home,' said Emma.

'Home? Not back to your work?' said Jonathan.

'No, I'm going home to lie down before you send me completely potty,' said Emma. Jonathan laughed. 'What's funny?' she asked.

'You are,' he said. 'Good for a laugh, you are,

Trudy, and laughing's right for people, it's like medicine. My dad's had fits of laughter all his life, and you never saw anyone healthier. Same with my mum. When Dad laughs, she laughs. So they never have to see a doctor.'

The two girls from another bench came by. They stopped and one said, 'What you got there, Jonathan?'

'A book,' he said.

'Why, is it for yer bedtime, then?' asked the other girl.

'With her readin' it to yer?' asked the first girl, and they both shrieked as they went on.

'I don't think much of your acquaintances,' said Emma.

'Don't let them worry you,' said Jonathan, nose in the book.

'Here, what d'you think you're doing?' asked Emma.

'Just reading a few lines of the first chapter,' said Jonathan.

'Well, that's not good manners,' said Emma.

'Couldn't help myself,' said Jonathan. He closed the book and gave it back to her, which made Emma feel a bit small.

'No, it's all right, you can read the first chapter, if you want,' she said. 'I'll just sit here.'

'I couldn't let you do that,' said Jonathan, 'it's up to me to get you talking.'

'I don't want you to get me talking,' said Emma.

'Best if you try,' said Jonathan. 'That'll soon put you in the way of talking naturally to all kinds of people.'

'Go on, read the first chapter,' said Emma, and returned the book to him. He opened it again, and Emma sat saying nothing while he entered the realms of the first chapter. Time went by and she still didn't say a word. She was watching him. He gave the book back to her again when he'd finished the chapter.

'That's going to be a really good story,' he said.

'Yes, it's marvellous all the way through,' she said.

'One thing about Scarlett O'Hara, she's hardly shy,' said Jonathan.

'More like a brazen hussy,' said Emma. 'Well, I've got to get back to my job now.'

'So have I,' said Jonathan. 'Will you bring some lunch here again tomorrow?'

'No, of course not,' said Emma, 'I go home to lunch when I don't go to Lyons. It was just the sunshine that made me buy a lunch box today. Still, I had a nice quiet time while you were reading.' She came to her feet. So did Jonathan. 'I'll say goodbye now.'

'Goodbye, Trudy,' he said, 'but don't be afraid to talk to people. All the best. Oh, and thanks for letting me read the first chapter.'

'That's all right,' said Emma.

They parted, Emma carrying her handbag and her book. Jonathan liked the way she walked, athletic and sure-footed. No one would have thought there goes a shy girl.

'Mr Adams, sir, I'm here,' said Emma, entering Boots's office a few minutes after her return from lunch. There was always some afternoon dictation as well as morning, since the midday post was never light. The other shorthand-typist was already taking dictation from Sammy.

'In a formal mood, are we, Miss Somers?' said Boots.

'Respectful,' said Emma.

'I'll accept that,' said Boots, who had been engrossed in details of a revised tender Sammy had roughed out for the Ministry of Defence. 'Sit down, respectful one.'

Emma smiled. Uncle Boots always went along with the little quirks of his nieces and nephews, and would always lend an ear to any of them.

'Could I tell you something, Uncle Boots?'

'I'm listening,' said Boots.

'I've met the oddest young man ever, he comes from Sussex and is as potty as a parrot.'

'Is that the one who deafened you on Monday?'

'Yes, that's him,' said Emma, and went into detail about her meetings with Jonathan Hardy and how he was trying in all kinds of peculiar ways to make her part of his life.

'Hold on,' said Boots, 'you told him you were shy?'

'Well, I had to discourage him,' said Emma, 'but instead it's made him think he ought to do a Boy Scout act and help to cure me.'

'How do you manage the shy business?' asked Boots.

'Lord knows,' said Emma. 'What d'you think's the best way of putting Jonathan Hardy off for good?'

Boots did a little musing. Her sister Annabelle had asked for his advice when she met Nick. She'd been seventeen at the time, as Emma was now.

'Well, if you don't put him off, Emma,' he said, 'what's Donald going to say?'

'Crikey, yes, I'd better put him right off,' said Emma. 'Well, I suppose I can do that by making sure he doesn't bump into me again. By the way, because he asked nosy questions I told him my name was Gertrude Potter.'

'You did what?' said Boots.

'Told him my name was Gertrude Potter.'

'Heaven help you, Emma,' said Boots.

'He calls me Trudy,' said Emma.

'Jesus give me strength,' said Boots. 'Shall we try to do some work?'

'Please commence, Mr Adams, sir,' said Emma, pencil poised over her notebook.

Boots smiled. Emma would survive, even if a certain Jonathan Hardy went under.

Chapter Eight

'*Gone With The Wind*, well, I never did,' said Jemima at suppertime.

'Nor me, I never did, neither,' said young Jonas.

'Don't be rude,' said Jane.

'Letting you read the first chapter, this girl must like you, Jonathan,' said Jemima, serving out hot rabbit pie.

Jane, receiving her plate of rabbit pie, new potatoes and a little green hill of steaming garden peas, said, 'What about the next chapter?'

'Oh, I'll have to wait till sometime in 1941 for that and the rest,' said Jonathan.

'Well, that's not right,' said Jane, 'she could let you read a chapter a day, this girl Trudy, couldn't she?'

'Only by arrangement,' said Jonathan.

'Well, you could make the arrangement with her, couldn't you?' said Jane.

'Not easily, unless I see her again,' said Jonathan.

'You mean you haven't even arranged that?' said Jane.

'I told you, she's shy about making friendships,' said Jonathan.

'She's daft,' said Jennifer.

'Sometimes,' said Job, 'a young man needs to be firm with a girl.'

'Maybe our Jonathan don't be a firm young man yet,' said Jennifer, 'just someone in long trousers.'

'Jonathan looks a firm young man to me,' said Jemima.

'Mums be soft about sons,' said Jennifer.

'Mum's not soft about me,' said young Jonas, 'whacked me bottom with a brush yesterday.'

'Only after you knocked her best basin off the table and broke it,' said Jane.

'I didn't break it,' protested young Jonas, 'floor did.'

'The film will be showing in the West End,' said Jemima.

'What film?' asked Job.

'*Gone With The Wind*,' said Jemima with a sweetly sly smile.

'Ah,' said Job, 'that's a hint to Jonathan, I reckon.'

'Not much of one, seeing the film probably won't be showing till next year,' said Jonathan.

'Still, you could ask her if she'd like to go with you when it does come out,' said Jane.

'I'll wait,' said Jonathan, 'and if I happen to run into her sometime next year, I'll ask her then. Will that suit all of you?'

'I'm sure you'll see her before then,' said Jemima.

'Girl like that and all,' said Job.

'Like what?' asked Jennifer.

'Like it's the first one Jonathan's ever talked about,' said Job. 'Must be a bit special, eh, Jemima?'

'Must be,' said Jemima.

'Look, we're not that kind of friends,' said Jonathan. 'It's all one to her whether she sees me again or not.'

'Like to be good friends, though, would you, Jonathan?' asked Jemima.

'Not much good if he's too much of a skinflint to ask her to the pictures,' said Jane.

'I don't reckon Jonathan be that,' said Job. 'He's been brought up to put his hand in his pocket when it's called for, like a right-minded chap should. Don't hold with skinflints in my family. Don't mind saucy girls too much, nor ones that go kissing chaps under the mistletoe when Christmas has gone by.'

'Dad, I never did,' said Jane.

'Saw you,' said Job. 'In the parlour with young Joe Morgan from down the street well after Christmas was over.'

Blushing, Jane said, 'Not fair, looking.'

'But I said I didn't mind too much, didn't I?' smiled Job. 'Jemima, you reckon Jonathan ought to ask this girl of his to come and have Sunday tea with us?'

'Oh, I'll make her welcome whenever Jonathan wants,' said Jemima.

'Can't I make it clear to everyone that Trudy isn't my girlfriend, just someone I know?' said Jonathan. 'And that I'm not likely to see her again? Haven't I already said all that?'

'Well, so you have, Jonathan,' said Job, 'so you have.'

'Jane's waiting to be asked to the pictures,' said Jennifer.

'Me?' said Jane.

'Jane might ask her mum if she could go, if young Joe Morgan asked her,' said Job, and laughed. Young Joe Morgan, seventeen, was an improvement on Alfie Hardcastle. 'Tidy old problem we've got here, Jonathan wanting to ask a girl that he might not see again, and Jane not being asked when she wants to be.'

'Mantelpiece be rocking, Dad,' said young Jonas.

'Little old devil's awake, is he?' said Job.

'Sounds like he wants to be asked himself,' said Jonathan, and got up just in time to save things sliding off the mantelpiece. 'That was a tidy load of old rhubarb you just spoke about me and Jane, Dad,' he said.

Job roared with laughter, and that started everyone else off. The kitchen vibrated familiarly.

There was a knock on the street door as the supper things were being cleared from the table. Jennifer answered.

'Watcher, Jennifer,' said young Joe Morgan from down the street, 'is your mum in?'

'What for?' asked Jennifer.

'What d'yer mean, what for?' asked Joe, a respectable young working bloke.

'What d'you want to know if she's in for?'

'I want to ask her if I can take Jane to the Kennington flicks in fifteen minutes,' said Joe.

'Well, I'm blessed,' said Jennifer, and turned. 'Mum,' she yelled, 'can Joe Morgan from down the street take Jane to the Kennington pictures in fifteen minutes?'

'That's it,' said Joe, 'let ev'ryone in Walworth know.'

Jemima appeared from the kitchen, Jane behind her.

'What's this, young Joe?' she asked.

''Ello, Mrs 'Ardy, how's yourself?' said Joe. 'I see Jane's lurkin' behind you there. Might I cart her off to the Prince's Picture Palace in Kennington? I cashed a postal order from my Aunt Glad today, and as that's made me a bit flush, I'd be pleased to treat Jane.'

'She's still at school,' said Jemima. 'Still, do 'ee want to go, Jane?'

Jane considered the offer.

'He's come up with it very sudden,' she said.

'Don't want to go, then?' smiled Jemima.

'Well, I could get ready in time if it'll please him,' said Jane.

'It'll please me fine,' said Joe.

'Come in, Joe, and wait in our kitchen while Jane's getting ready,' said Jemima.

Ten minutes later, Joe and Jane were away to the cinema, and Job was saying to Jonathan there you are, some young girls didn't mind a bit about being asked out to the pictures.

Depends on the girl, said Jonathan.

Later that evening, Susie spoke to Sammy.

'Mr Winston Churchill hasn't replied to my letter yet, Sammy.'

'Well, it's only been a few days,' said Sammy, 'and I daresay he's a bit busy. Give him time.'

'Our *Daily Mail* says Hitler has done some good things for Germany.'

'Such as, Susie?'

'Such as doin' away with unemployment in Germany,' said Susie.

'Well, I suppose that's good,' said Sammy.

'Yes, but what's he doin' for the people in Czechoslovakia?' asked Susie.

'Susie, you're gettin' a bit political lately,' said Sammy.

'I'm gettin' worried, you mean,' said Susie.

'Well, I tell you, Susie, Hitler's not good for business.'

'Or for all our families,' said Susie.

Susie's sister Sally was also worried. She'd been married to Horace Cooper for four years. They had a three-year-old son, William, and she was expecting their second child in four months. Horace was a professional cricketer with the Surrey County cricket team at a salary of two hundred and fifty pounds a year. Princely. Anything like a war would be doom and gloom. For a start, there'd be no county cricket. And Horace, not yet twenty-nine, would probably be called up, even though he was a husband and father. Blow that, thought Sally.

She refrained from talking to Horace about her worries. He seemed to have none himself. Whenever he referred to Hitler, he did so in his

cheerful way, putting him on a par with an intoxi-
cated trapeze performer due to fall off the high
wire and break his neck any day now.

They often entertained Freddy and Cassie to
Sunday tea, along with Chrissie and Danny
Thompson, and Nick and Annabelle, and all the
children. Chrissie, known as Dumpling, and as
roundly endowed as ever, never considered Hitler
worth a mention. She was still mad about football.
She was the mother of two boys, one four and the
other two, which she complained had come about
because Danny couldn't always keep his mind on
things that really mattered, like her beloved football team. He had too many soppy moments, the
kind that had ruined her own footballing career.
However, she was still on the football team's
committee, and had been made secretary, which
was a sort of dream come true for her and a happy
consolation for what Danny had done to her when
she had her eyes shut, good as.

At these Sunday teas, she treated everyone to all
the latest news concerning the Browning Street
Rovers, and that always included sad references to
the fact that Nick had resigned from the team on
account of family commitments. Football had lost
a really heroic team captain, she said, a bloke who
was naturally bossy and made to order people
about.

Dumpling didn't allow anyone to mention
Hitler. Danny made the mistake of doing so once,
and Dumpling thumped him when she got him
home.

Dumpling had her head buried in the sand.

Down there she could only see images of her football team and herself playing centre forward.

One thing she was sure of. Hitler would never have made a footballer.

In the handsome Red Post Hill house occupied by the senior Adams family, General Sir Henry Simms, still on the active list at a spruce and sprightly sixty-four, was received that evening by Boots and Mr Finch.

'Where can we talk?' asked Sir Henry.

'In the study?' suggested Mr Finch.

'Your den? That'll do,' said Sir Henry.

'With some malt whisky?' said Boots.

'I'm your man,' smiled Sir Henry, his regard for Boots always high, his knowledge of Mr Finch something that made him aware of his value to the country in times like these.

In the study, each man with a whisky, Sir Henry outlined the Army's attitude to the danger posed by Hitler's ambitions. War, he said, was now inevitable. Inevitable, yes, said Mr Finch, if Hitler decided to put Case White into operation. Case White was Hitler's secret memorandum detailing how Poland would be invaded and crushed in the shortest possible time, with the German *Luftwaffe* destroying the major cities in advance of the German Army. Mr Finch, along with the top echelon of British Intelligence, knew of Case White. He had helped to secure a copy. Prime Minister Neville Chamberlain preferred to pray that after Czechoslovakia, even Hitler would not invade Poland. All the same, he had pledged support for Poland, which would mean Britain going to war with Germany in the event of Case White being implemented. Chamberlain hoped the pact with Poland would deter Hitler.

Sir Henry said whatever the hopes and prayers of the Prime Minister, the Army had no illusions. It had to prepare for war, and wanted new tanks, guns and other assault weapons by the hundred. It also wanted an impressive intake of listed officers and Territorial NCOs with experience of the Great War. Such men would be in their forties now.

'You're one such man, of course, Boots,' said Sir Henry, 'and you're on Officers' Reserve.'

'Are you suggesting I've got something special to offer after years at a desk?' asked Boots.

'Give me credit, Boots, for knowing something about you that doesn't relate to your desk,' said Sir Henry. 'It's been eighteen years since we first met.'

'And it's been longer than that since you and I first got to know each other, Boots,' said Mr Finch.

'So you both know me,' said Boots. 'Is there an implication there's something in the wind that's going to surprise me?'

'I'm supposed to be retiring in September,' said Mr Finch.

'Supposed to be?' said Boots.

'That's being delayed,' said Mr Finch. 'I shall be going to France and then to Poland. I'll be leaving next month. Your mother will almost certainly want both of us to write a letter of protest to the Prime Minister, and when that doesn't work, she'll expect you, after I've left, to visit Downing Street, knock loudly on the door of Number

Ten and beard the Prime Minister personally. Unfortunately, that won't work, either. What has been asked of me, I shall do.' He smiled. 'Must do,' he added. 'Since I'm fit enough and in the right frame of mind, I've no reservations about undertaking one more service abroad for this old but admirable country of ours.'

That was spoken without effort, although, as Boots knew, he was German-born, a man who had been an agent for Imperial Germany before and during the Great War, mostly as a brilliant undercover man in England. But he became disillusioned with Germany, and eventually, after much heart-burning, he changed sides. He became a British national and entered British Intelligence as a master of his craft. His loyalty and devotion to his adopted country had never wavered. Nor had his feelings for Chinese Lady and her family.

Of all of them, Boots alone knew his stepfather's secrets.

'I can't say your orders surprise me, Edwin,' Boots said, 'but looking at the three of us, are we representative of the best the country can offer?' His smile had its familiar whimsical touch. 'I mean, we're a little aged, aren't we?'

'We'll exclude you,' said Mr Finch.

'You could, if I were twenty, or even thirty,' said Boots.

'For the moment, for the next year or two, age is irrelevant,' said Sir Henry. 'It doesn't, in my judgement, affect what we have to offer. Boots, allow me to suggest you go into uniform next month.'

'Good God,' said Boots, 'is the Army that hard-up?'

'If the war arrives this year,' said Sir Henry, 'I hope to be given command of a corps, mainly because of my Great War record. I escaped the odium of being classed as a butcher.' Sir Henry indeed had been almost alone among the generals in criticizing Haig to his face for sending thousands of men to be slaughtered in the mud of the trenches. For that he had lost all chance of being promoted to a higher command. 'I'm in my sixties, but have remained on the active list, despite attempts to put me in a wheelbarrow and deposit me on the rubbish heap of redundant generals. It's useful in any walk of life to have certain friends, and, in my case, a sympathetic Secretary of War. I count myself as mentally agile still. Further, I've contributed a paper on tank warfare which I feel updates the tactics of the Great War. Haig, unfortunately, never had much faith in tanks. They couldn't gallop and one couldn't put a saddle on them. General Ironside, our present Chief of Staff, has a different view. Where was I?' Sir Henry swallowed the last of his whisky. 'Oh, yes, I'd like you in uniform next month, Boots, or at least sometime early in August, since there'll be a place for you on my staff.'

'I thought this little meeting was meant to be serious,' said Boots.

'It is serious,' said Sir Henry, 'and I, personally, am damned serious.'

'Sir Henry,' said Boots, 'I've no experience of

being an officer, let alone experience of corps staff work.'

'Boots,' said Mr Finch, 'I've no experience at all of soldiering, either in the field or behind the lines, but since I think, as Sir Henry does, that a new war against Germany will be nothing like that of the Great War, your – um – ignorance means you'll be totally receptive to fresh ideas.'

'Precisely,' said Sir Henry. 'I want you on my staff, Boots, and mean to have you. But take a little time to think things over.'

'Emily won't like it,' said Boots.

'In a couple of months, Boots,' said Sir Henry, 'there's going to be all kinds of things the whole country won't like. We shall be at war, believe me.'

Sir Henry had left. Boots strolled into the garden, thinking. He saw Eloise, his French daughter, sauntering slowly around arm in arm with a young man. Eloise, twenty-two now, had acquired self-assurance, due to her life among the very self-assured Adams men and women, and to her employment at the French Embassy in London. Mr Finch had helped to secure the post. He owned the right kind of connections. The young man presently engaging her apparently earnest attention was the son of a British Foreign Office secretary.

'Oh, hello, Papa,' called Eloise. She was like her half-brother Tim, with her dark brown hair and grey eyes, and both in that respect were like Boots. She was also almost perfect in her command of English, which included command of every aspirate, previously a weakness. 'Andrew is just leaving. Then I will play cribbage with you for sixpence a game.'

'Watch how she deals the cards, Mr Adams,' said Andrew Worth, 'or she'll have the shirt off your back.'

'What a terrible lie,' laughed Eloise. 'Do you wish me to tell you not to come again?'

'No, I don't wish that,' smiled Andrew. He said goodbye to Boots, and after Eloise had seen him out, she rejoined her father, sitting down at the white-painted iron garden table with him.

'Now we're together,' she said, 'you can tell me why you and Sir Henry and Grandpa locked yourselves away in the study this evening.'

'We shared what was left in that bottle of malt whisky,' said Boots.

'And what else?' smiled Eloise, who liked being his only daughter while Rosie was away at college.

'Oh, a slightly sober look at the immediate future,' said Boots.

'Ah, I know, you have been talking about that dreadful man Hitler,' said Eloise. 'He will interfere with everyone's future, the monster.'

'Not yours, I hope, Eloise.'

'Everyone's,' said Eloise. 'France is very gloomy.'

'Do you mean the French Embassy is gloomy?' asked Boots.

'No-one can see how to stop the monster, I think,' said Eloise. 'He is cunning, isn't he? He knows no-one wants war except himself, and so he's always speaking loudly of it to frighten France

120

and Britain into giving him what he wants. Are you worried, Papa?'

'I dislike thinking of how a war will affect young people like you and Tim and Rosie,' said Boots.

'We will have to fight as you did in the Great War when you were young,' said Eloise. 'Tim will fight for his country, yes, I will fight for France and England, and Rosie—' Eloise paused and smiled. 'Rosie will fight for you.'

'For me?' said Boots.

'Of course, you first of all,' said Eloise.

'What makes you say that?' asked Boots.

'Because her life is what you have made it,' said Eloise. 'Everything that is most precious to her is here. She has never interested herself in any man, no, not one.'

'She has several interesting men friends,' said Boots.

'And that is all they will ever be to her, just friends, yes,' said Eloise. 'Her father will never take your place with her. She has spent years at university, and is now spending more at her teachers' training college, but always flies home the moment her vacations begin. Papa, is that fair?'

'Fair?' said Boots.

'Yes, that you should have such a hold on her affections as to make a prisoner of her,' said Eloise. 'How unfair that her home is her cage. Yes, Papa, she is a prisoner because of your hold on her affections. Aren't you ashamed?'

'I'm speechless,' said Boots.

'But not vexed with me because I have said these things?'

'No, not vexed, Eloise, astonished,' said Boots.

'Well, you must think about it,' said Eloise. 'One day, Papa, Rosie will want to break her chains, and you must break them for her.'

Tim came out. Nearly eighteen, he was tall and slim, and very much like his father had been at that age.

'Anything interesting going on?' he asked.

'Oh, only a little talk,' said Eloise.

'Good,' said Tim, 'because Mum would like us all to play "Monopoly".'

'Ah, the game one cannot win unless one owns Mayfair,' said Eloise.

Emily appeared, her dark auburn hair catching the evening light. She was carrying a cardboard box. She'd become addicted to 'Monopoly'.

'We're all goin' to play, aren't we?' she said.

'Nobody's busy doing anything else,' said Tim.

So they began the game in the warm air of the evening, and in a very competitive spirit. Neither Emily nor Tim would have dreamt that Boots was attempting to come to terms with all that Eloise had said about his relationship with Rosie, for he seemed his usual humorous self, even on the occasions when he was in gaol.

Rosie a prisoner in the family cage?

Rosie?

Emma collared her father in their garden. Ned, despite his artificial left leg, a metallic souvenir of the Great War, was effectively mobile as the family's chief gardener. He was hoeing at the moment.

'Daddy,' said Emma, 'what's your idea of a country yokel?'

'Country yokel?' said Ned.

'Yes, how do you see one?' asked Emma.

'By looking,' said Ned, forty-four and with little crow's-feet beginning to develop.

'No, I don't mean that, you silly,' said Emma, 'I mean, do you see one as a kind of simple bloke?'

'Far from it,' said Ned, 'real country people live close to the land and can't afford to be simple. They might not know how to run Battersea's power station, but they know how to keep the rest of us from starving.'

'I know someone from the country who seems to be trying to talk himself into becoming my best friend,' said Emma, and told her dad about Jonathan Hardy and his particular line of chat in his endeavours to pick her up.

'Well, he doesn't sound a simple bloke,' said Ned, 'he sounds a bit of a lad. Are you sure he's trying to pick you up?'

'Yes, of course I am,' said Emma, 'I won a bathing beauty contest at Salcombe last year, didn't I?'

'Granted,' said Ned. 'You met him in Lyons, you say?'

'He met me by sitting at my table and insisting on talking to me,' said Emma.

'You could put that down to the possibility that you were the first bathing beauty winner he'd ever seen,' said Ned. 'By the way, does Donald know that this young man from rural Sussex is following you about in a manner of speaking?'

'He knows about him,' said Emma, 'but if he

knew everything, he'd probably come up from the City one lunchtime and sort Jonathan Hardy out. Actually, though, it won't be necessary. I'm keeping out of the way in future. I just thought it might amuse you to know what's been happening to me at lunchtimes. When I told Mum ten minutes ago, she said she liked country people, but not the kind who try to pick girls up. As for Donald, now I've finished *Gone With The Wind*, I'll have to drop a hint to him about taking me to see the film.'

'Film?' said Ned.

'When it opens in the West End,' said Emma.

'Well, that seems the next natural step for the distant future,' said Ned.

'Yes, I'll phone Donald about it,' said Emma.

'Good hunting,' said Ned.

'You mean good hinting,' said Emma, and whisked away.

'Tommy,' said Mrs Vi Adams, 'did you know your nephew Bobby has just been made up to full bombardier in the Territorials? Lizzy told me so today.'

'Flamin' arrows of fire,' said Tommy Adams, a handsome stalwart of thirty-nine.

'Now, Tommy,' said Vi, 'you could say something nicer than that.'

'I could, but I don't feel like it,' said Tommy. 'Two stripes'll put Bobby smack in the front line with the regulars, if something nasty crops up. He'll probably get transferred from the Territorials straight into the regulars. And the way things are goin', I'm against any Adams havin' to 'suffer what Boots suffered in the Great War.'

'Bobby's a Somers,' said Vi.

'Same thing, seeing Lizzy's his mum and Ned's always been as good as an Adams,' said Tommy.

'I'm sure Ned would thank you for that compliment,' smiled Vi.

'I didn't originate it meself,' said Tommy, 'it came from Chinese Lady years ago. She's always been fond of Ned, and regards him as one of her own.'

'Anyway, Bobby won't have to fight in a war,' said Vi, 'because there won't be one.'

'What makes you so sure?' asked Tommy.

'Because I don't want one,' said Vi, 'and nor do all the other wives and mothers of this country.'

Tommy let that go. He didn't want to make Vi fret by advertising his pessimism.

Bobby, the elder son of Lizzy and Ned Somers, was in his nineteenth year. Tall, like his dad and his uncles, and his cousin Tim, he had broad shoulders, a sturdy ribcage and muscular limbs. His dark brown hair, a feature of the children and grandchildren of Corporal Daniel Adams, Chinese Lady's first husband, had the same deep tones as his mother's chestnut crown. His features promised to be rugged rather than handsome, and he was noted for the fact that he was as resolute as his square chin implied. Having targeted an objective, he would go for it with single-minded purpose. He was a natural as a Territorial.

He had been awarded the stripes of a full

bombardier at the drill hall ceremony last night, and this evening Lizzy was sewing them to the arms of his uniforms. Bobby had said he was supposed to do that himself. Lizzy said there were things a man had to do, and things a woman had to do, and anyone who tried to change that would only mess up the natural order of the Lord's world. That made Bobby grin, and it also made his dad, now in from the garden, hide his face behind his newspaper. Ned did a lot of hiding his face behind newspapers, simply because Lizzy was a bit of a scream whenever she chose to sound like Chinese Lady, Bobby's revered grandma. As far as Chinese Lady was concerned, sewing was one of the many vocations God ordered in a wife and mother, while husbands and fathers were born to provide, and the one should not interfere with the other. Bobby knew of his grandma's strict beliefs, and he also knew that his mum concurred with them, so he let her do the sewing.

Using her needle with expertise, Lizzy said, 'Your dad and me are quite proud you've earned two stripes, Bobby, but we want you to know you're not to take this sort of thing too serious. We both hope promotion only means you can enjoy playing at soldiers a little bit more.'

Bobby tottered.

'Playing at soldiers?' he said hoarsely. 'Playing?'

'Well, that's what the Territorials do, don't they?' said Lizzy.

'Mum, don't make me leave home,' said Bobby.

'Why, have I said something?' asked Lizzy. 'Have I, Ned?'

Ned buried himself deeper in his newspaper and croaked, 'What was that, Eliza?'

'Ned Somers,' said Lizzy, 'when Bobby joined the Territorials, you told me it was only like young men playing at being Boy Scouts.'

'Did I?' said Ned.

'I wouldn't have let him join if I'd thought there was anything serious about it,' said Lizzy. 'Bobby, you don't actu'lly fire guns or anything, do you?'

'Just water pistols,' said Ned.

'I'm askin' Bobby,' said Lizzy. She looked up. 'What d'you mean, water pistols? I'm not daft, I'll have you know.'

'I do know, Eliza,' said Ned.

'Bobby,' said Lizzy, 'I hope – where's that young man gone?'

'I think he slipped out,' said Ned.

'Well, I only wanted to know if being in the Territorials is serious or not,' said Lizzy.

Ned came out from behind his paper and looked soberly at his still extremely personable wife.

'I think you do know, Eliza,' he said, and Lizzy had a few quiet seconds.

'I try to think Hitler's a joke,' she said.

'So do I, Eliza, and don't we all?' said Ned.

Chapter Nine

'Emma, are you comin' home for lunch today?' asked Lizzy the following morning.

'Yes, Mum,' said Emma.

'Good,' said Lizzy, 'I'll do a nice ham salad just for you and me.'

'Thanks,' said Emma. 'I'm off now. 'Bye, Mum, see you lunchtime. Come on, Edward.'

'Come on?' said Edward. 'I happen to be pointed at the door and waiting.'

'Oh, you poor old thing, is it hurting your legs?' said Emma.

That morning, the spacious flat situated above two shops in Lower Marsh was the scene of a heated domestic disagreement. Mr Benjamin Goodman, bookmaker, and his wife Rachel were locked in verbal strife. Benjamin, although growing a little portly at thirty-nine, was quite an impressive-looking man. Rachel, nearly thirty-seven, was a lush and velvety beauty. Benjamin was a husband who, while he didn't favour a meek and mild wife, at least expected her to be compliant enough to fall in with any important decision it was necessary for him to make. In advising her that he had decided to apply on behalf of the family for entry into the USA as immigrants because of the infamous anti-Semitic developments in Europe, he had been prepared for a reasonable catalogue of ifs and buts. He had not been prepared for downright opposition.

With her two young girls at school, and her father, the renowned Isaac Moses, out on business, there was nothing to hold Rachel back from making her opposition heard in no uncertain fashion. She would not go, she said, nor would the children. If an entry visa comes through, said Benjamin, we will all go.

'We won't,' said Rachel.

'A man should listen to his wife paying no respect to his standing?' said Benjamin.

'I always pay respect to your standing,' said Rachel, 'but no-one of any sense would approve of my paying respect to your foolishness. Leave our home and our country to go to America? Are we poor people of Poland or Russia? Such people have always looked elsewhere, have always sought to escape their ghettos. Do we live in a ghetto, do we have no belongings, no friends, nor even running water? And are our children denied education?'

'My life,' said Benjamin, 'words come from a woman in dozens, where a man would make do with a few.'

'A dozen words from a woman are worth a hundred from a man,' said Rachel. 'We have more common sense. I am not going to America, nor are our children. I will chain myself and them to the statue of Nelson in Trafalgar Square first, and cry out to the people that this is what my foolish husband has made me do.'

'Woman,' said Benjamin, grinding his teeth, 'the people will laugh at you. They'll laugh because you'll have made a spectacle of yourself and because you are Jewish.'

'There are people in every country, even here, who are sick with ignorance and prejudice,' said Rachel heatedly, 'but in England I was born and in England I shall stay. So should you, for you are English-born too, and both of us can walk the streets and see many more friends than people of prejudice.'

'Rachel, Rachel, calm yourself, and listen to me,' said Benjamin. 'Europe will go up in flames before the year is out, and who will suffer most? Our people. It's always the same. We are blamed for wars and for every economic crisis. We'll be safe nowhere, so we must put ourselves a long way from all that we'll be blamed for. America is more open, more tolerant, and better for business.'

Rachel raised her hands and lifted angry eyes to the ceiling.

'Listen to my husband. Did any woman have a more blind one? There are a thousand closed doors to Jewish people in America. My life, don't you know that? Then speak to my father, who has relatives out there.'

'Your father has relatives everywhere,' said Benjamin sourly. 'Let's have the truth of your reluctance, woman. It's associated with Sammy

Adams. Don't think I don't know. You call me blind, but I haven't been as blind as that all these years. But I've said nothing, because should a man take a stick to a woman who has been a good wife and a faultless mother, even if she loves someone else?'

A flush surfaced to spread over Rachel's face, but her eyes did not drop, and nor did she weaken in any way.

'I've known Sammy Adams longer than I've known you,' she said, 'but nothing in all that time has ever happened that would cause me to cover my head in shame for a single moment.'

'Now I should listen to you absolving yourself of the guilt of loving another man?' said Benjamin. 'But no, I don't quarrel with you over that, only over your disobedience as my wife.'

'Disobedience?' said Rachel.

'What else does your attitude mean?' asked Benjamin. 'You speak of our life in England—'

'I speak of it because I love my country,' said Rachel.

'And Sammy Adams.'

'Leave him out of it,' said Rachel.

'England is the country of Mosley's Blackshirts,' said Benjamin, 'and his Blackshirts will do to our people here the same kind of thing Hitler's Nazis are doing to our people in Germany. Mosley's Fascist thugs are fighting running battles with the Jewish people of the East End every day.'

'But the British police are not standing by as the German police do,' said Rachel, 'and nor will the British Government tolerate the Blackshirts indefinitely. Parliament is already demanding an outright ban. Benjamin, we live in the birthplace of democracy, not in a dictatorship. My father will never leave the country he was born in, and nor will I. If a war comes, do you think I would want to be in America? No, I should want to be here, so that I could fight for England in my own way.'

Benjamin figuratively tore his hair at having to endure such rebelliousness. Was it right, he said, that a good Jewish wife should put her misguided interests before the sensible family plans of her husband? He pointed out, loudly, that Britain was in no position to fight a war with Germany, that if such a war came, Britain would lose, and the Jewish-hating Himmler would swamp the country with men of the Gestapo. Mosley and his Blackshirts would help them to root out every Jewish person in the land. There were terrible stories coming out of Germany about what the Gestapo did to captive Jews, young and old along with all others. Did Rachel wish their daughters to fall into the hands of such barbarians?

Rachel requested him to stop shouting at her. Benjamin responded that he was applying for exit visas to America for all of them, that all would go and that was that. So saying, he left for his office, slamming doors behind him.

Rachel looked at the clock. The time was coming up to ten. At twelve noon, her daughters would arrive home from school for their midday meal.

At half-past ten, Emma went into her Uncle Sammy's office.

'Uncle Sammy, Mrs Goodman would like to see you,' she said.

'Mrs Goodman, the female married person?' said Sammy, up to his eyes as usual, and committed, at eleven-thirty, to making a journey to the firm's second factory in Shoreditch.

'Yes, that's the lady, Uncle Sammy,' said Emma.

'Ask her to step in,' said Sammy.

In came Rachel, and Emma closed the door on her Uncle Sammy and the lady who had been his one and only girlfriend during the days of his youth. Sammy came to his feet.

'Mrs Goodman, I presume?' he said.

'Correct, Sammy,' said Rachel, superb in a light summer costume and brimmed hat.

'Take a pew,' said Sammy, and Rachel sat down. 'Upon me soul,' he said, 'might I point out you're as decorative as ever was?'

Rachel, who thought in turn that he was just as electric in his looks and vitality, made a little face and said, 'I don't feel decorative, Sammy, I feel desperate.'

'Desperate?' said Sammy.

'Desperate for help,' said Rachel. 'And since I know my father will tell me, however reluctantly, that a good wife must go along with her husband's wishes, I'm here in the hope you can think of a way out for me.'

'A way out of what?' asked Sammy.

'Emigration to America,' said Rachel. 'Benjamin has set his mind to it for all of us.'

'Here, hold on,' said Sammy, shocked, 'you're a valuable shareholder and director, and what's more, a fam'ly friend. You can't go to America, Rachel. It's full of cowboys, buffalo and film stars, not your style at all. Or mine.' He looked at his wristwatch. 'I'm pressed, of course, and it's against my principles, of course, to come between a married wife and her married husband, but could you give me the details in a few short words, Rachel?'

Rachel gave them, eloquently rather than briefly, such was her need for Sammy's understanding, although she said nothing about the accusation from Benjamin that it was Sammy she had always loved.

'I can't go,' she said at the end, 'my life and all my dearest friends are here. Sammy, if there's a war, you don't believe the Germans would win, do you?'

Sammy was silent for a while. While Boots for several years had been giving deep periodical thought to political developments in Europe, Sammy had been inclined to ignore the rise of Nazi Germany on the grounds that he couldn't afford to worry about Hitler while he had an ever-expanding business to run. He was forced now to concentrate seriously on Rachel's question before answering it. When he did so, his answer was honest.

'No, Rachel, I don't believe the Germans would win, because I don't believe they could carry out a successful invasion,' he said. 'I don't believe they could get past the Royal Navy, which they'd have to do to make any kind of worthwhile landin'. Napoleon thought about it, and ducked it. I learned that much at St John's Church School.

Might I pass you a consoling thought, Rachel? Which is that Chinese Lady has always believed the Lord made the English Channel to keep us safe from foreigners. Mind you,' he said, with a slight smile, 'that's only if we don't turn into heathens. We're all right while some of us still go to church and obey a fair percentage of the Ten Commandments.'

'Sammy, you're like two large spoonfuls of curative medicine,' said Rachel, 'but I still need help.'

'Well, Rachel me old and remarkable friend,' said Sammy, 'since Germany ain't goin' to get one jackboot over the white cliffs of Dover, Benjamin doesn't have to worry about us bein' swamped by the Gestapo. He can just keep his bookie's business running in line with the gee-gees.'

'I could deliver that information into his ear,' said Rachel, 'but it won't convince him. He's made up his mind that the Jewish people of this country are in as much danger as those in Germany.'

'Poor old Benjamin,' said Sammy. 'Nice bloke, but forgetful.'

'Forgetful of what?' asked Rachel.

'That he's got a good business, a remarkable lady wife, two fetchin' girls, and a chance of makin' a name for himself in the ranks of the ARP, which organization, I believe, is goin' to be formed to keep us out of the way of German bombs, if a war does arrive.'

'So how can we make him stay?' asked Rachel.

'Well, Rachel,' said Sammy, picking up the phone, 'suppose we ask Boots to do some of his renowned thinkin' for us?'

'Do that, Sammy,' said Rachel, and Sammy got through to Boots and requested the pleasure of his immediate company. Boots arrived in quick time.

'Hello, Boots lovey,' said Rachel.

'Same to you twice over,' said Boots, and kissed her cheek, and Rachel thought of all the Adams men and women, and of other Gentile friends like Polly Simms and Ned Somers and the Brown family. In the same way as Mr Eli Greenberg, she cherished them. 'Something's up, Sammy?' said Boots.

'A small problem,' said Sammy, looked at his watch again, and put Boots concisely in the picture.

'Tricky,' said Boots.

'That's not a good start,' said Sammy.

'Still tricky,' said Boots, 'husband and wife scenario.'

'Could you say that again?' asked Sammy.

'Husband and wife scenario,' said Boots. 'Decidedly tricky.'

'Sometimes,' said Sammy, 'I get a feelin' that that school we sent you to over-educated you. Don't use words like that when Rachel's got a nasty headache.'

'The point is,' said Boots, 'would it be fair or even halfway decent to do a friend's husband down?'

'No need to write a book about it,' said Sammy. 'Givin' Benjamin Goodman the chance to make a name for himself in a fight to the finish with Hitler is all of decent.'

'Granted, Sammy,' said Rachel with a faint smile.

'But could it be done, Boots?'

'It could if the American Embassy turned down Benjamin's application for an entry visa,' said Boots. 'In any case, America doesn't hand out visas like peanuts to would-be immigrants. It's the world's favourite place for immigration, and has to have quotas. I think there may be a way of persuading their Embassy to include Benjamin's application among those they turn down.'

'Boots, I've a feeling he's already applied,' said Rachel.

'Oh, it'll take time to process it,' said Boots. 'I'll have a word.'

'Holy Joe,' said Sammy, 'with the Embassy?'

'Hardly,' said Boots, 'I'm not acquainted with their Ambassador, Joseph Kennedy. I've someone else in mind. However, there's still the fact that it's going to be an attempt to give your husband a smack in the eye, Rachel. D'you want that?'

'I want us all to stay here, not to run off to America,' said Rachel, 'and I'll be able to shut my eyes to foul play, Boots.'

'Then leave it with me,' said Boots, and Rachel departed smiling and hopeful. Boots, looking at Sammy, said 'It's no go, of course.'

'No go?' said Sammy. 'But you told Rachel—'

'I know,' said Boots, 'but we can't interfere to that extent between husband and wife. On the other hand, we've known Rachel a long time, and I didn't want to give her an outright no. I didn't think I needed to, since I've an idea the American Embassy might issue a negative. But that kind of hope would only have been a straw in the wind for

Rachel. She needed something more positive in her present state of upset. Yes, as I said, I'll speak to someone.'

'What someone?' asked Sammy.

'Someone who'll know whether the answer's going to be definitely in her favour or not,' said Boots.

At lunchtime, Jonathan ate his sandwiches in the Green, along with acquaintances. There was no sign of Trudy all through his break. He quite missed her. He hadn't minded that she'd been on the defensive so much, or that she didn't see him as a promising friend. It had simply been enjoyable trying to be a help to her and bring her out socially. A girl like her could get to be a popular social asset. Funny about her shyness. Well, it never actually showed.

He thought about the buff envelope with its buff contents that had arrived for him by the first post this morning. It was a Government order to attend for a medical in the Southwark drill hall next Wednesday. He'd have to get time off for that. The medical, of course, was in connection with his call-up. His parents hadn't been too pleased, and his sisters had gone a little quiet, although Jane did say perhaps he'd fail the examination. The family all looked at him then, as if hoping to find he'd got a weak and hollow chest. Then his dad said, 'Well, this militia just be a precaution, I reckon.'

Jonathan, having told sniffy Spinks about it, decided the man looked happy for a change.

I think I've got life in the Army coming up, he

told himself. Hope it doesn't get rough and noisy.

Apart from that, he was philosophical about it, and it wouldn't break his heart to leave his job. Just one thing, though. He'd probably have to take his name off the library list for *Gone With The Wind*.

He went out for his lunch break on the dot the following day, ignoring the look cast at him by Mr Spinks. He didn't think he needed to take much further notice of that old geezer. He made for the Green, carrying a tin which contained a wrapped pork pie and two tomatoes, plus a little knife. There were some empty benches available, and he made himself comfortable on one, while leaving room for any acquaintances who might turn up. It was another fine day, with June still bestowing sunny light. Ladies' hats nodded behind tram windows, bus windows picked up golden dust, and blinds were drawn to shade shop windows. A chimney-sweep, looking no different with his black overalls, black bowler and sooty face, from the sweeps of his father's day, passed by pushing his barrow of canes and brushes.

Jonathan unwrapped his pie, placed it back in the tin and cut it into sections. His mum had said she didn't like to think of him eating it whole like a Walworth navvy, especially not in public. He ate a section with a bit of tomato.

A girl came in through the gate, carrying a handbag and a shopping bag. She had a very sprightly walk and looked attractive in a snowy white blouse and dark skirt. Hatless, her chestnut hair, springy with natural curls, caught the light of the sun. She passed Jonathan by without a glance.

'Hold on, isn't that you, Trudy?' he called.

Emma stopped and turned.

'Pardon?' she said.

'Still shy, are we?' smiled Jonathan.

'Oh, blow, it's you,' said Emma.

'Don't mind, do you?' said Jonathan.

'We weren't supposed to meet again,' said Emma.

'Yes, hard luck, I reckon,' said Jonathan. 'Still, now you're here, like to join me?' Emma looked at an empty bench. 'I wouldn't sit there if I were you,' said Jonathan, 'you'll get picked up.'

'It seems to happen all the time,' said Emma.

'Nowhere's safe for some girls,' said Jonathan, 'except where I am.'

'Except where you're not, you mean,' said Emma, 'but all right, I'll sit with you, as long as you understand I don't need talking to.'

'Yes, you do,' said Jonathan, as she sat down beside him. 'Any girl who spends her time trying to avoid people needs talking to. I suppose you nearly died, did you, when I joined you at your Lyons table last Monday?'

'Well, I did almost faint,' said Emma. 'What's that you've got in your lunch tin?'

'Pork pie,' said Jonathan. 'Like a piece?'

'No, thanks,' said Emma, 'I've got another Lyons lunch box.' She took it out of the carrier bag and opened it. In it were two sandwiches and an apple.

'You've got afters again,' said Jonathan.

'It's only an apple,' said Emma.

'Seems ages since I last saw you,' said Jonathan.

'It's only since Wednesday,' said Emma, beginning her first sandwich.

'What's today?' asked Jonathan.

'Friday,' said Emma.

'Feels like next week to me,' said Jonathan.

'Oh, dear, you do have trouble thinking straight, don't you?' said Emma.

'Well, you have your own troubles,' said Jonathan.

'I'm sure I'll get over them one day,' said Emma. 'By the way, I saw a real old-fashioned chimney sweep a few minutes ago, and he bowed to me.'

'I saw him too, when he was passing the Green,' said Jonathan, 'but he didn't bow to me.'

'Oh, I'm sorry,' said Emma.

'I'm the wrong shape, I reckon,' grinned Jonathan, still enjoying his pie.

Emma, finishing her first sandwich, said she supposed there'd always be chimney sweeps unless someone invented a chimney cleaning machine. Jonathan said that was a thoughtful remark for a girl to make. Emma said she didn't know she'd made it thoughtfully, it was just a remark. Jonathan said if an inventor had heard her, it could have given him the idea of inventing the right kind of machine. But that would put all the chimney sweeps out of work, said Emma. That's an even more thoughtful remark, observed Jonathan. Interesting, in fact. It's just common sense, declared Emma.

Jonathan said his mother had any amount of common sense, and Emma said most mothers did. It's my sincere opinion, said Jonathan, that it would be difficult to do without mothers.

'Oh, what a thoughtful remark to make,' said Emma, and Jonathan laughed.

'Came back at me there, didn't you, Trudy?' he said, 'You're getting better every day.'

'At what?' said Emma.

'Talking to a strange country chap,' said Jonathan, and laughed again.

'It's not all that funny,' said Emma.

'It's promising, though,' said Jonathan. 'Tell you what,' he went on blithely, 'I'll walk you back to your office when we've finished our sandwiches, and on the way we'll stop people and ask them what the time is or do they know where Denmark Hill is – something like that – and then get you chatting to them.'

'That's daft,' said Emma.

'Sounds sensible to me,' said Jonathan. 'Do you any amount of good.'

'You might think so, I don't,' said Emma.

'Still, we'll have a go.'

'We won't,' said Emma, eating her apple.

'Now, Trudy, you shouldn't turn down an offer of help.'

'Some help,' said Emma.

'We might not see each other again,' said Jonathan.

'It was an unfortunate accident, meeting today,' said Emma.

'There you are, then,' said Jonathan, 'this might be my last chance to let you see people like being talked to. We'll start the walk in five minutes.'

'You must think I'm as barmy as you are,' said Emma.

'It's a nice day for it,' said Jonathan.

'Blow that,' said Emma.

'In five minutes,' said Jonathan.

'Not in five minutes, nor ten, nor ever,' said Emma.

'Four minutes now,' said Jonathan, and finished the last of his pie.

An imp of a smile touched Emma's mouth for a fleeting moment.

Chapter Ten

Meanwhile, Boots had also found company for lunch. Or, rather, the company had found him. He was in the handsome saloon of the pub opposite the firm's offices, and had just ordered a glass of beer and a chicken sandwich from Joe, the white-hatted barman-chef, when someone slipped into the wall seat beside him, someone who brought a hint of delicate scent.

'Hello, darling,' murmured Polly Simms, neatly elegant in a tailored black costume and white blouse, with a little hat.

'You'll get me talked about,' said Boots, 'and why aren't you at school?'

'Oh, teachers have a lunch break too, old top,' said Polly, 'and we earn it and need it. I dashed over in the car in the hope you'd be here.' She knew Boots often took a light lunch in this pub by himself. Sammy, more often than not, indulged in business lunches. This was by no means the first time Polly had sneaked in on one of Boots's light pub meals. 'You're thrilled to see me, of course?'

'Overwhelmed,' said Boots. 'I hope it won't show when I get back to my office.'

Joe arrived with his beer and sandwich.

'I'll have the same,' smiled Polly, 'except a dry cider instead of a beer.'

'Will you oblige the lady, Joe?' asked Boots.

'Certainly, Mr Adams,' said Joe, and returned to his bar, where the white stands containing cold roast joints stood on the marble counter. The Edwardian-style saloon, favoured by Camberwell businessmen, was nearly full, but Polly felt cosily shut off with Boots.

'What's brought you here?' he asked.

'You, of course,' said Polly.

'After all these years,' said Boots, 'I'd have thought—'

'Don't mention years,' said Polly, 'I'm carrying too many, and agonizing over the fact that I'll soon be forty.'

Boots, who knew she was forty-two, smiled and said, 'The pain won't last, Polly.'

'It'll last for ever if it gives me wrinkles,' said Polly. 'Damn it, can't you grow a few in sympathetic advance?'

'I think a multitude are going to rush on me before the year's out,' said Boots.

'I know what you mean,' said Polly. 'Listen, old darling, have you decided to go into uniform next month?'

'You know about your father's conversation with me?' said Boots.

'Of course, every word,' said Polly, 'and I'd like to have an answer to my question.'

'I haven't spoken to Emily yet,' said Boots, 'so I haven't made a decision.'

'Oh, Emily,' said Polly.

'We usually decide things together,' said Boots.

'Stop talking like a stuffed shirt,' said Polly. 'Ye gods, why I'm still willing to be your favourite concubine is a mystery to me. Worse, in any case, is the fact that at my age I've gone past being voluptuous. That's compulsory in concubines, isn't it, O Sultan of a Thousand Nights? Are you laughing? I'm not.'

'Here's your sandwich and cider,' said Boots. Joe arrived with Polly's order. Boots paid him, added a generous tip, and Joe said once a gent always a gent, Mr Adams.

'About getting into uniform,' said Polly after a mouthful of cider, 'would you like to know I'm leaving my teaching job at the end of this term to attach my valuable self to the Army?'

'Say that again, Polly.'

'I'm going into the Auxiliary Territorial Service,' said Polly, 'since the Government's come off its *derrière* and is signalling its belated recognition of women and their worth in the event of another war.'

'I thought you'd had all the war you wanted in 14–18,' said Boots.

'That war, yes, up to here, old darling,' said Polly. 'This one is different. Hitler's the four horsemen of the Apocalypse rolled into one, and his Nazis are the world's worst swines. God, I pity the Germans for what they've done to themselves in falling for the oratory of Adolf Hitler, their mad Führer. They're helpless now. There's no way out for France and Britain except to stand up and fight sooner or later. It's going to be bloody, I know, but there's one thing that's comforting me.'

'And what's that?' asked Boots.

'Well, this time, in this new war, wherever you are, I'll be right behind you,' said Polly with her brittle smile.

'The balloon hasn't gone up yet,' said Boots.

'But it will,' said Polly.

'Yes, it will,' said Boots soberly.

'So you'll have to tell Emily you're getting into uniform, won't you?'

'It looks like it,' said Boots.

A warm hand pressed his knee, the hand of a woman who had never forgotten her comradeship with the Tommies of the trenches during the Great War. He thought of that war and the unimaginative commander, Haig, who had never been anywhere near the front line or ever visited a single hospital to talk to wounded men who had survived the slaughter he himself had initiated. It was as if he had never wanted to experience the discomfort of seeing the unspeakable conditions of the front or of coming face to face with the men of whom he continually asked the impossible.

If any new war was conducted by a similar type, thought Boots, a wholesale mutiny would be the only way of getting him replaced.

Emma and Jonathan were leaving the little oasis of Camberwell Green and entering the crowded walks close to the junction.

'Listen,' said Emma, 'you're not really going to stop people and get me to talk to them, are you?'

'Only one or two,' said Jonathan.

'Well, you'll be on your own,' said Emma.

'Where's your offices?' asked Jonathan.

'A little way up Denmark Hill,' said Emma, 'but I'll find my own way there.'

'Don't back out now,' said Jonathan, 'be brave. You're not going to die talking to people in the street about the price of coal or nightshirts.'

'Me do what?' said Emma.

'You'll find people interested in prices,' said Jonathan, with Emma wondering if he ought to be certified. 'Especially people in Walworth and Camberwell.'

'Me talk to strange people about the price of coal and nightshirts? Me?' said Emma.

'It needn't be nightshirts,' said Jonathan. 'Try the price of butter, say.'

'I'm glad this is definitely the last time I'm going to let you bump into me, because I could get to hate you,' said Emma.

'Don't see why, when I'm trying to help you,' said Jonathan, and stopped the next person who came their way, a large lady carrying a large shopping basket.

'Excuse me, missus,' he said, 'my friend be looking for Denmark Hill. Where by be it, do 'ee know?'

'Well, I ought to know,' said the large lady, and beamed at Emma. 'I've lived in Camberwell all me life, so's me old man, and Denmark Hill's still where it always was from when we was both born. My, 'ave yer come up from the country, young miss?'

'Me?' said Emma.

'Well, yer friend spoke a bit countrified, I thought.'

'Oh, well, yes, he's come up from darkest Sussex, poor chap,' said Emma, 'but I haven't.'

'Always liked Sussex, me and me old man,' said the large lady, 'specially Brighton. I see yer friend's got a Sussex complexion, sort of a bit russet, like. That's what I call it, russet. Is 'e yer country cousin?'

'No, he's just somebody's friend,' said Emma, with Jonathan giving her an encouraging look.

'Well, everyone ought to 'ave friends except that man 'Itler,' said the large lady. 'He ought to be trod on by elephants. Do 'im good, that would. Let's see—'

'My friend be wondering if coal's a mite expensive round this way,' said Jonathan.

'Well, I never,' said the large lady. She beamed again at Emma. 'My, fancy a girl like you already worrying 'erself about the price of coal. Well, it costs me and me old man a bit more than we can afford in the winter, and that ain't no lie. Is it the same with yer own fam'ly, might I hask?'

'Well, no,' said Emma. 'I mean, I've never heard them complain.'

Jonathan smiled, and the large lady said, 'Well, some people don't know 'ow to complain, ducky. Them mine-owners know that, they know a lot of people just put up with their prices. There ought to come a day when ev'ryone complains, and out loud. Well, I hasks yer, one and fourpence an 'undredweight and all.'

'Oh, yes, that does seem a lot,' said Emma.

'And you've got to burn fires in the winter or get terrible sharp pains in yer chilblains,' said the large lady. 'You got chilblains yet, ducky?'

'No, not yet,' said Emma.

'Well, I'm gratified for yer, I don't like girls your age to suffer,' said the large lady.

'Oh, she's a mite short on suffering, being young and healthy with a tidy old appetite,' said Jonathan. 'All she be bothered by is that she don't rightly know where she is.'

Emma struggled against hysterics.

'This is Camberwell Green, ducks,' said the large woman kindly. 'And let's see, where was it you wanted?'

Emma, fighting a good fight, managed to say, 'Oh, Denmark Hill.' Jonathan, she could see, was trying not to grin all over, the beast. 'Are we somewhere near it?'

'You're near it all right, dearie. There it is, just across the junction, right in front of yer eyes. My, ain't yer got big eyes too?'

'Better than a big head,' said Emma.

'Beg yer pardon?' said the large lady.

'Thanks, you've been very kind,' said Emma.

'Bless yer, and you with yer friend that's up from the country and all,' beamed the large lady, and went on her way.

'That didn't hurt, did it?' said Jonathan.

'You'll hurt, and all over, if I push you under a bus,' said Emma.

'Trudy, you spoke up just like any normal girl,' said Jonathan.

'Oh, I'm near to normal, am I?'

'Yes, nearly,' said Jonathan, and they crossed the junction into Denmark Hill.

'Don't stop anyone else,' said Emma, 'or you'll find yourself nearly dead.'

'Just this one,' said Jonathan, and stopped a bloke in a brown bowler hat. 'Excuse me,' he said, 'but my friend wants to know if buses go up Denmark Hill.'

'Want to catch one, do yer, girlie?' said Brown Bowler, giving Emma a grin.

'My friend's going to catch something in a minute, and it won't be a bus,' said Emma.

'Takin' yer name in vain or something, is 'e?' grinned Brown Bowler. 'Anyway, see that?' he said, pointing. 'That's a bus.'

'Thanks,' said Emma, 'but I do know what a bus is.'

'Yerse, that's one,' said Brown Bowler, chuckling in a manner that reminded Jonathan of his dad. 'And it's goin' up this hill, which is Denmark Hill. A number 68. Is that what yer want, a number 68?'

'I don't exactly want it now,' said Emma, who thought a good kick would take the grin off Jonathan's face.

'She be thinking later on maybe, don't 'ee, Trudy?' he said.

''Ello, 'ello, is yer friend a country lad?' asked Brown Bowler.

'Yes, and one of the backward kind,' said Emma.

'Ain't one of them village idiots, is 'e?' whispered Brown Bowler.

'Well, no,' said Emma, 'he's not actually a village idiot.'

Jonathan laughed.

Brown Bowler whispered again to Emma.

'Sounds like one, though, poor bloke.'

'Yes, it's sad for his mother,' said Emma.

'Well, you sound all there yerself, girlie,' said Brown Bowler, and departed like a man who had just enjoyed a couple of comical minutes.

'Blow me if you weren't a surprise packet, Trudy,' said Jonathan, 'nor far short of being a saucy baggage.'

'Baggage?' said Emma. 'Baggage? Me?'

'Little devil you were, calling me a village idiot,' said Jonathan. 'Still, you showed what you can do when you try talking to people. You had a rare old chat about coal with that woman.'

'Oh, you think so, do you?' said Emma. 'Kindly do me the favour of not crossing my path again.'

'Well, if it should happen accidentally again,' said Jonathan, 'we'll do some more stopping of people and getting you to talk to them, shall we?'

'Not if I can help it,' said Emma.

'Shall I walk you as far as your offices?' asked Jonathan.

'No, we'll say goodbye here,' said Emma.

'All right, Trudy, so long, then,' said Jonathan.

'So long,' said Emma, and turned to go, only to turn back. 'Oh, I forgot that I brought the book to read the last chapter once more,' she said. 'I won't bother now, so d'you want to borrow it?'

'Pardon?' said Jonathan.

'D'you want to borrow it?'

'You offering honestly?' said Jonathan.

'Yes, of course,' said Emma.

'Well, I'm really touched,' said Jonathan.

'I'm only loaning it for a week,' said Emma, 'then I suppose I'll simply have to meet you again, after all, today week, in the Green.' She brought the book out of the carrier-bag and handed it to him.

'I don't know how to thank you,' said Jonathan.

'I'll only meet you so that you can give it back,' said Emma.

'Well, that won't take long,' said Jonathan.

'About five seconds,' said Emma.

'You sure you don't mind lending it?' said Jonathan. 'I mean, an expensive book like this, suppose I didn't turn up?'

'You'd better,' said Emma, 'or I'll come into your firm's offices and get you the sack. Well, that's all. Goodbye.' She went off then, leaving Jonathan in grateful possession of the much-coveted book.

She reached the door to Adams Enterprises at the same time as Boots.

'You're looking bright,' said Boots.

'Yes, can I come up to your office with you for five minutes?' asked Emma.

'For any special reason?' asked Boots, climbing the stairs with her.

'Yes, very special,' said Emma, 'I'm going to have hysterics.'

'Can't you have them in your own office?' asked Boots.

'No, I need a kind shoulder,' said Emma.

'Some kind shoulders are available in office hours,' said Boots.

But Emma, of course, didn't have hysterics. What she did have was a series of giggles as she acquainted Boots with details of how that peculiar young man, Jonathan Hardy, had made her talk to people. Boots said she seemed to have found quite a character in young Mr Hardy. Emma said she didn't find him, he'd just popped up into her life and was driving her potty.

'Well, I must already be weak in the head to let him push me into talking to people about the price of coal and whether buses went up Denmark Hill or not.'

'Fascinating,' said Boots.

'Fascinating? Bats in the belfry, more like,' said Emma. 'I'm ditching him.'

'Best thing, I suppose,' said Boots, studying his midday post.

'Yes, I've got to be fair to Donald,' said Emma, refraining from mentioning she'd lent *Gone With The Wind* to the young man who was driving her to drink in a manner of speaking.

'Fetch your notebook, Emma,' said Boots.

'Yes, Uncle Boots,' said Emma.

Chapter Eleven

The corporation watercart stood outside the Hardy house in Stead Street. Job had had a bite to eat at home, and was just about to leave.

'Ah, by the by, Jemima,' he said, 'had a look at Aunt Matty's old grandfather clock. Still a good 'un, he is, but pendulum wants straightening, so I'm taking same to the Walworth clock shop, it being work for an expert.'

'All right, Job, though you're an expert yourself,' said Jemima.

'Not at clocks,' said Job.

'No, at gardening and other things,' said Jemima.

'Ah, I'm not too old for other things, maybe,' said Job.

'Be off with you,' said Jemima, and laughed.

Outside, little street kids were gawping at the watercart.

'Gi's a ride, mister, will yer?' said one.

'Unfortunate to say, Oliver, it don't be allowed,' said Job.

'Well, could yer turn the water on for us so's we can see?'

'Wait there,' said Job. He climbed up, started the engine and switched on the water. Out it gushed into the gutter, and as Job drove the vehicle away, the little kids were splashing about in the running stream. From an open door, a mum yelled.

'You Oliver, I'll drown yer in the copper if you don't come out of that gutter!'

'It's an 'ard life,' gloomed little Oliver to his mates.

Well, it was for all little Walworth kids who liked to paddle in puddles with their boots on.

That evening, Jemima was doing some sewing in the light of the kitchen window, Job was doing a bit of work in the back yard garden, Jennifer was having a scrap with young Jonas in the passage, Jonathan was reading *Gone With The Wind* in the kitchen, and Jane was at the gate taking in the sunshine while also wearing a frock almost as pretty as her best Sunday one.

Out came Alfie Hardcastle from the house next door, and from another house out came Joe Morgan. Alfie turned left, large ears catching a light breeze, and went past Jane, while Joe advanced from the opposite direction. Jane blinked. Alfie stopped. Joe stopped.

'Alfie, you're standin' in me way,' he said.

'And it ain't accidental, either,' said Alfie.

'D'you mind moving?' said Joe.

'Yus, course I mind, so I ain't goin' to,' said Alfie.

Joe tried a sidestep. Alfie blocked him.

'Turn it up,' said Joe.

'I notice you've just come out from indoors,' said Alfie.

'Highly observant of you,' said Joe.

'Might I recommend goin' back indoors?' said Alfie.

'Who, you or me?' said Joe.

'You,' said Alfie.

'Well, Alfie,' said Joe, 'I 'aven't come out just to go back in. I'd feel a twerp.'

'A natural feelin',' said Alfie. 'Might I hask if what you've come out for is to interfere with a relationship I've got with Jane 'Ardy?'

'What sort of relationship is that?' asked Joe.

'Intimate,' said Alfie.

Jane, looking and listening, thought she ought to hold her breath because the atmosphere was dramatic. Bless my dad's watercart, they're going to bash each other over me.

'On behalf of the honour of Miss Jane 'Ardy,' said Joe, 'I must request you to take back the word intimate.'

'I ain't goin' to,' said Alfie. 'Intimate I said, and intimate it is.'

'Well, sorry, Alfie,' said Joe, 'but Miss Jane 'Ardy bein' an unmarried girl, intimate is illegal and accordingly I don't believe yer. Miss Jane 'Ardy is a lady. Young, I grant yer, but still a lady, and wouldn't go in for anything illegal.'

'I ain't talkin' about illegal,' said Alfie, ears twitching, 'just about me relationship with 'er, which I ain't allowing you to interfere with.'

'Well, if you don't get out of me way, Alfie, I'll 'ave to cop you a packet,' said Joe.

'And if you don't get back indoors,' said Alfie, 'I'll 'ave to break yer legs and carry you in.'

''Ave you noticed Miss Jane 'Ardy herself is lookin'?' asked Joe.

Alfie turned his head and Joe stood on his foot. Alfie yelled and hopped.

'Oh, yer bleedin' git,' he bawled, 'you've broke me big toe.'

Out came neighbours to gawp and to ask questions.

'What's up with Alfie 'Ardcastle?'

'Yes, what's he 'opping about for?'

'He's had a little accident,' said Jane.

'Fell over, did 'e?'

'No, something dropped on his foot,' said Jane.

'It ain't 'alf makin' 'im bawl.'

'And it's turned 'is ears red.'

'Yes, I think his foot's hurting,' said Jane.

Up came Joe.

'Evening, Jane,' he said.

'D'you want to come in?' invited Jane. 'Just in case?'

'In case of Alfie?' said Joe.

'He might recover in a minute,' said Jane.

'Best if I do come in for a minute, then,' said Joe, and Jane took him into the house, locking the door by pushing the catch down.

'Just in case,' she said. 'We can go in the parlour, if you like.'

'Who be that?' called Jemima.

'Joe Morgan, Mum,' called Jane, 'and we're going in the parlour to be out of the way.'

'Whose way?' called Jemima.

'Alfie Hardcastle's,' called Jane.

'Oh, that be a good chap to be out of the way of,' said Jemima.

Something sounded from upstairs.

'What's that?' asked Joe.

'Oh, just one of the bedroom doors rattling,' said Jane.

'Oh, that,' said Joe.

'Yes, it be our Irish leprechaun,' said Jane.

'Don't you find 'im a bit too lively sometimes?' asked Joe.

'Oh, we don't mind,' said Jane.

'Your grandfather clock's stopped,' said Joe.

'Yes, Dad's taken the pendulum off to get it seen to,' said Jane. The street door vibrated. 'Here, what's that?'

'That's Alfie,' said Joe.

'Thought it weren't our little Patrick,' said Jane.

Boots and Emily were seating themselves at the garden table, and Emily was looking suspicious.

'You've brought me out here to tell me something,' she said.

'Well, you know I'm on the Officers' Reserve list,' said Boots.

'Your mum's still wondering how that happened,' said Emily. 'She's mentioned more than once that there's never been an officer in her fam'ly or the fam'ly of your late dad. Still, she's nearly over the shock. Anyway, what d'you want to tell me?'

'That I'll be going into uniform when we get back from our Salcombe holiday,' said Boots.

'Couldn't you have told me something else?' said Emily, the green of her eyes darkening a little.

'I could, but I'd still have had to come round to that,' said Boots.

'Will you have to go away?' asked Emily.

'Not out of the country,' said Boots. 'Sir Henry has a fanciful idea of taking me onto his staff. The Army's making quiet preparations, and setting up corps commands.'

'What's corps commands?' asked Emily. 'No, never mind, it's bound to be double Dutch to me. Sir Henry thinks there's goin' to be a war definite, Boots?'

'Only if Hitler goes completely off his head,' said Boots.

'Well, I'll keep hopin' he won't,' said Emily, 'but I've got a depressin' feeling he will.'

'Any other comments, Em?'

'Yes,' said Emily, 'I don't mind you goin' into uniform, not at a time like this, but I will mind if you go into any trenches. You did all your fightin' in the Great War. I don't mind you servin' with Sir Henry as long as you only have to salute him each morning and give him things to sign. I won't stand for anything dangerous if a war does come. I hope that's clear, Boots.'

'I'm totally in favour of nothing dangerous, old girl,' said Boots.

'You'd better mean that,' said Emily. 'Only I know you, and I wouldn't put it past you to do something you shouldn't. And war or no war, you've got to be home at weekends.'

'I'll—'

'Every weekend, d'you hear me, Boots?'

'Well, I hear you, Em, but—'

'Just let Sir Henry know that,' said Emily.

Boots smiled. Emily tried to look unassailable.

'I'll have a word with him,' said Boots.

'You'll have to have a word with Sammy too,' said Emily, 'because you'll be leavin' the business. Yes, and who's Sammy goin' to get in your place? It won't be easy, gettin' someone who holds everything together like you do. Sammy doesn't always realize what you're worth to the firm.'

'He'll work things out, Em.'

'He's still goin' to have a headache,' said Emily.

'Not if he puts you in my place,' said Boots.

'Me?' said Emily.

'You know all there is to know about the firm as secretary,' said Boots, 'so I'll be recommending you.'

'Boots, you really think I could be general manager?'

'Yes, I think so,' said Boots, 'and I know you'd like to give it a go.'

'Oh, not half I wouldn't,' said Emily, 'but I never thought you'd think I was good enough to be recommendable as general manager.'

'You're good enough,' said Boots. He knew her aptitude for office work as the firm's secretary, and how much she liked it. Further, Chinese Lady ran the household, which suited both her and Emily. 'Sammy won't argue, he'll prefer the job remaining with the family instead of bringing in an outsider.'

'Well, bless you, Boots, it's touchin' you've got faith in me,' said Emily.

Chinese Lady came out then, together with Mr Finch, Eloise and Tim. Eloise was carrying a tray laden with cups, saucers, a jug of warm milk and a pot of hot coffee. Eloise had managed to establish coffee-drinking times, one of which was after supper, although this had not prevented Chinese Lady from making a large pot of tea for the family later in the evenings.

'It is nice, isn't it, coffee in the garden?' said Eloise, placing the tray on the table and smiling at Boots. 'The weather is just like we have in France.'

Boots had his reservations about that as far as Northern France was concerned. He remembered too much about the liquid mud of the trenches.

'Boots has something to tell you,' said Emily as she let Eloise pour the coffee.

Boots brought forth his admission that he was going into uniform next month. Chinese Lady came stiffly upright in her chair, Mr Finch looked non-committal, Tim gave his dad a smile, and Eloise stared.

'Papa, why are you doing that?' she asked.

'In some way, Eloise, the country has to make preparations,' said Boots.

'But that is for younger men, not for you,' said Eloise. 'Speak to him, Grandmama.'

'I've spent most of my life speakin' to my only oldest son,' said Chinese Lady, 'and I can't remember it ever doin' any good. He went behind my back and joined up in 1914 when he knew I didn't hold with the war, and now he's done it again. What's goin' to happen to this fam'ly I'm sure I don't know, Boots goin' back into the Army and my husband not bein' able to retire like he should be because the Government's sendin' him to France. I've said I don't know how many times that someone should of done something to Hitler, but of course no one takes any notice of me.'

'Well, it's not too late, Maisie,' said Mr Finch.

'Plenty of time for someone to put a bomb under this chair while he's eating his cream buns,' said Tim. 'Imagine that, little bits of Hitler and his cream buns flying about all over his favourite mountain.'

Eloise shrieked with laughter. Mr Finch coughed. Boots looked at the sky.

'Em'ly,' said Chinese Lady, 'I hope that boy of yours isn't goin' to turn into a music hall comedian like his father.'

'He's already well on the way, Mum,' said Emily.

'I credit him myself with the makings of an excellent idea,' said Mr Finch.

'Oh, yes,' said Eloise, 'what could be more excellent than Hitler and his cream buns all flying about in bits?'

Chinese's Lady's firm mouth twitched.

'Dad, what regiment are you joining?' asked Tim. 'Is it your old West Kents?'

'I'm not havin' that,' said Chinese Lady, 'I'll go and see the Prime Minister first.'

'As things are,' said Boots, 'it looks as if I'll be on

Sir Henry's staff, which means that if the balloon does go up I'll be well behind the lines.'

'So that he can come home every weekend,' said Emily.

'Eh?' said Tim.

'Every weekend,' said Emily.

'Oh, it's all absurd,' said Eloise.

'Unfortunately, Hitler might make things serious for all of us,' said Mr Finch.

'He's a monster,' said Eloise, 'but he's also a clown and if France and Britain, and everyone else, laughed at him, perhaps that would turn him into a very little clown wishing to hide himself.'

'I don't feel like laughin' at him myself,' said Emily.

'I wonder what Rosie'll say, Dad, when she next phones and finds out from you that you're going back into the Army?' said Tim.

'She'll have a lot to say, I shouldn't wonder,' observed Chinese Lady severely.

Eloise wrinkled her nose.

Boots had a private word with Mr Finch later.

'Edwin,' he said, 'I've a favour to ask.'

'Well, in all the years we've known each other, Boots, you've asked very few favours of me,' said Mr Finch. 'I've had many from you in the most personal of ways.'

'Water under the bridge,' said Boots, and acquainted his stepfather with Rachel Goodman's problem. Mr Finch, having first met Rachel during the Great War when she'd been Sammy's one and only girlfriend, regarded her as the family did, as a faithful and long-standing friend. He agreed with Boots that one should think twice before interceding in a matter affecting the interests of a husband and wife. On the other hand, he said, if we go along with our belief that Germany couldn't mount a successful invasion of Britain, then we could also go along with Rachel's belief that there's no need for her family to emigrate.

'Yes, I think we could do that, Boots, go along with her belief and take no action. That would avoid presumptuous interference.'

'Live in hope for her?' said Boots, not entirely satisfied.

'Oh, a little more than that,' smiled Mr Finch. 'The fact is, the American Embassy has been overwhelmed with applications for entry visas, and has reached the stage where it's processing only those coming from Jewish people whose circumstances are desperate. I can't imagine they'll consider Mr Goodman and his family to be in that category. No, Boots, I'm sure they won't.'

'Did you get that piece of information from the American Ambassador?' asked Boots.

'Mr Joseph Kennedy?' said Mr Finch. 'No, indeed not, Boots. Mr Joseph Kennedy is a very sharp and successful businessman, but more pro-German than pro-British. He's quite the wrong man to be representing the United States in this country at this particular time. If it were necessary to ask a favour, I'd not ask it of him. As you know—' Mr Finch smiled again. 'As you know, I'm more English than the English. I might perhaps ask a few questions of someone else.

In any event, tell Rachel to be of good cheer.'

'Be of good cheer?' said Boots, and laughed. 'That's as English as anyone could get.'

'I like to be told that kind of thing,' said Mr Finch.

Chapter Twelve

At breakfast on Tuesday morning, Jemima addressed Jonathan with a smile.

'I never did know you to put your nose into a book like that one,' she said. 'All over the weekend—'

'Not every minute,' said Jonathan.

'Nearly,' said Jane, 'and dodging Amelia from next door by making Jennifer tell her you were ill in bed.'

'Ill in bed be a comfortable way of dodging Amelia,' said Job.

'Specially when Jonathan's found a girl nice enough to lend him her best book,' said Jemima. 'All over the weekend he had his nose in it, and last night as well.'

'In love with it, that's what he is,' said Jennifer.

'Has he kissed it yet?' asked young Jonas.

'Well, I haven't seen him do that,' said Jemima, 'I've only seen him cuddling it so far.'

'Seen some cuddling myself lately,' said Job.

'Where?' asked Jennifer.

'In the parlour,' said Job.

'What, Jonathan cuddling the girl's book?' asked Jennifer.

'No, young Joe Morgan cuddling our Jane,' said Job.

Jane blushed, Jennifer giggled and Jemima shrieked.

'Dad, it don't be fair, looking,' said Jane.

'Only through the keyhole,' said Job. 'Good cuddler, young Joe Morgan be.'

'Dad, you be a shocker,' said Jane, and Job winked at her.

'Did you see the girl Trudy yesterday, Jonathan?' asked Jemima.

'No, she wasn't in Lyons,' said Jonathan, 'and we're not supposed to meet, anyway, until Friday, when I've got to return the book to her.'

'It's your medical tomorrow,' said Jane.

'Yes, three in the afternoon,' said Jonathan.

'You might not pass if you had a lot of coughing fits,' said Jane.

'I'll practise some,' said Jonathan.

Jemima sighed a little.

Jonathan made his way to Lyons at lunchtime. His eyes wandered to the table where he'd first seen Trudy. She was there today. He passed her on his way to a vacant table for two.

'See you Friday, Trudy,' he said as he went by.

Emma watched him seat himself at the other table. She came to her feet and walked over.

'Are you sulking?' she asked.

'Me?' said Jonathan, looking up at her.

'Yes, you,' said Emma. 'Fat lot of good it was

lending you my book if it's making you sulk.'

'Excuse me,' said Jonathan, 'but I'm not, I just—'

'You could have said good morning and asked me how I was,' said Emma, and sat down at the table.

'I thought—'

'I'm all embarrassed at having to come over to tell you off,' said Emma.

Up came Trixie with her order block and pencil.

'Different table, I see,' she said. 'Still, one's as good as another when it's a table for two.' She smiled. 'What might I get you?'

'I'll have a ham salad, please,' said Emma.

'I'll have my Tuesday special,' said Jonathan, 'poached egg on toast.'

'Pleasure,' said Trixie, and away she went.

'Trudy, you sure you want to sit with me?' said Jonathan.

'Have you been reading the book?' asked Emma.

'You bet I have,' said Jonathan, 'I'm up to where Scarlett's dad, having gone off his rocker, has broken his neck trying to jump a fence.'

'You're more than halfway through the story, then,' said Emma.

'Yes, I'll finish it by Friday,' said Jonathan.

'Are you enjoying it?' asked Emma.

'Even more than I thought I would,' said Jonathan. 'It's so descriptive that reading it is like witnessing everything that happens, and, of course, what's happening is the gradual destruction of a whole way of life. It struck me that the people of Georgia lived a kind of gracious, unhurried existence that made them the aristocrats of America.'

'But it wasn't gracious and unhurried for the slaves,' said Emma.

'No, it wasn't,' agreed Jonathan. 'Perhaps if the plantation owners had freed them and paid them wages, there wouldn't have been a war and they could still have enjoyed the better part of their own way of life.'

'Well, I'm blessed,' said Emma, 'that's the first time you haven't sounded potty. I feel quite surprised you're appreciating the book, and making sensible comments about it. I thought, because of all your daft moments, that you'd say you still prefer to read comics.'

'Oh, I be past comics, I be getting into a tidy old way of reading and writing,' said Jonathan, and Emma gave him a pitying look.

'Stop talking that way, will you?' she said.

'Sometimes I can't help myself,' said Jonathan.

'Yes, you can,' said Emma, 'you do it just for a laugh.'

'No, it comes naturally,' said Jonathan. 'But might I mention my gratitude for the loan of the book? In return, I'm willing to walk you back to your offices again and to help you talk to some more people.'

'Oh, no, you don't,' said Emma, 'I'm not letting you drag me over the pavements again to make me talk to people about the price of coal. That's not a cure for shyness, that's a way of getting me to look retarded.'

'But you did a good job the other day,' said

Jonathan. 'Didn't it make you feel pleased with yourself?'

'No, it didn't,' said Emma.

'But you looked pleased,' said Jonathan.

'You're mistaken,' said Emma, 'that was my suffering look.'

'Give it another go,' said Jonathan. 'It needn't be about the price of coal again, it could be about train fares.'

'Never,' said Emma.

'Might do you more good,' said Jonathan.

'Might give you a laugh, you mean,' said Emma.

Trixie arrived with her tray then, and placed their lunches in front of them.

'There you are, miss, there you are, young sir,' she said. 'Havin' a nice talk, are you?'

'Not much,' said Emma.

'I know what you mean, some mothers do 'ave 'em, don't they?' said Trixie, and laughed as she left them to each other.

'Trudy,' said Jonathan, 'you sure you're shy?'

'I'm not listening,' said Emma, beginning her meal.

'Oh, all right,' said Jonathan, 'Let's just eat.'

The suggested silence didn't last long, however, and Emma found herself drawn into the usual kind of dotty conversation, much to her sense of helplessness. Worse was to come, for Jonathan talked her into leaving early so that he could again help her to chat to strangers. Emma suppressed all inclinations to push him under a bus in favour of hysterical inclinations to giggle herself silly when he stopped a little old lady and said his friend wanted to know if there was a zoo in Camberwell.

The little old lady, who still had a bit of a twinkle in her eye, said, 'A zoo?'

'Yes,' said Jonathan, 'this young lady be wanting to know if there's one in Camberwell. She be right gone on zoos.'

'Well, I never did.' The little old lady gazed enquiringly at Emma. 'Are you both up from the country, young lady?'

'I'm not, he is,' said Emma. 'It's not my fault he talks like that.'

'I seen 'is kind before, when I was a girl and 'ad holidays in the country,' said the little old lady. 'Terrors, some of them country boys, and saucier than Bermondsey dockers. Talk about a barn dance and makin' me show me petticoat. Is this one saucy?'

'That and other things,' said Emma, and the little old lady took a look at Jonathan.

'Looks like a reg'lar young devil to me,' she said. 'Has 'e got wicked ways?'

'Worse than Rhett Butler,' said Emma.

'Who's 'e, some bloke from down your street?'

'No, he's a bit farther away than that,' said Emma. 'It's this saucy country chap I'm worried about, he talks me into doing everything I don't want to do.'

'Ought to be in a zoo 'imself, then, in the monkeys' cage,' said the little old lady, whose granny bonnet smelled of camphor balls. 'What d'you want to know if there's a zoo in Camberwell for?'

'Well, I – well, is there?' asked Emma helplessly.

'Never 'eard of it,' said the little old lady. 'Can't you go to the London Zoo? They've got walkin' elephants there, and penguins. I never seen any in Camberwell. Where'd you come from, lovey?'

'Pardon?' said Emma.

'Forgotten, I shouldn't wonder,' said Jonathan. 'She be a mite forgetful about a lot of things.'

'Oh, the poor gal,' said the little old lady, 'that's worrying.'

'Don't listen to him,' said Emma, 'I'm not forgetful about anything.'

'Well, remember it's the London Zoo where you can see penguins, lions and walkin' elephants, not Camberwell,' said the little old lady. 'Camberwell's just got trams, buses and some poor people, but not a zoo. Now what 'ave I come out for? It must be for something or I wouldn't 'ave come out. I never do unless it's for something.'

'Perhaps it's for shopping,' suggested Emma.

'Yes, that's it, shoppin',' said the little old lady happily. 'Well, I'm glad I met you, young miss, or I might not 'ave remembered. Your country boy's lucky you're a bright gal.'

'Yes, he's a bit missing himself,' said Emma.

'It don't seem to stop 'im havin' a wicked look. Mind, they're all the same, saucy young blokes up from the country.' The little old lady winked and went twinkling on her way.

'Trudy,' said Jonathan, 'in helping you to talk to people, I don't expect you to make them think I'm not all there.'

'They don't have to think,' said Emma, 'it's obvious each time you open your mouth.'

'Further,' said Jonathan, 'stop insinuating I'm wicked.'

'How do I know you're not?' said Emma, walking with him.

'You can take my word for it.' Jonathan looked at his watch and stopped. 'I'm nearly past my lunchtime,' he said, 'I've got to get back. Still, I liked accidentally running into you again, Trudy. See you in the Green on Friday, when I'll bring back the book.'

'Yes, and we'll only have to meet then for five seconds,' said Emma.

They turned then at the sound of a yell.

'Oh, yer bleedin' Nazis!'

A dark-haired lad of about sixteen was on the ground, sprawled, and he was shouting at two men in flat caps, trousers, and black shirts. They were instantly recognizable to Jonathan as followers of Oswald Mosley, a fascist and an admirer of Hitler.

'Serve yer right,' said one man. 'Just watch where yer walkin', Jewboy.'

'I ain't a Jewboy, and I didn't walk into you, you did it to me!' yelled the lad, and scrambled to his feet. He was furious enough to aim a kick at the man. The man knocked him off his feet and sent him sprawling again.

Jonathan saw red. He rushed, took hold of the man by his arm, pulled him round and socked him with a clenched fist. The Blackshirt took the piledriver full on the jaw and crashed. Emma held her breath, and pedestrians gathered, some in happy expectation of a first-class punch-up. A policeman was approaching as the second

Blackshirt swung a fist at Jonathan. Jonathan ducked and the man closed with him. The policeman, brawny, pushed his way through, and forcibly separated the contestants.

'What's all this, then?' he asked. 'Don't you know public brawling's against the law?'

'Don't be a spoilsport,' called a bloke from the crowd, 'let 'em fight it out.'

'You're under arrest,' said the copper to Jonathan. 'So are you,' he said to the second Blackshirt. 'And him,' he added, as the first man came to his feet. 'You'll come along of me to the station – oh, no, you don't.' He reached out a long arm, took hold of the first man by his collar and yanked him back as he tried for a getaway. 'Now, names, if you don't mind. Yours, sir?' he said to Jonathan.

'Hold on,' said Jonathan, 'it's not like that. This sod knocked a boy down.'

'What boy?' asked the policeman, notebook out.

Jonathan looked around. The boy had slipped away in instinctive avoidance of getting mixed up with the arm of the law. That was instinctive in most cockney lads, whether innocent or not.

'He's gone,' said Jonathan.

'He ran off,' said a woman, 'so would anybody from them 'ooligans.'

'Disappeared like a dog's dinner,' said an old bloke.

'Makes no difference,' said the constable to Jonathan and the Blackshirts, 'a brawl on a public pavement is a chargeable offence. I want your names.'

'You can whistle for mine,' said the first Blackshirt, holding his swelling jaw.

'And mine,' said the second.

'Right, let's have you all down to the station,' said the copper. His colleague on the beat appeared then, and as soon as he was given details, the two constables escorted the accused to the Camberwell Police Station, leaving Emma wide-eyed and disbelieving among the other spectators.

At the station desk, a police sergeant took down details, the Blackshirts surrendering their names and addresses, and Jonathan giving his. Jonathan explained what had set him off, but he and the two Blackshirts were formally charged and held in cells to await a hearing at Southwark Magistrates Court at three-thirty.

Emma arrived. It had taken her quite a while to recover her senses and to realize what she simply had to do.

'Yes, miss?' asked the desk sergeant.

'Where's Mr Hardy?' asked Emma.

'One Mr Jonathan Hardy?'

'Yes.'

'He's in a cell, he's been charged with being involved in a public affray.'

'Don't be silly,' said Emma.

'Come again, miss?'

'It's ridiculous,' said Emma. 'Mr Hardy went to help a boy who'd been knocked down by those louts. You can't charge him for that.'

'Unfortunately, miss, he's been charged for takin' the law into his own hands. Might I ask if you want to bear witness on his behalf?'

'I certainly do,' said Emma.

'Might I have your name and address?'

Emma gave them, then said, 'Now what do I do?'

'Appear at Southwark Magistrates Court at three-thirty, when the case is bein' heard, Miss Somers.'

'I suppose you know Mr Hardy should be at work?' said Emma.

'Well, if he hadn't—'

'Don't bother,' said Emma, and walked out. She took herself off to Jonathan's employers, remembering who they were. She also remembered he had mentioned a Mr Spinks. She asked for him when she arrived, and was taken to his office. She saw him as a lean, fusty clerk in a black jacket and grey trousers with black stripes, his high collar starched. 'Mr Spinks?'

'Yes?'

'I think Mr Jonathan Hardy works here, doesn't he?'

'Yes, and I regret he's overstaying his lunch hour.' Mr Spinks spoke fretfully but without a sniff.

'He may not be back all afternoon,' said Emma. 'I'm a – I'm an acquaintance of his.' She went on to inform Mr Spinks that Jonathan had gone to the help of a boy who had been twice knocked down by two men wearing black shirts, that the two men had been arrested, and that Jonathan had been summonsed to appear in court with them this afternoon. She didn't say as a defendant, she said as a witness to the assault. She herself had been present at the time.

'Ah,' said Mr Spinks. 'Ah, very unfortunate. Thank you, Miss – ah—?'

'Somers,' said Emma.

'Thank you, Miss Somers, for coming here and letting us know.'

'It was just in case you thought of sacking him on the spot,' said Emma.

'I assure you, only if we had good reason to,' said Mr Spinks.

'I think there's good reason to give him a medal instead,' said Emma. 'Goodbye, Mr Spinks.'

'Yes – ah – goodbye, Miss Somers.'

Emma left, hoping she'd done Jonathan a good turn with his skinflint employers. He might have all the cheek in the world at the way he'd been trying to earn himself a place in her life, but he didn't deserve being arrested for bashing that brute of a Blackshirt.

Arriving back at the offices, she went straight to Boots's sanctum.

'Uncle Boots—'

'So there you are,' said Boots.

'Yes, here I am, and ever so sorry I'm so late,' said Emma. She explained, and at length.

'I see,' said Boots. 'So what does it mean, that this odd country bloke is reckless enough to rush in where angels fear to tread?'

'He just did it,' said Emma, 'he just went for those men, he didn't stop and ask himself if he was being odd or reckless.'

'Well, who could quarrel with that?' said Boots. 'Just a pity that the bobby showed up before he'd laid out both men. The fact that he's going to be up before the beaks later this afternoon is damned hard luck. And you're going to speak up for him, Emma?'

'I think I've got to,' said Emma.

'I thought you were going to give up running into him at lunchtimes,' said Boots.

'Yes, I was, not half,' said Emma, 'but he keeps coming after me. Uncle Boots, d'you mind that I'll have to take time off this afternoon?'

'I don't mind at all that you feel you've got to speak up for him in court,' said Boots.

'I should've gone home for lunch,' said Emma, frowning.

The court was in session, the three magistrates were on the bench, the accused in dock, the arresting policeman, Constable Roberts, on the stand and consulting his notebook. He declared he had witnessed the brawl himself, had seen one of the accused, Jonathan Hardy, strike another, Walter Russell, and knock him to the ground. He had further seen him engage in an immediate brawl with the other accused, Frank Galway, when Galway attempted to strike him.

'Is this evidence disputed?' asked the chairman of the bench.

'I'm not disputing it,' said Jonathan, ' but I'd like to point out—'

'Not yet, not yet,' said the chairman.

'A witness wishes to take the stand, Your Honour,' said the clerk.

Emma was called and took the stand in an admirably composed way. Jonathan blinked to see her. He blinked again when she confirmed her name was Emma Somers. Having taken the oath, she was requested to acquaint the bench with her evidence. A court of law was quite new to her, but she spoke clearly.

'I was with Mr Hardy at the time,' she said, 'and we heard a boy shouting. We turned and saw him on the ground, two men standing over him.'

'Do you see those two men here?' asked the chairman.

'Yes,' said Emma, 'they're with Mr Hardy over there. One of them referred to the boy as a Jewboy, and knocked him down again when he got up. Mr Hardy then struck a blow for justice, he punched the man in the jaw. If he hadn't, the boy would have been kicked in the ribs.'

'The arresting constable made no mention of a boy,' said the chairman.

'Well, he didn't arrive in time for that,' said Emma, 'he didn't arrive in time to see the boy on the ground. What he did see as he was approaching was Mr Hardy delivering his punch.'

'Is this correct?' asked the chairman.

'Beg to advise Your Honour I didn't notice any grounded boy,' said Constable Roberts. 'Beg to further advise there was mention of a boy by members of the assembled pedestrians, but no boy was around.'

'He disappeared,' said Emma. 'He was frightened and ran off.'

'I see,' said the chairman. 'Is this witness's statement disputed?' He looked at all three accused.

'Don't now what she's talkin' about,' said the man Russell.

'We was set on by this bloke,' said Galway.

'Were you indeed,' said the chairman, 'and for no reason, I suppose?'

'Search me,' said Galway.

'You may step down, Miss Somers,' said the chairman. Emma did so and found a seat in the court. The chairman conferred with his fellow magistrates, then addressed the defendants. 'We accept the evidence of the arresting constable, and also the statement given by the witness, Miss Somers. We find Russell and Galway guilty of common assault and Hardy guilty of misdemeanour. Hardy, you must not take the law into your own hands.'

'Well, I'll be blowed,' said Jonathan, 'all I did—'

'You may be blowed or not,' said the chairman, 'but you're certainly fined ten shillings, with fourteen days to pay. Russell and Galway, you are each fined twenty-one shillings, with seven days to pay.'

'Bleedin' swindle,' muttered Russell.

'What was that?' demanded the chairman.

'Nothing,' said Russell.

All three left the dock, and were escorted by a policeman to the clerk of the court, where the two Blackshirts paid up in scowling fashion, leaving Jonathan to explain he didn't have as much as ten bob on him. The clerk reminded him he had fourteen days to settle.

Emma was waiting outside the building as Jonathan left.

'Now look what you've done, getting yourself a

181

'conviction and me in a law court,' she said.

'Thanks for coming, Gertrude Potter,' said Jonathan.

'Pardon?' said Emma.

'Or should I say Emma Somers?'

'Oh,' said Emma. 'Oh, lor'.' She'd forgotten about Gertrude Potter. 'Well, I wasn't myself that time you first tried to pick me up, and anyway, I wouldn't ever give my right name to people I don't know.'

'All the same,' said Jonathan, 'thanks for being a witness, I'm touched.'

'It didn't save you from being fined,' said Emma.

'No, but never mind,' said Jonathan, 'that one punch was worth ten bob, even if it makes a hole in my savings. Now I've got to get back to the office and try to do some explaining.'

Emma went back to Camberwell with him, and on the way she let him know she'd called in and spoken to a Mr Spinks.

'I told him you had to go to court as a witness, I didn't say you'd been arrested. Well, I said I was an acquaintance of yours, and I didn't want him to think I acquainted myself with law-breakers.'

'I don't know how you've come to do me these good turns on top of loaning me *Gone With The Wind*,' said Jonathan, 'but I'm very appreciative.'

'Well, I understand why you punched that Blackshirt,' said Emma. 'You're a funny bloke, you're not all there most of the time, but I'm glad you thumped him.'

Jonathan said it was on the spur of the moment,

but it had felt good when the man went down. He talked about the Blackshirts, and supplied some reasons why, as supporters of Adolf Hitler, they all ought to be locked up until the dictator of Germany fell down dead. Emma said Hitler was getting boring, and so was all talk about him. Jonathan said good idea, then, to push him under the carpet, and save being bored.

At Camberwell Green, he thanked her again for being a regular sport in standing witness for him, and that the name Emma suited her a lot better than Gertrude.

Emma said, 'What's in a name?'

'In some, a few laughs,' said Jonathan.

'Well, see you on Friday,' said Emma.

'Just for five seconds?' said Jonathan.

'I think I can manage five seconds and a final goodbye,' said Emma.

She was frowning as she went back to the offices once more. She wasn't quite sure if she was going to succeed in getting him out of her life. She'd never met anyone more persistent in crossing her path.

Jonathan's belated return to work was noted sympathetically by Mr Spinks, who advised him that the firm fully understood why he had had to absent himself most of the afternoon. A young lady, a Miss Somers, had been kind enough to call and explain everything. What had been the result of the magistrates' hearing?

'The two men were fined twenty-one shillings each,' said Jonathan.

'Most gratifying,' said Mr Spinks. 'Now, perhaps

a little work before the office closes down for the day?'

*   *   *

At the teachers' training college near Bath, Rosie Adams, now twenty-four, was reflecting on the news that Boots, her adoptive father, was going into uniform. She understood why he was doing so. Even though the 1914–18 war had sickened and disgusted him, he was rigidly opposed to all that Hitler and Nazi Germany stood for. It disturbed Rosie to know that while Europe remained in a fractious state, he would be at the beck and call of the Army up to and beyond a possible declaration of war. It took the edge off her commitment to a teaching career, which began to look irrelevant.

And gave her cause to think.

Chapter Thirteen

Jonathan's family listened agog as he described the lunchtime events and his appearance in court, an appearance that put him on the wrong side of ten bob.

'Well, that's a cockeyed way of applying the law, durned if it isn't,' said Job.

'They fined you for going to the help of the boy?' said Jemima.

'With fourteen days to pay,' said Jonathan.

'What a sauce,' said Jane.

'Not fair,' said Jennifer.

'I'll put tuppence towards it, Jonathan,' said young Jonas.

'Good of you, young 'un,' said Jonathan.

'That girl went and stood witness for you?' said Jemima.

'Came up trumps,' said Jonathan, 'or I think I might have got the same fine as the Blackshirts, twenty-one bob.'

'I'm against them contrary Blackshirts,' said Job. 'I reckon they come up out of holes in the ground. Jemima?'

'Jonathan,' said Jemima, 'you can't afford that fine.'

'I'll dip into my savings,' said Jonathan.

'No, your dad and me will pay it,' said Jemima, 'I'll go to the court tomorrow.'

'It's my owings,' said Jonathan.

'It's ours,' said Jemima. 'Your dad and me like what you did, and it's no shame on you or any of us that the law can't see the difference between the good and the bad.'

'I don't know I should let you and Dad fork out ten bob,' said Jonathan.

'Jonathan, we can always find ten bob to support a good family cause,' said Job. 'Not as our duty, more our pleasure.'

'And it's nice the girl Trudy stood witness for you,' said Jemima.

'I expressed my appreciation,' said Jonathan, keeping her real name to himself for the moment. It saved a lot more tongue-wagging. 'When I see her on Friday to give her the book back, that'll be the last time I do see her.'

'Who said?' asked Jane.

'She did,' said Jonathan.

'Well, bless me,' said Jemima, and smiled.

The following day, Jemima visited the court and paid the fine, not without expressing disapproval of the law's treatment of her son. The law showed an impassive face.

In the afternoon, Jonathan had his medical under the supervision of an RAMC officer, who congratulated him on his physical fitness.

Jonathan asked if that meant he'd passed A1. The RAMC captain advised him that officially he could not give a verbal affirmative, but that his congratulations stood. Jonathan asked what life in the Army was like these days. Better than it was during the war, said the medical officer.

'There's a chance, then, that I'll come out all in one piece?' enquired Jonathan.

'Certainly, as long as there's no war. Do you have a preference for any particular branch of the Service?'

'Yes, one where I won't get shot at, sir,' said Jonathan.

'Fair comment.'

'What's my next move?' asked Jonathan.

'You can dress and leave.'

'And wait to hear, I suppose?'

'Correct.'

His family hoped on the one hand that he'd failed the medical. On the other hand, Job and Jemima didn't want to think they'd brought up a weakling. The kitchen floor moved about a bit during a discussion on the medical, which made young Jonas suggest the leprechaun might be thinking about following Jonathan into the Army.

'I wouldn't mind if he did,' said Jane.

'Give the rest of us a bit of peace and quiet,' said Jennifer.

'Yes, and me as well,' said young Jonas.

Jonathan was wading enjoyably through *Gone With The Wind* and the astonishing escapades of Scarlett O'Hara.

'Jonathan still at the book, I see, Job,' said Jemima.

'Aye,' said Job, 'labour of love, I reckon.'

'Well, it do look like he's breathing heavy over it,' said Jemima.

'That right, Jonathan?' said Job. 'Breathing heavy over it, are you?'

'Yes, I'm in labour,' said Jonathan.

Job roared with laughter and Jemima followed with a peal.

'Jane in the parlour with Joe again, is she?' asked Jemima on Thursday evening.

'I reckon,' said Jonathan.

'Jane be growing up fast,' said Job. 'Ought to be one day at a time, though.'

'Ought it?' said young Jonas.

'Yes, one day at a time's best,' said Jemima. 'I watched your dad, Jonas, and there he was, growing up every day, with all the village girls taking turns to measure him from his feet up to the top of his head. But I stopped that once he got to be eighteen and manly.'

'Why?' asked young Jonas.

'Well, I were thirteen and growing up fast myself,' said Jemima. 'More like a week at a time, not a day. Thirteen and growing fast be a terrible jealous experience for a girl.'

'How did you stop the other girls from measuring Dad?' asked Jennifer, agog.

'Pushed them in the duck pond,' said Jemima. 'Jonathan, you're growing up day by day, just like your dad. Some girl might like to start measuring you soon.'

'Some girl might be too shy,' said Jennifer.

'I were right shy as a growing young chap once,' said Job. 'Went into a shop to buy some new pants and there were two girls there, and I come over so shy I kind of shrunk.'

'Shrunk?' said Jennifer.

'That I did,' said Job, 'and durned if my trousers and old pants didn't fall down.'

The kitchen shook with laughter.

'But you pulled them up, didn't you, Job?' said Jemima.

'No, I were too shy to,' said Job, 'so I ran out of the shop.'

'With your trousers down, Dad?' asked young Jonas.

'That they were,' said Job, 'so I fell over in front of Mrs Barnard, the vicar's wife, didn't I?'

Jennifer shrieked.

'Your bedroom door's rattling, Mum,' said young Jonas.

'Growling as well this time,' said Jonathan. 'Taken umbrage at all this racket, I shouldn't wonder.'

'Vicar's wife took a tidy bit of umbrage herself,' said Job, 'me outside the shop flat on my face and showing a bare bottom.'

The family yelled.

Benjamin Goodman, home from a day on a race-course, opened a letter that had arrived by the midday post. Rachel watched him. She knew from the embossed envelope that it had been sent by the American Embassy. So did Benjamin.

'It's come quicker than I thought,' he said, pulling the letter out. He read it. Rachel stood by trying to compose herself. Boots had phoned last week, not to advise her of his conversation with his stepfather, but to tell her wheels were in motion and that she could now live in hope. My life, Rachel had said, but should I have a conscience about doing Benjamin down? We both should, said Boots, but as Sammy says he's filed his for the moment, let's do the same with ours. Boots, you are a darling, said Rachel. Boots asked if that applied to Sammy too. To all of you, said Rachel, and all of you are one of my chief reasons for not wanting to run away to America.

Benjamin read the letter twice.

'Well?' said Rachel, elbowing rebelliousness aside to show a pleasant wifely interest.

'You'll like this letter,' he said.

'Will I?' said Rachel. 'You mean they're granting us an entry visa?'

'What's all this, eh?' said Benjamin. 'Have you come round to my way of thinking, Mrs Goodman?'

'I've come round to recognizing I'm your wife, Benjamin,' said Rachel.

'Commendable,' said Benjamin, 'but in that case you won't like this letter, after all.'

'What d'you mean?' asked Rachel, lustrous brown eyes giving nothing away.

'I mean they've turned the application down,' said Benjamin.

Rachel quickened.

'For what reason?' she asked, not wanting to crow.

Benjamin quoted.

'"In view of the present unsettled situation in Europe, which has resulted in the Embassy receiving in the region of five hundred applications a week, no further requests for immigration visas can be considered unless the circumstances are exceptional enough to justify a humanitarian response."'

'How disappointing,' said Rachel.

'I should believe you mean that?' said Benjamin gloomily.

'I'm thinking of you and your hopes,' said Rachel. 'A wife must have some consideration for her husband and all his hopes.'

'Well, I won't tell a lie,' said Benjamin, 'I was shocked out of my skin to have you beat my brains out.'

'I forgot myself,' said Rachel. 'But there's still hope.'

'Is there?' asked Benjamin, a match for any other course bookie, but not always a match for the feminine subtlety of his wife.

Rachel smiled.

'My dear man,' she said, 'if, as you believe, Hitler will conquer Britain in the event of a war, you must apply again when his invasion is imminent and our fate accordingly promises to be frightening. The American Embassy will then grant the visa on humanitarian grounds.'

'What a wife I have, what a clever one, isn't she?' said Benjamin.

'So shall we swallow our disappointment for the time being?' said Rachel.

'It'll hurt on the way down,' said Benjamin, 'but I'll swallow it.'

Rachel omitted to point out that under the circumstances she'd outlined, all the Jewish people of Britain would probably besiege the American Embassy.

The following morning, when Benjamin was on his way to the racecourse and the girls were at school, Rachel phoned Boots at his office.

'Hello?' he said.

'Rachel here, Boots.'

'Tell me the good news first, if there is any,' said Boots.

'Oh, there's no bad news,' said Rachel, 'only the fact that the American Embassy has turned down Benjamin's application.'

'As my conscience is filed away with Sammy's temporarily,' said Boots, 'let me say I'm happy for you.'

'Bless you, Boots,' said Rachel. 'How you did it, I've no idea.'

'I merely spoke to someone,' said Boots, 'but it occurs to me now that perhaps it wasn't necessary, perhaps it was a genuine refusal.'

'Might it have been?' asked Rachel.

'Let's say it was,' said Boots, 'then we can all unfile our consciences.'

'My life,' said Rachel, 'what a happy thought.

Boots, will you pass the news to Sammy for me?'

'He's out at the moment,' said Boots, 'but I'll let him know.'

'Such lovely friends I have,' said Rachel.

'Hardy, where are you going?' asked Mr Spinks, his nose twitching.

'Out,' said Jonathan.

'Out? Out?'

'It's my lunchtime,' said Jonathan.

'I want the figures from the Lawson company's cash-book first.'

'Yes, I'll let you have them first thing after I've been half an hour back from lunch,' said Jonathan, and out he went, carrying Emma's book with him, together with a tin containing three of his mother's homemade sausage rolls wrapped in greaseproof paper. It was Friday, and he found a vacant bench in the Green. There, he waited for Trudy. Or Emma, or whatever.

He'd eaten all three rolls before she put in an appearance. She was wearing a light macintosh against the threat of rain.

'Hello,' he said.

'I'd have been here earlier,' she said, 'but I forgot, and I've only just remembered.'

'You forgot about the book?' said Jonathan.

'Yes,' said Emma.

'I can hardly believe you forgot about this particular book,' said Jonathan.

'Have you finished it?' asked Emma.

'Yes,' said Jonathan, 'and no wonder you want to see the film when it gets to London.'

193

'Yes, no wonder,' said Emma. 'Could I have the book back now, please?' Jonathan gave it to her.

'Thanks again for loaning it,' he said.

'That's all right,' said Emma. 'Well, goodbye.'

'Goodbye, Trudy. I mean Emma.'

He was a little surprised at her quick departure, even if they had agreed the meeting would be brief.

Emma felt she had to be fair to Donald.

Jonathan felt a little bereft at her determined departure from his life.

'The pendulum's back on Aunt Matty's clock,' said Jane at supper that evening.

'Yes, your dad came in lunchtime and fixed it back on,' said Jemima.

'It looks new,' said Jennifer.

'Well, it's as good as new,' said Job.

'How's your young lady, Jonathan?' asked Jane.

'Well, I think she's relieved she's got the book back,' said Jonathan.

'Ask her round one Sunday,' said Jemima.

'Can't,' said Jonathan, 'she's left me for good.'

'What, given you the push?' said Jane.

'It was never like that,' said Jonathan, 'it was just a lunchtime thing.'

'She's still not wanting to make proper friends with you?' said Jemima.

'Seems like it,' said Jonathan, who felt a little sad about the future state of his lunchtimes.

'Maybe she likes making haste slowly,' smiled Jemima.

'Well, Jonathan and a girl like that have got all

the time in the world for making haste slowly,' said Job. He grinned. 'Not like Joe Morgan and our Jane, they be making haste in a hurry in your parlour, Jemima.'

'I heard that, Dad,' said Jane.

'I notice you be changing into very pretty frocks of an evening, Jane,' said Jemima.

'Me?' said Jane.

'Joe Morgan likes pretty frocks,' said Jennifer.

'Well, I never seen him in one,' said young Jonas, 'not even on a Sunday.'

'Bless us, I should hope not,' said Jemima.

'By the way, the clock pendulum really does look new,' said Jonathan.

'Aye, and so it should,' said Job, 'it's had a little bit of straightening-up, and a wash and brush-up too. Good old pendulum, that is.'

Jemima smiled.

'The floors haven't been moving today,' said Jane.

'Nor the mantelpieces,' said Jennifer.

'And the doors haven't been rattling,' said Jonathan.

'Dad, nothing's been moving today,' said young Jonas.

'Well, I reckon that little old devil has gone on summer holiday,' said Job.

The family laughed.

The floor perceptibly moved.

'Back from his holiday already,' said Jonathan.

The street door opened to a pull on the latch-cord, and Amelia Hardcastle from next door was heard.

'You finished yer supper, Jonathan? Can yer come into me mum's parlour and listen to "Tiger Rag" on our gramophone?'

Jonathan vanished.

Into the garden.

And with the co-operative connivance of his family, he once more succeeded in keeping out of the Hardcastle parlour, which Jemima thought possibly saved him from being smothered. She was quite against Jonathan suffering that kind of fate at the hands of Amelia Hardcastle.

Jemima liked the sound of the girl Trudy a lot better than she liked the designing nature of Amelia.

Rosie Adams made one of her regular phone calls to her family that evening. Boots took his turn to speak to her, and she asked him if he still believed war was a possibility.

'What do you believe?' asked Boots.

'Oh, you know me,' said Rosie, 'I believe what you believe.'

Boots, thinking of the accusation made by Eloise, said, 'Don't do that, poppet. Make up your own mind about everything. Follow your own leanings, your own wishes, your own instincts. Don't encourage me to be too possessive with you.'

'What?' said Rosie in astonishment.

'You're a free being, Rosie, free to live your own life.'

'But I do live my own life,' said Rosie. 'What makes you think I don't?'

'Just a thought I had.'

'Well, you can chuck thoughts like that into the waste-paper basket,' said Rosie.

'Rosie, the future belongs to people of your age. Those of my age are creatures of our pasts.'

'That's not true,' said Rosie, 'you've always been a man of the present. As for being possessive, well, that's the very first time I've heard you well below your usual form. Have you got a headache or something?'

'No, I merely—'

'Never mention it again,' said Rosie. 'Now, I have to tell you that if there's a war, I won't want to be in a classroom. If Polly's leaving her teaching job to join the Auxiliary Territorials, I shan't be far behind.'

'I hope not,' said Boots. 'You know about Polly, do you?'

'We stay faithfully in touch,' said Rosie.

'Rosie, you don't intend to give up college, do you?'

'Sorry, Daddy love, just accept it can't be helped. Polly did her bit in the Great War, so I'm not going to be left out of a new one, especially if it's against Hitler. Oh, I'm putting another sixpence in, so may I talk to Nana now, and then to Tim?'

'Rosie—'

'United we stand, ducky, divided we fall,' said Rosie. 'There, there goes my sixpence, so be a sweetie and put Nana on the line.'

'Don't tell her what you've just told me,' said Boots, 'or she'll have my head.'

'Oh, it's just between you and me for the time being,' said Rosie, which was typical of Boots's adopted daughter. She shared with him, as she always had, all her feelings and all her secrets, important or unimportant.

Donald let Emma know he was to have a medical. It was the first step, of course, to being conscripted into the militia. Emma said she didn't think much of circumstances that made conscription necessary. Donald asked if his possible departure into the Army would break her heart. Emma, frank, said well, no, not at her age. Her relationship with him was pleasant and uncomplicated as far as she was concerned. There were no moments of troublesome emotions, just an acceptance that closer ties might come about if she fell in love with him. Give it a year, say, Donald had said recently. Certainly, Emma never thought about falling in love at seventeen, even if her sister Annabelle had. She simply enjoyed having a boyfriend as likeable as Donald.

Donald said it would be a bit of a blow if she didn't even miss him, so Emma said of course she would miss him, and that they could get together whenever he came home on leave. Donald said he hoped nothing would happen while his back was turned. Emma asked what he meant, and he said she might turn into someone else's girlfriend.

'Who's someone else?' asked Emma.

'Unknown quantity at the moment,' said Donald.

'Oh, if an unknown quantity turns up, I'll let you know,' said Emma.

Donald laughed.

Chapter Fourteen

Boots had a word with Sammy in his office on Saturday morning.

'Sammy, regarding my commitment to the Army in August—'

'Leave off,' growled Sammy.

'Can't be ignored,' said Boots. 'I'll be going into uniform immediately after returning from Salcombe.'

'Susie's goin' to talk to you,' said Sammy.

'She already has,' said Boots.

'She's goin' to use a hammer this time,' said Sammy. 'She seriously feels a bit of head-bashin' is the only way to knock some sense into you. You've done your soldiering, she says, and I concur.'

'So do I,' said Boots, 'so I'll be behind the lines if the balloon goes up again. The point is that when I leave, you'll need someone in my place.'

'Listen, don't grieve me,' said Sammy, 'I've already got a headache about that.'

'There's a cure,' said Boots.

'I'm off headache powders,' said Sammy.

'Give the job to Emily,' said Boots.

'Eh?' Sammy sat up.

'She's the obvious choice,' said Boots, 'she knows the office and our systems inside-out.'

'Mother O'Grady, you serious?' said Sammy. 'A female general manager?'

'And she's family,' said Boots.

'Oh, my aching soul,' said Sammy.

'Steady, Junior, you'll get heartburn next,' said Boots.

'I'm improvin',' said Sammy, 'my headache's gone. Em'ly, you said? So you did. Did you further say that that means keepin' the job in the fam'ly?'

'You've caught up, Sammy,' said Boots.

'Perishing Amy,' said Sammy, 'I feel like complimentin' you on your mental machinery, Boots, and not for the first time. Offer my congratulations to Em'ly on her promotion.'

'And her increase in salary,' said Boots.

'Sometimes, Boots, you grieve my considerate nature,' said Sammy.

'We've all got some sorrows,' said Boots.

By the time Boots was home from his morning's work, Rosie had unexpectedly arrived. She was staying until Sunday afternoon. Eloise noted the warmth of her reception by the family. One simply had to accept she had a very special place in everyone's affections, and also that she really was a beautiful woman, her blue eyes showing some of Uncle Sammy's electricity.

Over lunch she announced her intention of volunteering for the women's Auxiliary Territorial Service in the event of a war.

'Rosie, I won't have it,' said Chinese Lady. 'It's

bad enough that your father's going into the Army again.'

'Daddy has to go, Nana,' said Rosie, 'he's among the men of the Great War who have something special to offer. Oh, and I've heard from Major Charles Armitage. He's already back in the Army.'

Major Charles Armitage was Rosie's natural father. She visited him periodically and regularly corresponded with him.

'Well, I suppose some old soldiers have to go back,' said Emily, 'but I don't know you have to give up the college to join anything, Rosie. And I don't know we need to talk as if we've got to have a war, it's very unsettling.'

'I've never felt more unsettled,' said Chinese Lady, 'What with Edwin havin' to go to France on Monday, Boots goin' into uniform after our holiday, and now Rosie talkin' about leavin' college to join that women's brigade or whatever. I'll never hold with puttin' women into uniform, it's not natural. I don't mind them being Army nurses or ambulance drivers, but not soldiers. God didn't order that sort of thing for women.'

'Yes, you must stay at college, Rosie, and finish your studies,' said Eloise.

'I think Rosie's already made up her mind,' said Tim.

'Then it's up to Boots to unmake it for her,' said Chinese Lady.

'Dad could try putting his foot down with a heavy hand,' said Tim, 'but I don't know if it'll work.'

'We won't have any comedian talk, Tim,' said Chinese Lady, 'we just want your father to talk

Rosie out of being a lady soldier. There's never been any lady soldiers in this fam'ly, and we don't want to start now.'

'Well, for this afternoon,' said Boots, 'I'm going to suggest Rosie and Tim might like a game of tennis.'

'Lovely,' said Rosie.

'I'm playing cricket,' said Tim.

'We'll ask Annabelle and Nick if they can make up a four, then,' said Boots, 'and if not, Emma and her boyfriend Donald.'

'I can't believe my ears,' said Chinese Lady. 'With the fam'ly so unsettled and Rosie talkin' about joining the Army, tennis is all you can think about, Boots?'

'Assure you, old girl, there are other things on my mind,' said Boots. 'By the way, when I do go into uniform, Emily's taking my place as general manager of the firm.'

'What's that?' asked Chinese Lady.

'Congratulations, Emily,' said Mr Finch.

'Boots, has Sammy agreed, then?' asked Emily, showing excitement.

'The prospect cured his headache,' said Boots.

'Why didn't you tell me when you came home from the office?' asked Emily, who herself had Saturday mornings off.

'It slipped my mind,' said Boots.

'What, when it's the most important thing that's ever 'appened to me?' said Emily.

A little silence fell, and Chinese Lady frowned.

'Em'ly, you sure you should have said that?' she asked, and Emily, realizing she'd dropped a brick, hastened to make amends.

'Oh, I only meant in me workin' life,' she said.

'Well, it's wonderful for your working life, Mum,' said Rosie, doing her own bit to help Emily out of embarrassment. She felt her adoptive mother had spoken without thinking, which was an unhappy mistake when Polly Simms was waiting in the wings, as it were. Rosie was sure Polly would always be ready to take centre stage with Boots. Not that Boots would let that happen too easily. He was always very much in control of himself.

'One's working life is quite separate from one's family life,' said Mr Finch on a helpful note of his own.

'Mama, you are really going to take Papa's place?' said Eloise.

Emily, a little flushed, said, 'It seems like it.'

'Well, that's settled a bit of the unsettling,' said Tim.

Chinese Lady frowned again.

'Em'ly, you're a wife and mother,' she said.

'Yes, I do know that, Mum,' said Emily in further haste. 'I've been so lucky. Well, right back to when I was young I always wanted to be a wife and mother. Still, with Eloise and Tim and Rosie so grown-up now, they don't need me as much as the fam'ly firm does, and I do feel complimented that Boots and Sammy both agree I can do the job.'

'Mama, of course we still need you,' said Eloise.

'But it won't make any real difference,' said Emily, 'I do work nearly full-time as secretary.'

'I don't like it,' said Chinese Lady. 'Women should first of all be wives and mothers, not general managers or dustmen. You all know very well that's what is natural. I just don't know what the world is comin' to, and you needn't sit there not saying a word, Edwin.'

'Ah, is it my turn to speak again?' said Mr Finch. 'Well, let me say, Maisie, that the world is changing fast and has been since the end of the Great War.'

'I don't mind some changes,' said Chinese Lady, 'but I'll never hold with lady soldiers and women general managers. Of course, no-one ever takes any notice of me, and I just don't know why I ever bother to open my mouth.'

'It's no bother to listen, old lady,' said Boots.

'Rosie a lady soldier and Em'ly a general manager,' sighed Chinese Lady, 'it all seems upside down to me, and I'm sure Queen Victoria would never 'ave allowed it. Next thing, I suppose, some women will want to grow moustaches and wear trousers and braces.' Rosie and Eloise shrieked with laughter. 'I don't know I said anything funny, did I?'

'Well, Nana,' said Tim, 'Uncle Sammy says Aunt Susie's been wearing the trousers for ages.'

'That's different,' said Chinese Lady, 'that's marriage trousers, which is what God ordered for the good of marriage.'

Annabelle and Nick couldn't get away for tennis because of their children, and Donald wasn't at home. So Boots got hold of Emma and brother Tommy. When Tommy arrived at the Ruskin Park Courts, he embraced Rosie in his outgoing way and planted a warm kiss on her cheek.

'I like it, Rosie,' he said.

'Like what, Uncle Tommy?'

'Seeing you,' said Tommy. 'Always did, always will. You're a partic'lar kind of fam'ly treasure, Rosie.'

'Mutual, Uncle Tommy, and you're a dear,' said Rosie.

Just before the game began, with Emma partnering Boots against Rosie and Tommy, Emma told Boots that Donald was going to be called up.

'Hard luck,' said Boots.

'Is that all you wish to say?' asked Emma, as lissom as a gazelle in her short tennis dress.

'What more is there, chicken?' asked Boots, who had never felt Emma to be earnestly involved with Donald. At seventeen, she was not as susceptible as Annabelle had been. Annabelle's involvement with Nick had been life and death to her.

'But aren't you sad for me that I'll be without a boyfriend?'

'Shall I find you another, Emma?'

'What kind?' asked Emma.

'What kind would you like?'

'Not one out of a hat,' said Emma.

'Are you two awake?' called Tommy.

'Serve away,' called Boots.

Tommy prepared to serve. Emma prepared to receive. Tommy served. Wallop. Emma gave a yell as the ball whizzed beyond her flailing racquet.

'Uncle Tommy, blowed if you don't be a demon!' she cried.

Boots looked at her.

Emma, who never floundered, floundered.

'Emma?' smiled Boots.

'I've gone potty,' said Emma.

'Join the club,' said Boots, and the game went on in earnest. Emma came to, and she and Rosie gave exuberant support to their partners, everything else forgotten for the moment.

Emily and Eloise were on one of their favourite excursions, shopping in the superior area of Streatham. Tim was playing cricket. Chinese Lady and Mr Finch were sharing a pot of tea in the garden.

Annabelle and Nick were at home with their children. Sammy and Susie were having a lively family afternoon with theirs. Lizzy and Ned were at Sammy's Brixton shop, Lizzy buying a new dress with the advantage of family discount.

Horace Cooper was at Lord's, playing for Surrey against Middlesex. Sally and her son were enjoying afternoon tea with Horace's parents, Jim and Rebecca Cooper. Cassie and Freddy Brown were at home in Walworth, making a fuss of infant Muffin.

Outside Lord's, and in Streatham, Brixton, Camberwell, Walworth and elsewhere in London, news vendors were selling the afternoon editions of the evening papers. They all had similar placards:

'HITLER WARNS POLES. FINNS HURL RUSSIANS BACK'.

Which meant Hitler was foaming at the mouth again, and that Soviet Russia was having a humiliating experience in its war against little Finland. Joseph Stalin, a bear who with a brief wave of his paw had countenanced the murder of millions of

Russians, had decided to deprive Finland of a strip of adjoining territory. Finland decided to resist, and its small but efficient army had socked and rocked the bear not once, but several times. It all added to the uneasiness of Europe.

Bobby Somers was with his Territorial unit, and very aware of the presence of regular Army officers and NCOs. Territorials were having to take their duties that much more seriously than usual, and Bobby didn't need to be told that the country's reserve army would be expected to play an immediate part in the event of war, and the Territorials were being prepared for that. Weapon drill was more intensive, so was gunnery practice. And field exercises were more combative every weekend, when the unit entrained for country areas.

Just after four, Amelia from next door called in one more attempt to inveigle Jonathan out of his house and into her mum's parlour. Jennifer opened the door to her.

''Ello, how's yerself,' said Amelia, sporting a bright yellow Hollywood sweater, 'is Jonathan doin' anything?'

'No, but the upstairs doors are,' said Jennifer, 'they're rattling away like they never did before. D'you want to come in and listen?'

'Oh, me gawd, no I don't,' said Amelia, turning pale. 'I don't know 'ow you can live 'ere.'

'It won't hurt, just coming in and listening,' said Jennifer.

'Yes, it will, it'll freeze me blood,' said Amelia. 'I'll just wait on the step while you get Jonathan.'

'What d'you want him for?' asked Jennifer.

'I've got something to show 'im,' said Amelia, and Jennifer studied the bright Hollywood sweater.

'I don't think he's old enough,' she said.

'What d'you mean, not old enough?' said Amelia.

'He's only twenty,' said Jennifer, 'that's not old enough for looking.'

'Lookin' at what?' asked Amelia.

'What you want to show him,' said Jennifer.

'Oh, yer cheeky young ha'porth,' said Amelia, 'I just want to show 'im our new gramophone. It's electrified. Where is 'e?'

Jennifer turned and yelled.

'Jonathan! D'you want to go and see Amelia Hardcastle's new electrified gramophone that be in her mum's parlour?'

No answer from Jonathan. But Jane appeared, having recently returned from the market with her mum.

'Oh, hello, Amelia,' she said, 'what are you standing on the step for?'

'I ain't comin' in,' said Amelia, 'not while your upstairs doors are rattling. I was saying to Jennifer, I just don't know 'ow you can live 'ere without all yer hair turning white. Would you ask Jonathan to come and see our new gramophone?'

'Well, I would,' said Jane, 'only he's got a headache. It's just come on. D'you want to come through and bathe his forehead? The kitchen floor's moving a bit, it always does on Saturday afternoons, but it won't do you any damage.'

'Oh, yer all crazy,' breathed Amelia, paling again, 'it's what that ghost 'as done to yer. I ain't puttin' even 'alf a foot in this house, I'm goin' before I get 'aunted for life.' She rushed off.

'Well, I'm blessed, she's gone,' said Jennifer.

'She be a funny girl about little Patrick,' said Jane. 'Still, Jonathan can come out of hiding in the larder now.'

Someone knocked after supper that night.

'Could that be Amelia again?' asked Jennifer.

'More like young Joe Morgan come to sit in the parlour with Jane,' said Job. 'I see she's wearing a pretty frock, and durned if her every pretty frock don't seem to bring young Joe knocking. D'you want to answer the door?'

'I'll go,' said Jonathan. He found Mr and Mrs Hardcastle on the doorstep, together with a long thin man wearing a black frock-coat and a tall stovepipe hat. Mr and Mrs Hardcastle, parents of Alfie and Amelia, were both stout with a liking for a regular drop of what they fancied. Regularity had given them red faces and happy dispositions. Mr Hardcastle was a navvy, Mrs Hardcastle a cheerful collector of public house beer tumblers when the publicans weren't looking.

''Ello, Jonathan, howjerdo, eh?' said Mr Hardcastle.

'My, ain't yer growin' up 'andsome?' said Mrs Hardcastle. 'No wonder 'Melia fancies yer.'

'Yerse, why don't yer come and join 'er in the

parlour occasional, Jonathan?' invited Mr Hardcastle.

'I'll give that a bit of thought when I'm not helping young Jonas to stick stamps in his album,' said Jonathan. 'Anyway, what can I do for you?'

'Well, it's like this,' said Mr Hardcastle. 'We – 'old on, you ain't met Mrs 'Ardcastle's distant cousin Jarsper, 'ave yer?'

'No, I don't think I've had the pleasure,' said Jonathan.

'Well, 'ere he is,' said Mr Hardcastle, 'Mr Jarsper Galleymore of Stoke Newington.'

'Pleasure, Mr Galleymore,' said Jonathan.

'Mutual, I'm sure,' said Mr Jasper Galleymore, dark of eyes and cadaverous of features.

'Jarsper's come to do you and yer fam'ly a good turn,' said Mrs Hardcastle.

'That's nice of him,' said Jonathan. 'What good turn?'

'It's regardin' yer troubles,' said Mr Hardcastle.

'What troubles?' asked Jonathan.

'Well, you got demons, Jonathan, what's scarin' 'Melia to death and puttin' the wind up Alfie,' said Mrs Hardcastle. 'And nor ain't Bert and me, and some of yer other neighbours, none too 'appy. Would yer like to invite us in so's we can talk to yer fam'ly?'

'Well,' said Jonathan, 'I'll ask—'

'There y'ar, Jarsper,' said Mr Hardcastle, 'we can go in. Jonathan and 'is fam'ly's always welcomin'.'

'A happy virtue,' boomed Mr Galleymore.

'Yes, we'll go in the parlour, shall we, Jonathan?' beamed Mrs Hardcastle, and led the way. The entry of two stout bodies and a tall thin one had the effect of making Jonathan feel that the front door was suddenly trying to knock him off his feet. By the time he'd recovered his balance, all three callers were in the parlour.

'Yes, come in,' he said, closing the door. 'I'll fetch the family.'

'If you got a bottle or two, Jonathan, we won't say no,' called Mr Hardcastle.

Jonathan, returning to the kitchen, acquainted his family with the news that Mr and Mrs Hardcastle were making themselves at home in the parlour, along with Mrs Hardcastle's distant cousin, one Jasper Galleymore.

'Oh, Lordy, in the parlour, are they?' said Jemima.

'What for?' asked young Jonas.

'Mr Galleymore wants to do us a good turn regarding little Patrick,' said Jonathan.

'Eh?' said Job.

'Fact,' said Jonathan.

'Well, I be blowed,' said Job.

'What good turn?' asked Jane.

'Daft one, probably,' said Jonathan.

'Little Patrick won't like it,' said young Jonas.

'Kick up a rumpus, I shouldn't wonder,' said Jennifer.

'Well, best to be neighbourly and see what it's all about,' said Jemima.

'Aye, that's best,' said Job.

They presented themselves to the Hardcastles in the parlour, and were introduced to Mr

Galleymore, who removed his stovepipe hat and bowed to Jemima.

'Honoured to be 'ere, Mrs Hardy,' he boomed.

'Thank you,' said Jemima, 'but I be all of mystified.'

'Jarspers's an exorser,' beamed Mrs Hardcastle proudly.

'Come natural to 'im,' said Mr Hardcastle.

'What's an exorser?' said Jane.

'One that's got an 'oly touch,' said Mrs Hardcastle, 'and can get rid of little demons.'

'Modestly, I claim the power to exorcize a dwelling, to drive forth spirits of darkness, spirits of restlessness, and the tormenting 'ands of the unseen,' said Mr Galleymore.

'Told yer, Jemima,' said Mr Hardcastle, 'told yer Jarsper was a natural. Well, yer see, livin' next door to you and yer fam'ly like we do, I speak for self and the missus and Alfie and 'Melia in saying it ain't doin' our nerves much good. Mrs 'Ardcastle, me good lady, ain't beginnin' to sleep too well at night, thinkin' them little demons of yourn might take it into their 'eads to pay us a visit and then stay for good.'

'It's only an Irish leprechaun that got left behind when the house was built,' said Jane. 'He be harmless.'

'Does a bit of chuckling now and again, which be right harmless,' said Job.

'Might turn nasty one day, Job,' said Mr Hardcastle.

'Which is beginnin' to worry other neighbours,' said Mrs Hardcastle. 'And our 'Melia says every time she visits, the demon's at 'is tricks. She said she felt 'im tryin' to climb up 'er skirt one time, which ain't nice for a delicate girl like 'er. Anyway, Jarsper offered to come and exorse yer.'

'Well, I be in two minds about being exorsed,' said Job.

'We all are,' said Jane.

'So am I,' said young Jonas.

'What's the procedure?' asked Jonathan.

Mr Galleymore lifted his hands.

'My friends,' he boomed. He began a dissertation on wandering souls and imps of Satan that could find no rest, alas.

Then, alas again, tremors travelled through the floor, and the kitchen door rattled. Mrs Hardcastle jumped. Mr Hardcastle quivered. Mr Galleymore spoke in sepulchral tones.

'Begone, unhappy soul, begone, restless spirit, begone, imp of Satan. Begone.'

The parlour door itself rattled.

'Oh, me dear gawd,' breathed Mrs Hardcastle.

'Crikey,' said young Jonas, 'little Patrick don't like being told "begone".'

'Return whence you came, dark one,' boomed Mr Galleymore, extending a long arm and pointing a long finger westward. Jonathan supposed he had Ireland in mind.

The floor trembled and issued a series of creaks.

'That's him,' said Jennifer, 'giggling and all, would you believe.'

'Your mum had a fit of the giggles once,' said Job, as Mr Galleymore closed his eyes and muttered incantations. 'It were when she were fifteen and I were twenty. Down the lane she came with one of her dad's cows, and as it passed me it dropped a pat, and durned if I didn't step right into it.'

'Job, would yer mind givin' Jarsper a bit of quiet?' said Mr Hardcastle.

'Rods of 'eaven, iron-bound, beat the dark and lurking hound,' boomed Mr Galleymore, and executed circles with his hands.

'What's he doing?' asked young Jonas.

'He's drivin' yer little demon forth,' said Mr Hardcastle.

'Little Patrick don't be a demon,' said Jennifer.

'Jolly little chap, that he is,' said Jonathan.

'Well, Jonathan lovey,' said Mrs Hardcastle, still all of a tremble, 'it ain't very jolly for 'Melia and Alfie, nor me. Me blood's running cold this 'ere minute.'

'Could we 'ave some quiet?' complained Mr Hardcastle, happy disposition taking a back seat for once.

Mr Galleymore, awesome in his height and his long circling arms, declaimed.

'Seven times round the 'and of fate moves to circumnavigate, imps of darkness, shed your spell, begone ye demons, back to hell.'

'I don't think little Patrick will be liking that,' said Jemima.

The parlour door, ajar, rattled loudly. Mr Galleymore advanced, hands raised high.

'Begone, I say!' he boomed.

The door quivered and swung back, and Mr Galleymore, very unfortunately considering he was

214

only there to do the Hardy family a good turn, received it in shock. Well, it struck his chest and his nose. He emitted a muffled nasal yell.

'Oh, Lordy,' breathed Jemima.

'Told you,' said young Jonas, 'told you little Patrick wouldn't like it.'

Mr Galleymore, hand clapped to his bruised hooter, regarded the door balefully.

'Spawn of Satan, begone!' he hissed.

The quivering door swung again and clouted him. He staggered, tripped, and fell flat on his back.

'Bugger it,' he bawled, and the floor trembled beneath him. 'I ain't staying 'ere,' he hollered, 'it's bleedin' 'aunted.'

Job roared with laughter. Jemima pealed. Jonathan, Jane, Jennifer and young Jonas all exploded with mirth, and the parlour vibrated with loud merriment. Mr Hardcastle blinked, grinned, and then his own laughter bawled. Mrs Hardcastle stopped trembling and a little giggle arrived. Mr Galleymore scrambled up, grabbed his stovepipe hat and departed in a rush, intent on never returning.

'Oh, 'elp, poor Jarsper,' said Mrs Hardcastle.

''E ain't goin' to forgive us easy,' said Mr Hardcastle, wiping his eyes.

'Oh, well, 'e's only a distant cousin,' said Mrs Hardcastle.

'And 'e did talk 'imself into comin',' said Mr Hardcastle. 'Mind, I didn't know 'is 'ooter was goin' to cop a packet. Still, no 'arm to us, eh, Gladys?'

'Except it's give me a bit of a thirst,' said Mrs Hardcastle.

'Tell yer what, Job,' said Mr Hardcastle, ''ow about a drop of what some of us might fancy, eh?'

'You be right welcome,' said Job.

'Yes, come to the kitchen,' said Jemima, 'and Job will find a bottle or two.'

'Floor's not moving, Mum,' said Jennifer.

'And there's no doors rattling,' said Jane.

'And I daresay the mantelpieces are all behaving,' said Jonathan.

'Nice and quiet now,' said Job, escorting the visitors to the kitchen.

'Funny 'ow me blood ain't running cold no more,' said Mrs Hardcastle.

'That shows little Patrick's taken a fancy to you,' said Jonathan.

'Oh, 'ow kind,' said Mrs Hardcastle. 'I don't know why Alfie and 'Melia worry so much.'

On Sunday afternoon, Boots drove Rosie to Paddington and saw her onto her train. Standing in the door of the coach, Rosie said she was relieved he hadn't talked to her as his mother insisted he should.

'About your idea of volunteering for the Auxiliaries?' said Boots.

'Yes,' smiled Rosie.

'Are you going to tell me you've changed your mind?' asked Boots.

'No,' said Rosie.

'It seems hard on the years you've spent studying,' said Boots.

'Daddy old love,' said Rosie, 'you know me. You know me better than anyone. You hate war, you hate it for a very good reason. I hate it too. But if you're going to do your bit in the event of a new war, you don't seriously think you can leave me behind, do you? Polly won't be left behind. Neither will I. Neither will Bobby. That young man is going to make a fine soldier. He knows and you know, and so do I, that some of us have got to stand up to Hitler.'

The engine let off hissing steam. The guard was out of his van, his green flag in his hand. Latecomers were running along the platform. Compartment doors opened and closed.

'What I hate most, Rosie, is a spoiled future for you and all our other young people,' said Boots.

'And what I hate most, apart from Hitler and his Stormtroopers, is the fact that men like you are going to have to fight all over again,' said Rosie.

Porters were closing doors, and the guard had his whistle close to his mouth.

'Think of yourself, poppet, not of me,' said Boots.

'Stop worrying about me,' said Rosie. The whistle was blown and the green flag lifted as she bent her head. Boots kissed her. 'Bless you, Daddy old soldier,' she said.

'You'll wish you'd never joined,' said Boots.

The train began to move. Rosie, at the coach door, waved. Boots lifted his hand. She blew a kiss, then disappeared.

Driving home, Boots wondered why it was that his adopted daughter always seemed to mean a little more to him than all the other young people. It was unfair to all the others, and Eloise said it had fashioned a cage for Rosie, a cage that kept her from making a life of her own.

He grimaced.

Chapter Fifteen

Jonathan hesitated about going to Lyons on Monday. If Emma happened to be there, his arrival wouldn't be welcomed. He felt a little sad again about her insistence on finishing with him. Oh, well, grin and bear it.

He went into Lyons, anyway, and there she was, at her usual table. He took his life into his hands. He approached her and said, 'Like me to join you, Emma?'

Emma regarded him frowningly. She was thinking about what was happening to her friendship with Donald.

'No, you'd better not,' she said.

'I won't make a nuisance of myself.'

'Yes, you will,' she said.

'Not if we just talked about *Gone With The Wind*,' said Jonathan.

'Well, all right,' said Emma, and Jonathan sat down. 'No, you'd better not,' she said again. 'I should have told you first off that I've got a steady boyfriend.'

'No, is that a fact?' said Jonathan.

'Yes,' said Emma.

'Well, that's great,' said Jonathan.

'What d'you mean, great?'

'I thought you were too shy for that sort of thing,' said Jonathan.

'What sort of thing?' demanded Emma amid the rattle and buzz of Lyons.

'You know,' said Jonathan, 'kisses and cuddles. I mean, they must be blush-making for a shy girl.'

Oh, help, thought Emma, I'll giggle myself silly if he says anything else like that.

'How dare you accuse me at my age of letting someone be familiar with me?' she said.

'D'you mean kissing and cuddling?' said Jonathan. 'Don't you do that, then, with your chap?'

'Certainly not,' said Emma, 'that's only for when I'm engaged to be married.'

'Well, I'm fair amazed,' said Jonathan. 'My sister Jane goes in for a lot of that with her young chap, and she's not engaged.'

'What your sister does is her own affair,' said Emma.

'Still,' said Jonathan, 'I've got to say it's good that you've got a boyfriend. It means you're normal.'

'I'm what?'

'I mean, you're not so shy that you don't have a bloke,' said Jonathan. 'That's really good, Emma, I was afraid you might end up as a wallflower.'

'A wallflower?' Emma could hardly believe the old-fashioned stuff that frequently came out of his mouth.

'Yes,' said Jonathan. 'As it is, I honestly couldn't be more pleased for you.'

'D'you want me to hit you with the cruet?' asked Emma.

'No, I don't, not here, not in Lyons.'

'You're the one who's not normal,' said Emma, 'you've got more bats in the belfry than anyone else I ever met, and what's more, you've got wicked eyes, which is what that little old lady said about you. I don't suppose even Rhett Butler had wickeder ones. Anyway, it's not your business to be pleased for me because I've got a steady boyfriend.'

'Well, you don't think I could be cross, do you?' said Jonathan. 'I mean, it shows you've got happy prospects, and that's something for both of us to be pleased about, isn't it?'

'It's nothing to do with you,' said Emma.

''Ello, you two, what's it to be today?' Trixie had arrived.

'Just a poached egg on toast for me,' said Emma. 'And he can have poison,' she said under her breath.

'I didn't catch that, miss,' said Trixie.

'I only want something light,' said Emma.

'Yes, poached egg on toast,' said Trixie.

'Then a cup of coffee, please,' said Emma.

'And what can I get you, young sir?' asked Trixie.

'I'll have poached egg on toast too,' said Jonathan, 'and college pudding and custard for afters.'

'Reckless again, are we?' smiled Trixie, and bustled away.

'Can we get it straight, Emma?' said Jonathan. 'If you're being courted—'

'Dated,' said Emma distantly.

'Yes, same thing—'

'No, it isn't, and don't be so old-fashioned. I told you, no one says courting any more. It's died a death.'

'Funny thing, it was my mother who courted my dad,' said Jonathan. 'Dad was only the village handyman and didn't feel he was in a position to court any girl, so Mum did all the courting. She said she'd drown herself if he didn't marry her, so of course Dad said he'd give her bottom a rare old pasting if she ever did anything as daft as that. Well, Mum—'

'I'll scream, d'you hear me?' breathed Emma. 'I'll scream out loud.'

'What for?' asked Jonathan.

'Because you're driving me potty,' said Emma.

'Be a bit embarrassing, if you screamed out loud in here,' said Jonathan. 'Listen, on account of you being a normal girl and having a boyfriend, I suppose it would only be fair if I did sit somewhere else. I can understand what you mean, it might get back to him that you've been seen with me, and I'd be bowed down with sorrow if I caused any upset.'

'Bowed down with sorrow?' Emma nearly choked. 'D'you have to talk like someone ninety years old?'

'No, I don't have to,' said Jonathan, 'and I didn't think I did.'

'Well, you do,' said Emma, much as if she was determined to fight him. 'And it's too late to go and sit somewhere else when you've already been seen with me hundreds of times.'

'Hundreds?' said Jonathan.

'That's what it feels like,' said Emma, 'and someone will tell Donald eventually, I suppose.'

'That's his name?' said Jonathan.

'Yes,' said Emma.

'Emma and Donald,' said Jonathan. 'Well, I think that's a fine old example of names going together. Emma and Donald, yes, they suit each other, I reckon.'

'Oh, they do, do they?' said Emma.

'Yes, and would you like me to sit somewhere else before Trixie brings our food?' asked Jonathan.

'I told you, it's too late,' said Emma. 'But don't keep making eyes at me.'

'I'm not,' said Jonathan.

'Yes, you are,' said Emma.

'Emma, believe me, I'm downright pleased about you and Donald,' said Jonathan, who wasn't, of course. But he didn't want to be a sourpuss.

'Oh, it's made you as happy as a lark, has it?' said Emma.

'Well, I'm—'

'Never mind,' said Emma.

Trixie brought their poached eggs on toast.

'There we are,' she said. 'Things goin' a treat for you two?' she said, and away she went again.

'Emma, d'you want to talk about Donald?' asked Jonathan.

'No,' said Emma.

'Did you have a nice weekend?'

'I always have a nice weekend,' said Emma.

'Dating, I suppose,' said Jonathan.

'Are you dating when you're not trying it on with me?' asked Emma, as they began their light meal.

223

'Well, I'm like Dad was,' said Jonathan, 'I'm a bit underfunded due to my stingy bosses, and you have to have something in your pocket if you want to take a girl out.'

'Why do you?' asked Emma.

'Well, a girl expects—'

'I don't think much of any girl who wants to know how much you've got in your pocket before she goes out with you,' said Emma. 'There's one you do treat when you can, is there?'

'Not that I know of,' said Jonathan, 'there's just the girl next door who wants to get me into her mum's parlour to listen to their new electrified gramophone.' Emma choked on a mouthful of egg and toast. 'Went down the wrong way, did it, Emma?'

Emma struggled against a whole army of rising giggles. It wasn't a brief struggle, either. It took her quite a while to win.

'What's she like, the girl next door?' she asked.

'Not like you,' said Jonathan, 'she's not half a yard shy. She wears Hollywood sweaters and they—' He decided not to go on.

'Yes?' said Emma.

'No, she's not shy,' said Jonathan. 'What's Donald like?'

'Well, I can tell you one thing about him,' said Emma, 'he doesn't drag me into crowds of people to make me talk to strangers.'

'No, well, he likes kissing and cuddling better, I suppose,' said Jonathan. 'Can't say I blame him.'

'Oh, not that again,' said Emma. 'What a daft way of putting words together. Kissing and cuddling.

You sound like someone's grandmother. I expect you're thinking about dragging me off again as soon as you've had your afters, are you?'

The college pudding arrived, and so did Emma's coffee. Trixie smiled as she set them down on the table.

'You two still gettin' along? That's nice,' she said, and whisked away again.

'Emma, I wouldn't dream of dragging you into the crowds again,' said Jonathan, 'especially now I know about Donald.'

'I'll just have to put up with it,' said Emma.

'Emma, I don't think you need to talk to people, after all.'

'No, you win,' said Emma. 'I suppose it might be good for me, and you'll only keep on if I don't let you. I'll just have to grit my teeth.'

'Well, you be a rare old funny girl,' said Jonathan.

'Yes, don't I be,' said Emma, looking forward to having hysterics again.

'Excuse me, sir,' said Jonathan a little later, 'but this young lady be wishful to know where the parish church is.'

'Eh?' said an old bloke with mutton chops.

'The Camberwell parish church,' said Jonathan, with Emma killing herself.

'Eh?' said the old bloke again.

'My friend wants to do a bit of praying come Sunday,' said Jonathan. 'If you could talk to her about the church and where it is, she'd be grateful.'

The old bloke scanned Emma. Emma did her terrible best to look churchified.

'What d'yer want to do praying for?' he asked.

'Well, I – well, I've got a sick cousin in the country,' said Emma. 'She's ill in bed.'

'Can't 'er old lady pray for 'er?'

'Oh, she can't get to church,' said Emma, 'she's crippled.'

'Ain't we all,' said the old bloke, 'it's an 'ard life that does it and a useless Government.'

'Yes, life is awful burdensome,' said Emma.

'Are yer Roman Cath'lic?' asked the old bloke.

'No, she be young and healthy,' said Jonathan.

'Bein' Roman Cath'lic ain't strickly a complaint,' said the old bloke, and scanned Emma again. 'Mind, I believe yer, I never seen anyone younger nor more 'ealthy. Walkin' out with 'er, are yer?'

'D'you mean courting?' asked Jonathan.

'That's it, courtin',' said the old bloke.

'No, she doesn't do courting,' said Jonathan.

'Too young, I s'pose,' said the old bloke. 'She does prayin', though, don't yer, young lady?'

'Yes, I'm praying now,' said Emma.

'For yer sick country cousin?'

'No, for a load of bricks to drop on someone's head,' said Emma.

''Ello, 'ello,' said the old bloke, 'got it in for that barmy Adolf 'Itler, 'ave yer?'

'Yes, not half, and for someone just as barmy,' said Emma.

'There ain't many as barmy as 'Itler, yer know,' said the old bloke.

'There's one,' said Emma, 'and it's my bad luck

that I'm personally acquainted with him.'

''Ave yer tried rat poison?' asked the old bloke.

'Not yet,' said Emma.

''E won't last long after a dose of that in 'is tea,' said the old bloke, 'but don't leave any finger-prints. About this 'ere parish church that yer want to do some prayin' in, I ain't able to 'elp yer. Never been in no church in my life, except when I was baptized, and yer can't do much about it at that age. I don't go to church, never 'ave, so I can't tell yer where any of 'em is. I can tell yer where the gasworks is, and you could do yer praying there, if you ain't too partic'lar.'

'You're very kind,' said Emma.

'Of course, I ain't done any prayin' meself at the gasworks,' said the old bloke, 'but when I was a lad and Maggie Perryman lived next door, I used to take 'er there for a bit of 'ealthy kissin' and cuddlin'.'

'I've been hearing a lot about that sort of thing lately,' said Emma.

'We did it round the back, of course,' said the old bloke. 'You remind me of Maggie, yer know. Born for kissin' and cuddlin', Maggie was, and I trust I ain't offendin' yer when I say you look like you was born for it too.'

'I think my young friend prefers praying,' said Jonathan.

'A bit of prayin' now and again won't 'urt yer, young lady,' said the old bloke, 'but kissin' and cuddlin' is a sight more 'ealthy. It's natural, yer see. Well, give me regards to yer sick country cousin, and I'll do a bit of prayin' for 'er meself in me backyard. Good afternoon to yer.'

Emma stood quite still as he went off.

'Anything wrong?' asked Jonathan.

'Yes, I can't move,' breathed Emma.

'Can't move?' said Jonathan.

'No. If I do, I'll go off bang,' said Emma.

'I can't think why,' said Jonathan, 'you had a rare old chat with the bloke.'

'Don't speak, don't say a word,' breathed Emma. 'I'll scream if you do. Did you hear him say what I was born for? The saucy old devil. Oh, you're really wicked, you are, Jonathan Hardy, putting me in all my modesty up against an old devil like that.'

'Well, I did say I didn't think you needed to talk to people in the street, after all.'

'Don't make excuses, you – you worm,' said Emma, letting people flow by. 'Oh, what a sad day I had when I met you.'

'Tell you what,' said Jonathan, 'let's try stopping a lady with a kind face, someone who'll make up for the old bloke. I'll ask her if she knows the Camberwell Palace, and if they want a girl contralto as a variety turn. Everyone likes the theatre. Can you do contralto?'

'If you don't go away, I will scream, d'you hear?' said Emma.

'I don't know why you get so upset,' said Jonathan.

'I'm going back to my work this minute,' said Emma, 'and I'll be bringing sandwiches tomorrow while you go to Lyons. Is that clear?'

'Actually, I was thinking—'

'Is that clear?'

'Well, yes,' said Jonathan.

'Then farewell,' said Emma dramatically, and left at a fast pace. She had to. She was splitting her sides.

Funny girl, thought Jonathan. But it had been uplifting to be with her again, even if she did have a steady date. Did I tell her I was pleased about it? I think I told a lie.

Jemima was intrigued to know Jonathan had seen the girl Trudy again. She was very fond of her firstborn, who was like his good-looking, happy-go-lucky dad, who had helped her escape her grim and gloomy parents. Jemima had never forgotten Job's brave rescue act, for it took a lot to defy her father. And because Jonathan was like Job, only over her dead body would a tarty girl like Amelia Hardcastle get her painted fingernails into him.

She was naturally very curious about the girl Trudy, and didn't think Jonathan's casual references to her meant his feelings were casual.

For some reason, Jemima liked the sound of Trudy more each day.

What she didn't like, naturally, was the thought of Jonathan being called up. Or the further thought that it might mean him going to war.

Emma, replacing a split pearl button on one of her office blouses, had trouble with her sewing needle that evening. It pricked her thumb.

'Oh, blow, what a fool I be,' she said.

'Do what?' said Bobby.

'What's that you said, Emma?' asked Lizzy.

'Nothing,' said Emma, sucking her thumb.

'A funny nothing,' said Bobby, 'sounded like Cornish.'

'Cornish is Celtic,' said Ned.

'Not Cornish English,' said Edward.

'Ar, tiddly bit of Cornish English Emma spoke then, me dears,' said Bobby.

'I don't know what you mean,' said Emma. Horrors, she thought, I'm going native as well as potty. Oh, that Jonathan Hardy has got a lot to answer for. I've a good mind to run into him in Lyons tomorrow so that I can let him know what I really think of him.

Jonathan, however, didn't appear in Lyons the following day, so she ate her lunch without being bothered by him for a single moment.

Wednesday. Lunchtime again. She had sandwiches. And she sat in the middle of a bench with her handbag to her right and a carrier bag to her left to discourage strangers from sitting beside her.

Jonathan appeared, his lunch-tin in his hand. Emma, spotting him out of the corner of her eye, sat up challengingly. Up he came.

'Hello, Emma,' he said.

'You can't,' she said.

'Can't what?'

'You can't sit here.'

'Don't want me to?'

'There's no room.'

'Well,' said Jonathan, 'if you'd move that carrier-bag—'

'I won't,' said Emma.

'Or your handbag—'

'No.'

'I could sit right at the end,' said Jonathan.

'I need that space for my book,' said Emma.

'You haven't got a book,' said Jonathan.

'I had a nice quiet time in Lyons yesterday,' said Emma.

'I had sandwiches here to keep out of your way,' said Jonathan, and sat down.

'What d'you think you're doing?' asked Emma.

'I'm sitting,' said Jonathan.

'Yes, and on my carrier-bag,' said Emma.

'There's nothing in it,' said Jonathan.

'My sandwiches could have been,' said Emma.

'They're on your lap,' said Jonathan.

'Never mind that,' said Emma, 'stop sitting on my carrier-bag.'

'How's Donald?' asked Jonathan, opening his lunch-tin.

'Lucky for you he's not here,' said Emma. 'What sandwiches have you got?'

'Tongue,' said Jonathan

'I like tongue,' said Emma.

'Have one,' said Jonathan, offering.

'I've got ham,' said Emma.

'I like ham,' said Jonathan. 'Is there mustard?'

'A smidgeon,' said Emma, and they made an exchange of one sandwich each. 'Yours is brown bread.'

'Yes, Hovis,' said Jonathan.

'As soon as we've finished eating,' said Emma, 'you can go.'

'I was thinking of staying,' said Jonathan.

'Well, you can't,' said Emma. 'I might be engaged to be married by this time next year.'

'Well, I'm blowed,' said Jonathan, 'I'm fair amazed again. No, wait a bit, I thought you said you were only dating.'

'That doesn't mean I won't be engaged to be married by this time next year,' said Emma, 'so I've got to put a stop to you meeting me like this.'

'Hold on, I've never actually tried to push myself.'

'Yes, you have,' said Emma. 'What about all the times you've made eyes at me? By the way, did your mother make your sandwiches?'

'Yes.'

'Well, this one's very nice.'

'Glad you like it, and the ham sandwich is good,' said Jonathan. 'About your marriage—'

'About my what?' said Emma.

'I'd like to wish you all the best,' said Jonathan.

'I didn't say I was going to be married, only that I might be engaged,' said Emma.

'Well, one thing leads to the other,' said Jonathan.

'And you're as happy as a lark again for me, are you?'

'You must be happy yourself that you've got prospects of being a bride and not a wallflower,' said Jonathan. 'When we first met I thought it can't be right, young Trudy shaping up to be a wallflower all her life. Of course, I didn't know about

Donald at the time. Would you be able to accept a wedding present from me? What would you like, if it's not too expensive?'

'I'd like an ambulance to take me to hospital,' said Emma.

'Hospital? What for?' asked Jonathan.

'I need an operation,' said Emma.

'Operation?'

'Yes, on my head,' said Emma.

'What's wrong with your head?'

'Everything,' said Emma, 'or I wouldn't be here.'

'I think you're having a game with me,' said Jonathan.

'Have you finished your sandwiches yet?' asked Emma.

'Not yet,' said Jonathan. 'Is Donald well-off, by the way?'

'I don't know, I haven't asked him,' said Emma.

'About a wedding present—'

'I'll have a horse,' said Emma, 'I've always wanted a horse.'

'Don't they come a bit expensive?' asked Jonathan.

'I don't mind a second-hand one,' said Emma.

'Be a funny old wedding present, a second-hand horse,' said Jonathan.

'I couldn't accept it, anyway,' said Emma, 'not without it putting Donald into an awful rage.'

'He's a jealous bloke?' said Jonathan.

'Oh, he be terrible jealous, me dear,' said Emma, and Jonathan laughed.

'I don't think you're shy any more,' he said.

'Yes, I am.'

'No, you're not.'

'How do you know?'

'You're a bit cheeky, I reckon.'

'You've got wicked eyes,' said Emma.

'That's not the first time you've said that.'

'Well, you're still sitting on my carrier-bag,' said Emma. 'Have you finished your sandwiches now?'

'Yes, all gone, and I enjoyed the ham,' said Jonathan.

'Well, then?' said Emma.

'All right,' said Jonathan, getting to his feet, 'I'll push off now.'

'I'd better leave too,' said Emma, 'I need to buy some toothpaste from the chemist's shop – oh, look at what you've done to my carrier-bag.'

'It's only a bit wrinkled,' said Jonathan.

'It wasn't wrinkled before you sat on it,' said Emma. She put her sandwich wrapping into the bag, and they left the Green to cross the road to the chemist's shop. Once there, Emma said, 'Well, goodbye.'

'Is that final?' asked Jonathan.

'Well, there's Donald, isn't there?' said Emma.

'He doesn't have to be terrible jealous,' said Jonathan.

'Yes, he does,' said Emma.

'No, he doesn't,' said Jonathan, 'he's got nothing to be jealous about.'

'Don't think I don't know you're trying to date me yourself,' said Emma, 'and if Donald knew he'd explode into a dreadful temper.'

'Serve him right,' muttered Jonathan.

'What's that you said?'

'Emma, have I ever asked you for a date? Have I ever?'

'It won't be long coming,' said Emma. 'If I stayed here talking to you for just five more minutes, I bet you'd ask if you could take me to see the film of *Gone With The Wind* when it comes out.'

'No, I wouldn't,' said Jonathan.

'Yes, you would,' said Emma, 'you're shameless enough not to have any respect for the fact that I might be engaged to be married by this time next year.'

'Well, I'm blowed,' said Jonathan, 'didn't I say I was pleased for you? I reckon that was showing respect, wasn't it?'

'Don't make excuses,' said Emma. 'I'm going home to lunch every day from now on in case Donald finds out about the way you keep meeting me. I suppose you'll bring sandwiches again tomorrow, will you?'

'Yes, I have to save a bit of money each week,' said Jonathan.

'Don't we all,' said Emma. 'Well, goodbye.' Into the shop she went, leaving Jonathan fishing aimlessly about in search of his head. Well, he felt it wasn't where it should have been. That was what came of cross-talk with Emma.

In the shop, Emma purchased a tube of toothpaste.

The lady assistant, who knew her, asked, 'Was that your young man you were talking to outside?'

'No, just a country chap,' said Emma.

'A country chap?'

'Yes, he be that all right,' said Emma.

She was smiling when she left the shop.

But the smile had become a frown again by the time she reached the offices.

Chapter Sixteen

At supper that evening, Jemima said, 'Did you see Trudy again, Jonathan?'

'I wasn't supposed to,' said Jonathan, 'but I did bump into her.'

'Why wasn't you supposed to?' asked young Jonas.

'She's got a steady chap,' said Jonathan.

Everyone stopped eating steak and kidney pie to look at him.

'Don't like what that means,' said Job, 'I were beginning to get fond of that Trudy.'

'Dad, you've never met her,' said Jane.

'Can't help that,' said Job, 'I liked the sound of her. Nice shy girl, with nice ways, I reckon, like standing up for Jonathan in that court.'

'Jonathan, what did you say to Trudy when she told you she had a steady young man?' asked Jemima.

'I said I was fair amazed but told her I was pleased for her.'

'And what did she say?' asked Jane.

'Goodbye,' said Jonathan. 'But I still bumped into her again.'

'And she didn't mind?' said Jemima.

'Gave me a rocket,' said Jonathan, 'but didn't mind exchanging one of her ham sandwiches for one of my tongue.'

'Ah,' smiled Jemima.

'After which she told me she might be engaged in a year's time,' said Jonathan.

'Oh, Lordy, were that a blow to you?' asked Jemima.

'Well, I asked her if I could give her a wedding present, and she said a horse, and I said horses come a bit expensive, and she said a second-hand one would do.'

Job's laughter erupted and Jemima shrieked.

'Oh, that girl, Jonathan,' she said, 'she be after pulling your leg something comical.'

'She can't be all that shy,' said Jane.

'More comical than shy,' said Jennifer.

'Comical girls aren't shy at all,' said Jane.

'Maybe her telling Jonathan she might be engaged next year were wishful thinking,' said Jemima.

'No, I don't think she goes in for wishful thinking,' said Jonathan. 'Too pretty to have to.'

'Ah,' smiled Jemima, 'I thought somehow she were pretty.'

'And she's not engaged yet,' said Jane.

'Summat else might happen first,' said Job.

'Yes, it be funny the way she keeps letting Jonathan bump into her,' said Jemima.

'It's not funny to me, it's nerve-racking,' said Jonathan.

'Fond of her, are you, Jonathan?' said Jemima.

'So-so,' said Jonathan guardedly.

'Funny our Jonathan hasn't been called up yet,' said Jennifer.

'Maybe he failed the medical,' said Jane.

'Got a weak chest, d'you think?' said young Jonas.

'Don't look like it from here,' said Job.

'Ah, well,' said Jemima, 'we'll see.'

The front door opened to a pull on the latch-cord, and Alfie Hardcastle was heard.

''Ave yer finished yer supper yet, Jane?'

'Oh, lor',' said Jane.

'Come in directly, Alfie,' called Job, 'kitchen floor's only moving a mite.'

'Then I ain't comin' in at all,' shouted Alfie. 'Can't Jane come out?'

'Not directly,' called Job, 'she be having supper.'

Young Jonas lifted his voice.

'Is that the front door rattling, Alfie?'

Alfie jumped a mile.

'Perishin' Amy,' he bawled, 'it'll be yer roof next!'

Then there was silence.

'Shame about Alfie not liking little Patrick,' said Jemima.

'Joe Morgan don't mind him,' said Jennifer.

'Young Joe's got sense,' said Job, 'he knows a rattling door don't count for as much as walkin' out with our little Jane.'

'Oh, Dad, you soppy ha'porth,' said Jane, 'I'm not little.'

'Well, look at that, nor you're not,' said

Jonathan. 'Grown up all at once right in front of our eyes, Dad.'

'So she has,' said Job. 'How did that come about, I wonder?'

'Second helpings of rice pudding,' said young Jonas.

'Emma, you're hardly comin' home to lunch at all these days,' said Lizzy the following morning. 'It's not like you to keep takin' sandwiches.'

'Well, it's just that the weather's so nice,' said Emma, 'and I enjoy eating the sandwiches in the Green.'

'Well, all right, lovey,' said Lizzy. 'I remember years ago when I worked at Gamages in their dress department, I used to take sandwiches and eat them in St Paul's churchyard. I've got fond memories of those days.'

'And fond memories of being dated by Daddy?' said Emma.

'Not dated,' said Lizzy, 'I don't like dated, it's one of these modern words that don't mean anything special.'

'Walking out, that's what you used to call it, Mum,' said Edward, gulping tea and looking at the kitchen clock.

'Well, yes, when you were walking out it meant you were goin' steady, like Emma is with Donald,' said Lizzy, pouring herself more breakfast tea.

'I'm not actually going steady, Mum,' said Emma, getting up from the table.

'Well, goin' out with him,' said Lizzy. 'Anyway,

I've put your sandwiches in greaseproof in a bag with an apple.'

'Thanks, Mum,' said Emma. 'Come on, Edward, if you want to ride on the bus with me.'

'What a thrill,' said Edward, rising to his feet. 'There's another speech by Hitler in the paper, Mum.'

'That man's always got his mouth open,' said Lizzy. 'Something horrible ought to drop into it one day.'

'Like a bus,' said Emma.

'Yes, it's big enough for two buses,' said Lizzy, who was sorry for Emma that Donald was obviously going to be called up.

Sniffy Spinks was quite decent to Jonathan during the morning, finding little fault at all with him. That sent Jonathan out to lunch in a better frame of mind. The sky was blue, the day hot, and a welcome little breeze frolicked playfully, causing the hems of girls' summer dresses to flutter coyly. In the Green, all the benches had been taken.

Lunchtime acquaintances made themselves heard.

'Seen you with a girl lately, Jonathan.'

'Seen you with 'er lots, Jonathan.'

Wish they wouldn't shout, thought Jonathan, Donald might get to hear.

Someone came up behind him.

'There she is, Jonathan.'

He turned and Emma regarded him coolly.

'Now see what you've done by following me about,' she said.

'Emma, Camberwell Green's a small place,' he said.

'Yes, and here it's crowded out,' said Emma. 'We'll have to sit on the grass.'

Jonathan noted that for once she was out of her office blouse and skirt. She was wearing a lovely summer dress of primrose. Hatless, the springy curls of her chestnut hair tickled his fancy. He wanted to touch them.

'Will Donald mind?' he asked.

'Well, you're here now,' she said, 'and I know I shan't be able to stop you sitting with me, not unless I call a policeman. That'll make the second time you've been arrested.'

'Don't talk about it, it's painful,' said Jonathan.

'Oh, well, let's sit over there,' said Emma.

They found a patch of warm dry grass, and sat down, Emma with her legs tucked sideways. In apparent primness, she made sure her knees were covered.

'That's a pretty dress,' said Jonathan.

'You're looking,' said Emma.

'Is there a charge, then?' asked Jonathan.

'You've got very looking eyes,' said Emma.

'We all have, haven't we?' said Jonathan.

'Not like yours,' said Emma, opening up her little white lunch bag. Inside she found her sandwiches, together with two tomatoes as well as an apple.

Jonathan, opening his tin, uncovered two split rolls with a cheese filling and a section of cold apple pie.

'What's yours today, Emma?' he asked.

242

'Two chicken sandwiches, two tomatoes and an apple,' said Emma.

'Like one of my cheese rolls, would you?' said Jonathan. 'They be rare crisp and new, with a tidy old filling of cheese filings.'

'If you're going to talk like a daft country yokel, I'm going home,' said Emma. 'Still, I don't mind one of your rolls. I like cheese put through a grater. Here's one of my sandwiches, and a tomato.'

They exchanged. Jonathan gave her a curious glance. Emma smiled.

'Are you sure Donald won't mind us having a picnic lunch together?' he asked.

'He'll mind you looking at my legs,' said Emma.

'Can't see them from here, can I?' said Jonathan.

'Oh, dear, hard luck,' said Emma.

'Seems to me as if you've lost your shyness,' said Jonathan.

'There's my natural modesty,' said Emma, 'you don't pay much respect to that when you make me listen to saucy old devils talking about low life at the back of the gasworks.'

'Dead comical old bloke, he was,' said Jonathan.

'Wicked, like you,' said Emma, and made healthy and enjoyable inroads into the cheese roll, while Jonathan decimated the sandwich. 'If my mother knew what a devil you were, she'd faint.'

'So would my mother,' said Jonathan.

'I suppose you realize what an awful conscience I've got letting you sit here with me,' said Emma.

'You've got Donald in mind?' said Jonathan. 'Well, I could lock myself away in our office filing cabinet every day until you get married and no one can split you and Donald asunder.'

'Very funny, I don't think,' said Emma. 'Are you going to eat the tomato?'

'Yes,' said Jonathan. Emma watched as he used his teeth to bite all the way through it without letting it get the better of him at all. She took out the other tomato and eyed it cautiously.

'Tomatoes can bite a girl back,' she said.

'Shall I cut it up for you?' asked Jonathan. He produced a penknife and opened its sharpest blade. Emma gave him the tomato. He closed his lunch tin, placed the tomato on its lid and cut it into four sections. 'There we are,' he said.

'Well, thanks,' said Emma. 'I saw into your tin, then. You've got what looks like a slice of apple pie.'

'Like half of it in a minute?' said Jonathan.

'Yes, that's only fair,' said Emma. 'By the way, exactly what is it that makes you follow me about?'

'I don't follow you about.'

'You're not lovesick, are you?' said Emma.

'Eh?' said Jonathan.

'My Uncle Sammy was lovesick once, according to what another uncle of mine told me,' said Emma. 'It was over a divine young lady called Susie. He was lovesick for ages, but didn't realize it. He had awful headaches and couldn't sleep at night. He used to lie awake tossing and turning and groaning. His eldest brother told him in the end why he was suffering, so he married Susie and all his headaches and groaning stopped. D'you groan at night and have headaches?'

'No, I don't,' said Jonathan.

'Still, you must be a bit lovesick to come

after me nearly every day,' said Emma.

'Emma, I'm not lovesick and I don't come after you,' said Jonathan. 'We just happen to meet now and again.'

'Yes, and that's making it very awkward for me,' said Emma, frowning. 'Oh, I'll have my piece of apple pie now, thanks.'

Jonathan cut the slice in half and they shared it.

'I've got a feeling you're trying to get my goat,' he said.

'I'm sure I don't know what you mean,' said Emma. 'Did your mum make this apple pie? It's lovely.'

'Yes, she's good at cooking and baking,' said Jonathan.

'Does she know you're after me?' asked Emma.

'If I were, she'd guess I was,' said Jonathan, 'but I'm not. It wouldn't be right when you're expecting to be engaged.'

'Not yet I'm not,' said Emma, 'I'm only seventeen.'

'It beats me, a girl only seventeen having as much to say for herself as you do,' grinned Jonathan.

'Crikey, you can talk,' said Emma. 'Anyway, I'm not going to complain to Donald about you as long as you don't take advantage of me.'

'Now how would I take advantage of you?' asked Jonathan.

'There's all kinds of ways,' said Emma, 'especially as I'd faint to start with.'

'That'll be the day,' said Jonathan, and laughed.

'What's funny?' asked Emma.

'You are, you be a real comical girl,' said

Jonathan, 'and a laugh a minute at home, I shouldn't wonder. My dad's like that. He fell out of a tree once, and didn't half land with a wallop. A woman rushed to see if he was hurt, and there he was, sitting up and laughing. She asked him why he was laughing, and Dad said it weren't any use crying now the damage had been done. What damage? asked the woman. Split me breeches, said Dad, and I daresn't get up till you go away.'

'Any more hysterical stories?' asked Emma.

'Well,' said Jonathan, 'there was the one about the Hollywood actress who liked her tenth husband so much she decided to keep him for an extra fortnight.'

'And?' said Emma.

'Give over,' said Jonathan.

'Was that all of it?' asked Emma.

'Yes, all of it,' said Jonathan.

'I see,' said Emma. 'When do I laugh?'

'Anytime you like,' said Jonathan, 'laughing's good medicine.'

'I think you said that before.'

'Well, it's worth saying twice.'

They went on like this for quite a while, and then Emma said, 'I'm going to Lyons now for a cup of coffee. Are you going to follow me?'

'I'll spare you that,' said Jonathan.

'Goodbye, then,' said Emma, standing up. 'Will you be having lunch in Lyons tomorrow?'

'No, I usually only go Mondays and Tuesdays, and not even Tuesdays sometimes,' said Jonathan, rising.

'Still, you'd better go tomorrow,' said Emma, 'as

246

I'll be eating sandwiches here again. We simply have to stop seeing each other sometime, and, after all, it's not my fault you fancy me. I've never given you the slightest encouragement.'

'I'm not sure if I'm cockeyed, or if you are, or if we both are,' said Jonathan. 'I think it's you. If you want some help about it, I'll do my best. I've read it up. First, you lie on a couch—'

'I do what?' said Emma.

'You lie on a couch—'

'Oh, you really do have wicked ideas, Jonathan Hardy.'

'Then I ask you to speak all your deepest thoughts.'

'You wouldn't like that,' said Emma, 'all my deepest thoughts are about how potty you are. I'm not the one who needs a doctor, it's you. Well, I'm going now. Thank your mother for the apple pie, and don't forget to avoid me tomorrow.'

Jonathan laughed out loud. Emma gave him a look and left.

Alfie Hardcastle was in the way again, planted purposefully on the doorstep of the Hardy home when Joe Morgan called on Jane that evening. Alfie's legs were stiffly purposeful, so was his chest and so were his large ears.

'What d'you want, Joe Morgan?' he asked.

'I want to knock on the door,' said Joe amiably.

'What for?' growled Alfie.

'To see Jane,' said Joe.

''Oppit,' said Alfie.

'D'you mind if I don't?' said Joe.

'Course I bleedin' mind,' said Alfie. ''Oppit.'

'You fancy Jane, do you?' said Joe.

'None of yer business,' said Alfie.

'Tell you what,' said Joe, 'either we fight for who knocks on her door, or we spin a coin. Take yer pick, Alfie.'

'Well, just for this once, spin a coin,' said Alfie.

'Right,' said Joe, and fished out a penny from his pocket. 'Heads I win, tails you lose. Fair?'

'Think I'm daft, do yer?' said Alfie.

'My mistake,' said Joe. 'All right, tails I win, heads you do. That fair?'

'No, it ain't,' growled Alfie suspiciously, 'tails I win, get me?'

'Got you, Alfie,' said Joe, and spun the coin and let it drop on the doorstep. It tinkled, ran, wobbled and fell on its side. The King's head showed up. 'Right?' said Joe.

'No, it ain't, it's bleedin' 'eads, which is wrong to me,' said Alfie, 'so I'm still goin' to fight yer.'

'All right, mitts up,' said Joe, and Alfie's fists came up at the ready, and he started to ferociously shadow-box in a pretty good attempt to frighten Joe to death. Joe, who didn't want to draw blood on Jane's doorstep, trod hard on his left foot. Alfie bellowed with agony.

'Oh, yer bleeder, you done me ruddy big toe in again!'

He hopped around in pain and anguish. Joe gave him a bit of a nudge. It collapsed him. Well, he was only standing on one leg.

A Mrs Carpenter passed by, then stopped, came back and looked.

'What's that Alfie 'Ardcastle rolling about for on Mrs 'Ardy's doorstep?' she asked.

'He's 'urt his foot,' said Joe.

''E always was clumsy,' said Mrs Carpenter. 'Bless me soul, ain't he hollerin' fit to wake the dead?'

'Oh, me foot,' bawled Alfie.

The door opened and Jane appeared. She stared at the rolling Alfie.

'What's all the noise about, and what's Alfie doing down there?'

''E's 'urt his foot,' said Mrs Carpenter.

'Oh lor', oh dear,' said Jane.

''E needs sweeping up,' said Mrs Carpenter, ''e's makin' yer mum's doorstep look very untidy, Jane. I'll knock on 'is door and ask 'is dad to bring a broom.'

'Oh, thanks,' said Jane. 'Come in, Joe.'

Joe went in, Jane closed the door, and Alfie used several very violent words.

'Oh, 'ow dare you, yer common 'ooligan,' cried Mrs Carpenter, and conked him with her handbag. 'Even me Uncle Gabriel never used words like that, and 'e was a sailor.'

'Sod yer Uncle Gabriel,' bawled Alfie, ''ope he drowned at sea!'

''Ere, 'ave another one,' said Mrs Carpenter, and conked him again.

Alfie gave up.

Meanwhile, from all that Jonathan had said about his lunchtime interlude today, Jemima had a feeling that the girl Trudy was driving him up the wall. Jemima thought it very interesting.

Chapter Seventeen

The following day, Jonathan had just eaten the last mouthful of the cheapest snack in Lyons, baked beans on toast again, when a vexed voice accosted his ears.

'What are you doing here?'

He looked up. There she was, Emma who had once been Trudy.

'You asked me to come here today to save us bumping into each other again,' said Jonathan.

'How was I to know you would when you said you didn't?' asked Emma. 'You said only Mondays and Tuesdays.'

'But you said you were bringing sandwiches today.'

'And I did, and I've eaten them,' said Emma, 'and I'm here to have a cup of coffee.' She sat down. 'Heaven knows how we're going to stop meeting if you carry on like this.'

'We needn't meet now,' said Jonathan, 'you can sit somewhere else.'

Trixie appeared.

''Ello, miss, you got here bit late today, I see,' she said.

Emma composed herself and said, 'Well, I've only come in for a cup of coffee.'

'I'll have one too,' said Jonathan.

'Crikey, a shipping order,' said Trixie, departing.

'If Donald came in here for tea and a bun,' said Emma, 'Trixie could tell him all about how you've been meeting me.'

'Does Trixie know Donald and that you might be engaged to him in a year's time?' asked Jonathan.

'No, but—'

'Then I'm going to say something.'

'What?' asked Emma.

'Blow Donald,' said Jonathan.

'I beg your pardon?' said Emma.

'Blow Donald.'

'Well, thanks very much, I don't think,' said Emma.

'And I'm going to say something else.'

'You'd better not,' said Emma.

'I've had Donald up to here,' said Jonathan, touching his chin.

'Well, I'm blessed,' said Emma, 'you just don't care what you say to people, do you? Still, I'm not perfect myself. What was it you said your father did when he was living in Sussex?'

'He did odd jobs as the village handyman,' said Jonathan.

'And what did your mother do?' asked Emma.

'Mum was a farmer's daughter, but gave all that up when she married Dad,' said Jonathan. 'Might I ask if this is leading up to something I won't like?'

'Never mind that,' said Emma. 'Did you say—'

She stopped as Trixie brought the coffees, gave her a smile and departed. 'Did you say your dad wouldn't marry your mother because he didn't have much to offer her?'

'Well, as the village handyman he didn't have much at all,' said Jonathan.

'But he married her in the end, didn't he?' said Emma.

'Yes, didn't I tell you? Mum said she'd drown herself if he didn't. And she was as good as her word. She chucked herself in the village pond.'

'She did what?' said Emma.

'Chucked herself in the village pond,' said Jonathan.

'Like Ophelia?' said Emma.

'Who?' said Jonathan.

'You know, in *Hamlet*,' said Emma. 'She drowned herself out of despairing love for the Prince of Denmark.'

'Well, I don't know that Dad reckoned he was any Prince of Denmark,' said Jonathan. 'He was just the village handyman. Anyway, he dived in after Mum.'

'Dived in?' said Emma. 'Into a village pond? Didn't he hit his head on the bottom?'

'I don't think you're taking this seriously,' said Jonathan.

'Yes, I am,' said Emma. 'Then what happened?'

'He pulled Mum out, and told her if she did it again he'd smack her bottom.'

'And did she and did he?' asked Emma.

'No, she didn't have to,' said Jonathan. 'Dad reckoned it was best, after all, to marry her. He

252

didn't want to spend his life pulling her out of the pond every time she felt despairing.'

'Priceless,' said Emma.

'Might I ask why you're suddenly interested in my family?' enquired Jonathan.

'I'm just trying to act as if this is the first time we've met,' said Emma. 'I don't want to think about how we've been meeting like this.'

'Donald wouldn't like it, you mean?' said Jonathan.

'Well, he wouldn't, would he?' said Emma.

'Durned old woman, then,' said Jonathan under his breath.

'What did you say?' asked Emma.

'What?' said Jonathan.

'Yes, what?' asked Emma.

'Search me,' said Jonathan.

'You mumbled something,' said Emma accusingly.

'Did I? What was it about?'

'How do I know?' said Emma. 'It was just mumble mumble. Rhett Butler never mumbled once all through *Gone With The Wind*.'

'Well, as far as I could make out, he had a good set of teeth,' said Jonathan. Emma, coffee cup to her lips, choked on a mouthful. I'll kill him, she thought, I'll kill him. 'Coffee gone down the wrong way?' said Jonathan.

'Some of it,' she said. 'Did you say if you had brothers and sisters?'

'What's the idea?' asked Jonathan.

'Pardon?' said Emma.

'Come off it,' said Jonathan, 'you're cooking

something up, asking questions about my family. I reckon you're a bit of a caution, Emma Somers.'

'No, I'm not,' said Emma. 'I'm not as scheming as some people, I haven't lived long enough.'

'Still, you're growing up very nicely,' said Jonathan.

'I hope that's not a personal remark,' said Emma.

'Well, it's my own personal opinion,' said Jonathan.

'It's out of order,' said Emma, 'and I think we'd better work something out to make sure we definitely never meet again.'

'We've already tried that,' said Jonathan, 'and we still keep bumping into each other.'

'Well, you're always where you're not supposed to be, like today,' said Emma. 'I don't know what Donald would do if he knew.'

'Blow a fuse, I shouldn't wonder, and electrocute himself,' said Jonathan.

'Oh, you'd like that, I suppose,' said Emma. 'You'd feel free to do your worst, wouldn't you?'

'Yes, I would,' said Jonathan, 'and I'm a terrible daunting chap when I'm doing my worst with a girl.'

Emma struggled with a rising urge to have hysterics, emerged victorious and looked at her watch.

'I've got to go now,' she said. 'Will you be here on Monday?'

'Will you?' asked Jonathan.

'Yes, if you won't,' said Emma, 'I've got to be fair to Donald.'

'Yes, I suppose you have,' said Jonathan.

'It's goodbye, then,' said Emma.

'Yes, goodbye, Emma.'

'Goodbye,' said Emma, but didn't get up.

'Something keeping you?' said Jonathan.

'Yes, I don't like your eyes following me,' said Emma.

'All right, let's leave together,' said Jonathan, and a couple of minutes later, after settling their bills, they were out on the busy pavement.

A girl, passing by, stopped for a moment and looked at them.

'Oh, hello, Emma,' she said.

'Oh, hello, Ivy,' said Emma.

'See you,' said Ivy, and went on.

'There, that's one of our office typists,' said Emma, 'and she's seen you with me. I'll get talked about. It's definitely goodbye now.'

'Is that for ever?' asked Jonathan.

'Goodbyes are always for ever,' said Emma.

'Well, I wish you luck,' said Jonathan, 'and if I do see you in Lyons, I'll look the other way. Goodbye, then.'

'Goodbye,' said Emma, and went. She had an urge to laugh because conversation with Jonathan was so droll. Goodbye indeed, she'd bet he wasn't going to let that stop him, she'd bet he'd turn up again.

Then she thought of Donald, and she frowned. She wasn't being fair to him. Although she'd mentioned Jonathan, it had only been in a dismissive way. Donald had no idea she was spending so many lunchtimes with the barmy country chap.

255

And why was she? She could easily have avoided him, she knew that. Well, she'd made an effort to say a definite goodbye to him this time.

The point was, would he take any notice of the definitive?

Emma, a very straightforward young lady, didn't like feeling she was being unfair. On the other hand, it wasn't as if there was anything serious about her friendship with Donald. Well, at her age, who wanted to get serious when life was a wide-open arena of excitement and fun?

Even so, she carried her frown with her all the way back to the offices. There, she had a word with her Uncle Boots.

'I can't get rid of him,' she said.

'Who?' asked Boots.

'That country chap,' said Emma. 'He's always there at lunchtimes.'

'Where's there?'

'Everywhere,' said Emma.

'Is it a problem, Emma?'

'Yes, of course it is,' said Emma.

'A serious problem?' said Boots.

'No, hysterical,' said Emma, and laughed.

This time, her frown didn't appear.

Susie had received a reply from Britain's bulldog, Mr Winston Churchill, by the midday post. It was addressed from the House of Commons.

> *My dear Mrs Adams,*
> *I must thank you for your kind letter and its very frank and pertinent comments.*

I assure you I shall continue to use whatever influence I possess to help offset the threat Hitler poses to the peace of Europe. His evil intentions are now perceived to be brutally obvious, and His Majesty's Government will undoubtedly honour its pact with Poland in the event of that unfortunate country being attacked by Nazi Germany.

Be confident that the Prime Minster is resolute in his conviction that Hitler must be stopped. Further, I am sure it will give you some satisfaction to know he is just as resolute in his belief that well-loaded firearms must supersede umbrellas.

I am, Yours Sincerely,
Winston S. Churchill.

Well, I'm blessed, said Susie to herself, what a lovely man.

She rang Sammy and read the letter to him, and told him to tell Boots about it. Sammy said what a great bunch of bananas for Susie to get a letter from Winston Churchill himself. It's nothing to do with bananas, said Susie. Coconuts, then, said Sammy. If you don't pull yourself together, said Susie, something you won't like will happen to you. Things are serious, not funny. Yes, I know, Susie, said Sammy, but now that the family's got Winston Churchill for a friend, that's put some cheer into our seriousness. I want you and Boots to do something about making him our Prime Minister, said Susie. Well, we will, said Sammy, we'll do wonders, if possible, and meanwhile I'll get on with buying up all the material and fabric I can from mills and wholesalers just in case a crisis pops up from somewhere. Sammy Adams, breathed Susie over the line, are you after cornering the market in material like you did once before? It's a thought, said Sammy, and glad you're in favour, Susie. Sammy Adams, said Susie, you know I don't believe in that sort of thing. Well, normally, it's against my own principles, said Sammy, but in a crisis it's good business. I'll give you good business, said Susie, just wait till you get home. There's a lot more to be thought about than good business, she said, there's dear Mr Churchill. Sammy asked how he came to be dear to her. Because I want him to be Prime Minister, said Susie, so you and Boots had better do something about it.

Sammy spoke to Boots.

'Susie's had a reply from Winston Churchill,' he said, and gave the gist of it.

'I'm impressed,' said Boots.

'You won't be,' said Sammy, 'not when I tell you we've got an order from Susie to set about making Churchill Prime Minister.'

'Is an order from Susie on a par with an order from Chinese Lady?' asked Boots.

'Well, I tell you, old mate,' said Sammy, 'it is as far as I'm concerned. Susie delivers her orders with one hand on her frying-pan.'

'Figuratively?' said Boots.

'Leave off,' said Sammy, 'I'm not up with that kind of educated word.'

'Not much,' said Boots. 'Just tell Susie we're with her all the way and will recommend Winston Churchill to all our friends. We've both got several.

But first, of course, you'll have to get rid of our present Prime Minister, Neville Chamberlain.'

'Me do what?' said Sammy.

'Your privilege, Sammy, as Susie's husband,' said Boots.

'Might I be informed as to how I can manage it?' asked Sammy.

'A bomb?' suggested Boots.

'A whatter?' said Sammy.

'You've got it, Sammy,' said Boots, 'blow him up.'

'Tonight?' said Sammy. 'Or can it wait till tomorrow?'

'Ask Susie,' said Boots.

'She'll come round and see you,' said Sammy.

'Always a pleasure,' said Boots.

'With her frying-pan,' said Sammy.

On arriving home that evening he informed Susie of his conversation with Boots.

'Wait a minute, Sammy, he said what?' asked Susie.

'That we'd first got to get rid of Neville Chamberlain.'

'With a bomb?' said Susie.

'Yes, and that it was my privilege to deliver it in a brown paper parcel to Number 10 Downing Street,' said Sammy.

'Bless the man,' said Susie, 'what a lovely idea. But poor Mr Chamberlain, does he deserve a bomb? I'm sure he thinks he's doing the best for the country. Still, we do need Mr Churchill, so yes, all right, Sammy.'

'Pardon?' said Sammy.

'Yes, go ahead, Sammy love,' said Susie, 'only

259

make sure you don't blow yourself up as well. We'd all miss you.'

'I think I'm goin' to take to drink,' said Sammy.

Boots had received a communication from the War Office notifying him of when and where he was to present himself to receive his commission. Eloise made faces about it, Chinese Lady frowned, Emily accepted it as a resigned wife, and Tim congratulated his dad.

'That's all very well,' said Chinese Lady, 'but at his age, your father didn't ought to be goin' into any army. That man,' she added with a touch of acidity.

'What man?' asked Tim. 'D'you mean Dad?'

'No, Hitler,' said Chinese Lady, 'it's all his fault. I don't know there was ever a worse time than the day he came into the world.'

'One could put up with him much better if he didn't talk as much or shout as much,' said Eloise. 'Ah, if only he had a train set or toy soldiers to play with, that might keep him quiet, Grandmama.'

'So it might if he fell off his soap-box and broke his neck,' said Chinese Lady tartly.

'Well, that's a happy thought, Mum,' said Emily.

'We'll hang on to it,' said Mr Finch.

'And think about collapsing soap-boxes,' said Tim.

'We'll hang on to that as well,' said Boots.

'One can always hope,' said Mr Finch, who was due in a week or so to take himself off to Poland on behalf of a certain Government department.

* * *

Polly rang Boots at his office on Saturday morning and received news from him of the notification.

'Ye gods, old love, your second call to arms,' she said.

'I'm hoping this one will call me to a desk,' said Boots.

'You're hoping nothing of the kind,' said Polly. 'You're at your office desk every day, and the last thing you'll stand for is to be stuck at an Army desk. By the way, I've applied to join the Auxiliaries, and am making myself available as soon as the school breaks up for the summer holidays, when I'll be leaving the profession.'

'What will be your rank?' asked Boots.

'What's your guess, old sport?'

'Sergeant-Major?' said Boots.

'Miserable beast,' said Polly, 'one needs a big bosom for that job so that one can bellow, and you know it.'

'Is yours wanting, then?' asked Boots.

'I'll say it is,' said Polly, 'it's wanting a cuddle. Can you help?'

'Not over the phone,' said Boots.

Polly laughed.

'Well, call in on your way home from the office,' she said.

'Unfortunately—'

'Don't say it, old sport, I know all about unfortunately. It's been my most frustrating companion since I met you. I bear a hundred scars. But I'll never let go. There'll come a day.'

'So long, Polly.'

'So long, iron man.'

261

Chapter Eighteen

'I think it's come,' said Jemima when Jonathan arrived home from his Saturday morning's work. 'By the midday post.'

They were all there, ready for Saturday lunch, and all eyes were on Jonathan as he slit open the buff envelope and extracted the form that instructed him, on behalf of H M Government, to present himself at Taunton railway station on Monday, July 3rd, for transport to the Royal Artillery training camp. A railway warrant was enclosed.

'Yes, this is it, it's Monday week, third of July,' he said, and let the family read the command for themselves.

'That's it, then, Jonathan,' said Job soberly.

'The Army's got him,' said Jane.

'Rotten old Army,' said Jennifer.

'It don't be rotten old Army, Jennifer love,' said Jemima, 'it be rotten old Hitler. He's the cause.'

'I don't mind going with Jonathan,' said young Jonas.

'You can't, not till you're asked,' said Jane, 'and you won't be asked till you're old enough.'

'Blow that,' said young Jonas.

'One thing,' said Job, 'the artillery don't be as dangerous as the infantry. You'll be a gunner, you will, Jonathan, and as you did a bit of trigonommery at school—'

'Trigonometry,' said Jonathan.

'Aye, that were it, trigonommery,' said Job. 'Useful, that'll be, for a gunner. Might get you to be an officer.'

Jemima regarded her first-born with a silent sigh. She didn't think much of losing him to the Army. But there it was, it was the turn of today's young men to keep the country safe, and they all knew their fathers had done their bit in the Great War. It was a hopeful thing that most people didn't think there could possibly be another one, but the Government had already called up some young Walworth men. Now Jonathan was going to follow them.

'Let's sit down to our meal,' she said, 'it's ready.'

'When weren't any meal ever ready once you moved into that old cottage kitchen, eh?' said Job. 'Showed me a thing or two about how to use an oven, that you did, Jemima.'

'I were born for it, Job,' said Jemima. 'Just for your oven, though.'

Over the meal, Jonathan said he was going to spend next week at home, that he'd go in on Monday morning to let his firm know he was leaving there and then. Job pointed out they might ask for a week's notice. Jonathan said they'd have to do without it, that he wanted to enjoy the time at home. He'd got a tidy bit of savings and he'd use some to treat the family to outings, say a day trip by train to Brighton on Tuesday, and a day on the ocean waves from Westminster Pier to Southend on Thursday. Jane, Jennifer and young Jonas could skip school on those days.

'Oh, they'll excuse us for those days as you're going into the Army, I'm sure,' said Jane.

'Crikey, Brighton and Southend as well,' said young Jonas.

'Jonathan, that be spiffing,' said Jennifer.

'Mum will come too,' said Jonathan, 'but I don't know if you can get time off, Dad.'

'I don't reckon,' said Job, 'but that's no worry. You take the family, your mum as well, and I'll do a mite of cooking for when you all get back in the evenings.'

'Jonathan, spending some of your savings, though,' said Jemima.

'Well, I shan't have to fork out for new clothes. while I'm in the Army,' said Jonathan, 'so let's go on the binge to Brighton and Southend.'

'Jonathan, you be thinking of getting drunk?' said Jemima.

'On account of you won't see that girl Trudy any more?' said Jane.

'Oh, I'll grin and bear that,' said Jonathan, 'and won't take to drink till I've met my first sergeant-major.' He refused to mention he was a bit sad about no more lunchtimes with Emma. 'And listen, Jane, as it's a nice day, how about a ride to Ruskin Park this afternoon, where I'll treat you and Jennifer, and young Jonas, to tea and fruit buns in the park tea-room?'

'Oh, you bet,' said Jennifer.

'We'd love that,' said Jane.

'So would I,' said young Jonas.

'And you can bring Joe Morgan, if you want, Jane,' said Jonathan.

'Oh, I'll ask him,' said Jane, 'thanks ever so, Jonathan.'

'Chance for our Jane to put her Sunday frock on,' said Job, 'even if it still be only Saturday.'

'Did I hear a door rattle?' asked Jemima.

'I think little Patrick wants to come too,' said Jennifer.

'He probably will,' said Jane, 'and if the park gates rattle when we go in, we'll know he's with us.'

For her part, Jemima felt it a shame Jonathan had seen the last of the girl Trudy. Somehow, she had formed a likeable picture of her and her funny little habit of letting Jonathan bump into her. And that picture hadn't been changed by her telling him she had a steady young man.

Well, it hadn't been changed in Jemima's mind.

Joe was pleasured to be asked to join the outing to Ruskin Park, and doubly so when he saw Jane in her Sunday dress.

The five of them took a bus to the park, and Joe earned a nice mention from Jane by insisting that as Jonathan was standing treat for tea and buns, he'd pay everyone's fare, which he did. On arrival, it was agreed they'd sample the recreational atmosphere of the park before taking to the sociable atmosphere of the tea-room.

They strolled. The park wasn't as well patronized

as it was on Sundays, when the young people of Walworth and Camberwell were there in their scores, but the summery weather had brought more than a few promenaders out to enjoy the sunshine, the look of colourful flower-beds, and the freedom of open spaces. Peabody's Buildings, rows of terraced houses, shops and back-street factories, often made some Walworth residents feel hemmed in by brick and stone. On the other hand, it made others feel the closeness of neighbours, and all that neighbours meant. Rough-and-ready kindness, doorstep chats, and a shoulder-to-shoulder stand against trouble. Mind, it could also mean the occasional trouble-some drunk, fleas from someone's dog and the lightning-like spread of something infectious.

Ruskin Park was green and very open. Jennifer danced on the forbidden grass and then fled to hide herself behind Jonathan on the approach of a park-keeper, who peered darkly at the hallowed turf.

''Ere, who's left footmarks, eh?' he asked.

'Some girl,' said Jonathan, 'but she's gone now.'

'Yes, she went that way,' said Joe, pointing back.

'I'll skin 'er alive,' said the park-keeper.

Jennifer, still hiding herself, breathed, 'Oh, help.'

'Mister, what'll you do with the rest of her?' asked young Jonas.

'Boil 'er in oil,' said the park-keeper.

'That reminds me,' said Jonathan, 'did you hear about the cannibal who toasted his mother-in-law at his wedding dinner?'

'That's a good 'un,' grinned the park-keeper, and the young people resumed their stroll. Except for Jennifer, that is. She'd run for her life and was now safe from being boiled in oil.

'Jonathan, that were terrible corny, that joke,' said Jane.

'Saved Jennifer from bein' skinned alive, though,' said Joe.

On the way back, their leisurely walk took them past the tennis courts. Jonathan stopped.

'Oh, come on,' said Jennifer, now back among them.

'Catch you up in a tick,' he said, and she went on with the others. He watched a mixed doubles in play. A very elegant-looking woman was partnering a tall man against a young man and a girl, and all four players were good. Jonathan had stopped because he'd recognized the girl, a picture in her white tennis dress. Emma Somers. Her partner, a good-looking young man, hit a sizzler of a forehand drive that was unreturnable.

'Lovely shot, Donald, you stinker,' called the elegant woman.

'My pleasure,' said Donald.

Emma's mouth dropped open then. Facing the wire perimeter from the far side of the net, she'd spotted Jonathan. Jonathan made no gesture, except for a smile of acknowledgement, and then he turned away and walked to catch up with the others. He felt a little sad again, sad that he'd seen her for the last time. He'd also seen her steady date, Donald, for the first and probably only time.

On the court, Donald asked, 'What's up, Emma?'

'Nothing, I just thought I saw someone I knew,' said Emma. She and Donald were playing against Boots and Polly. 'Yes, ever such a lovely shot, Donald.'

The five young people had a very enjoyable time in the tea-room of the park, and Joe said he wouldn't have minded being called up himself alongside a decent bloke like Jonathan. Jane said that as she minded about Jonathan being called up, could they talk about something else, like swans and marmalade cats.

'Why?' asked young Jonas.

'I like swans and marmalade cats,' said Jane, 'and besides, talking about the Army don't be doing our fruit buns any good.'

'Nor mine,' said young Jonas.

Tommy Adams and his wife Vi were sharing a pot of tea in their garden with Vi's parents. Their children, Alice, David and Paul were all out with friends. Tomorrow, Tommy was driving his family to Brighton for the day. While there, they were going to select a hotel and reserve rooms for their fortnight's summer holiday. Vi liked Brighton. So did the kids.

'One of the posh hotels on the front,' said Tommy. 'No expense spared, eh, Vi?'

'We can afford to cast our pennies to the wind these days, Tommy,' said Vi, soft of voice and eye. Tommy liked that in his equable wife. Vi had always been soft-spoken and very feminine. Tommy considered her the best of the wives. He thought Emily a little sharp of tongue sometimes, and Susie a little bossy.

Vi's parents, known to the families as Aunt Victoria and Uncle Tom, looked at each other, Aunt Victoria showing a touch of maternal satisfaction. She turned to her son-in-law, the handsomest of the Adams brothers.

'Well, I must say you've worked hard to come up in the world, Tommy,' she said. In earlier years, she had hoped Vi would marry Boots, the gentleman of the Adams family and now very distinguished in his looks. Aunt Victoria had always had a particularly soft spot for Boots, but she'd come to be very fond of Tommy, and never failed to let her neighbours know what a prosperous businessman he was, owning his own car and a lovely house with a gardener. 'My, one of those select Brighton 'otels – hotels, Vi.' Aunt Victoria always corrected herself if she dropped an aitch. She aspired to be on correct conversational terms with the local vicar and his wife. 'It's gratifying to me and your father that you can afford it.'

'What's money if you don't spend some of it?' asked Uncle Tom, a likeable old buffer. Vi's equable nature had been inherited from her dad. Sixty-six now, he had been retired for a year, and was touched to the quick when, on his retirement day, Tommy and Vi presented him with the freehold deeds of the Camberwell house he'd been renting for many years. Tommy and Vi had purchased the house in his name for three hundred and fifty pounds. It meant that for the rest of his days he wouldn't have to worry about paying rent. The gift fair brought moisture to his eyes, and even Aunt Victoria, never one to show emotion, was so overwhelmed that she'd had to blow her nose not once but several times. 'Do you and Tommy and the kids a world of good, a posh 'oliday at Brighton, Vi,' said Uncle Tom. 'Mind, I don't know if Brighton's cockles and whelks are as juicy as what you get at Southend.'

'Southend's common,' said Aunt Victoria, 'and Brighton's got a Royal Palace.'

'I think it's the Royal Pavilion, Mum,' said Vi, who was thinking that if a war did happen, the Brighton holiday might be the last one her family would have for quite a while. That reminded her of something, something that wasn't as down-casting as thoughts of a war. 'Oh, would you believe,' she said, 'Susie phoned this afternoon to say she'd had a letter from Mr Winston Churchill.'

'That's right, so she did,' said Tommy, and the hint of a grin touched his mouth.

'Susie had a letter from Mr Churchill?' said Aunt Victoria, all agog.

'I like that bloke,' said Uncle Tom. ''E's got a bit of fire in 'is—' He stopped himself from saying belly, knowing discretion would save him from getting a talking-to for being common. 'In 'is water.'

'What?' said Aunt Victoria sharply.

'In 'is chest,' said Uncle Tom, having boobed, after all.

'Yes, Susie likes him too,' said Vi, and went on to

inform her parents of how Susie had written to him, and how he'd written back to tell her that he and Mr Chamberlain and the Government were doing everything they could about the evils of Hitler.

'My, fancy him writing personal to Susie,' said Aunt Victoria, thinking of how she could impress her neighbours. 'It makes me proud of our relatives.'

'Oh, and what d'you think?' said Vi. 'Susie told Sammy that he and Boots must do something about helpin' to make Mr Churchill our Prime Minister.'

'I didn't get left out, either,' said Tommy. 'Susie informed me everyone's got to help. Bothered if I know how to help make anyone Prime Minister. Mind you, it seems Boots told Sammy that someone would 'ave to get rid of Mr Chamberlain first, and that Sammy could do it with a bomb.'

Aunt Victoria paled and went faint. Uncle Tom cleared his throat of a frog. Vi glanced at Tommy, giving him a look that said, 'Don't you dare.' But Tommy went on, the devil.

'The idea being to blow him up.'

'Oh, I've got palpitations,' gasped Aunt Victoria. 'A bomb, you said, Tommy, a bomb?'

'No, it's what Boots said.' Tommy was straight-faced.

'Always knows what 'e's talkin' about, does Boots,' observed Uncle Tom with suitable gravity.

Aunt Victoria groped about, found her teacup, clasped it, looked into it, found it empty and said faintly, 'Where's my smelling-salts? I can't believe this of Boots. He's told Sammy to throw a bomb at Mr Chamberlain?'

'Seems like it,' said Tommy.

'At Mr Chamberlain?' gasped stricken Aunt Victoria.

'It'll be quick,' said Uncle Tom, ''e won't feel anything.'

'But it'll be criminal,' said Aunt Victoria hoarsely.

'I think Susie mentioned it'll be in a good cause,' said Tommy.

'Well, you've got to admit Nigel Chamberlain can't cope with 'Itler like Winston Churchill could,' said Uncle Tom.

'It's Neville Chamberlain, Dad,' said Tommy, receiving a kick from Vi under the table.

A moan issued from Aunt Victoria.

'I think she's fainted,' said Tommy.

'You Tommy, now see what you've done,' said Vi.

'Someone tell me I'm dreamin',' begged Aunt Victoria.

It took Vi only a little while to convince her that no-one was going to throw a bomb, least of all anyone in the Adams family. Later, it wasn't Uncle Tom who received a talking-to, it was Tommy. Tommy took it easily. Well, a talking-to from Vi wasn't much more than being walloped with a powder puff.

Something brought Job out of his sleep that night, something that emanated from the adjacent room, the parlour. He sat up, and the movement awoke Jemima.

'Job?' she whispered.

'Someone in the parlour, I reckon,' whispered Job.

'Jonathan, maybe?'

'Not him. Don't 'ee make any sound, Jemima, just listen.'

'But aren't you going to see who it is, Job?'

'No need. It'll be cousin George, I'll lay to it. He'll be at that old grandfather clock, after biding his time since Belle called a while ago.'

Whoever it was had entered the house by using the latchcord. In the parlour, he now had the grandfather clock illuminated by the beam of a torch. He opened up the clock, then stayed still to listen. He heard nothing apart from a steady tick-tock. Job and Jemima, in the adjoining room, stayed quiet, Jemima holding Job's warm hand. If any hand was comforting to Jemima, it was Job's.

Cousin George resumed work in a careful endeavour to silently remove the clock's pendulum and to replace it with another.

The clock stopped ticking.

Clever old Aunt Matty, thought cousin George, what a way of smuggling gold out of Africa by getting it turned into a pendulum. The crafty old biddy, bless her button-up boots. Well, it had been either her doing or the doing of Uncle Ethelbert, her late brother. He'd been out in Africa with her. In any case, she knew all about it. She'd made notes about it and kept them among her old letters and papers. And she'd kept the pendulum for a rainy day, I daresay, only it never rained hard enough for her to need the money it was worth. Then she got too old to bother with it. She probably even forgot about it in her dotage, or she might have had it converted to help out cousin Job and Jemima when they fell on their hard times. Still, she didn't forget to leave Job the clock. A bit of luck it was that Job didn't know the secret of the pendulum. It could put me and Belle in clover, that it could.

Got you, me lovely.

His fingers caressed the smooth·surface of the pendulum before he placed it with great care in a bag in which lay the replacement job. He fished out the latter. It was wrapped in cloth, and he opened it up. He'd got to get it fixed so as to leave Job and his family in ignorance. An unfinished business wouldn't do, it would make Job ask questions, and he might start with Belle, seeing it was Belle who, following a casual look through Aunt Matty's old papers, came here to discuss a possible purchase of the clock. She couldn't have offered a tidy old sum for it, not without arousing some suspicion in Job, who was nobody's fool.

Accordingly, cousin George was set on completing his work without giving any of the family cause to look twice at the old timepiece.

At that point, just as he was about to fix the substitute, the floor moved beneath his feet as if a little undulating wave was running through its solidity. Cousin George stiffened and tested the floor with a shuffle of one foot. That didn't bring reassurance, for as sure as chicks came out of eggs, the floor moved again, and there was a series of tiny little creaks, merry little creaks. Only they weren't merry to cousin George.

What the durned devil was happening?

The parlour door gently rattled.

Cousin George took up the torch and swept its beam of light around the room, but picked out nothing except furniture.

'Blast my backside, who's there?' he breathed, and listened again, intently. Not a sound came to his ears, but he wasn't convinced he was alone. He used the torch again, and its light played over the half-open parlour door. The door stayed still, and the house was quite silent. Yet he had a feeling he'd be wise to depart before every hair on his head stood up stiff and straight and turned him into the thin half of Laurel and Hardy.

However, he gritted his teeth, illuminated the clock again, steadied his fingers and fixed the substitute pendulum. The disc might need adjusting, but he'd have to chance that. He moved the pendulum gently to and fro, and the clock began to tick. He checked his pocket watch and set the minute hand of the clock to the correct time.

In the bedroom, Job whispered, 'Ought to be about finished by now.'

'Job, you sure it be cousin George?' whispered Jemima.

'I be sure it's not cousin Belle,' whispered Job. 'Not a woman's work, don't you see, but she knew we had a latchcord cousin George could use. She mentioned it were a temptation, so she did. That were to make me think of a burglar in case the old clock went missing.'

In the parlour, cousin George began to tidy up, but the floor moved again, and something fell off the mantelpiece. He froze. Save his soul if the parlour door didn't start a crazy rattling that was like the sound of the devil dancing on his cloven hooves. He nearly dropped the bag and its precious contents. The floor positively trembled, and more little creaks ran under his feet.

He shot out of the room. The front door was open and he rushed out, going at speed, hair on end, the torch and the bag travelling with him. In the bag was the detached pendulum, worth its weight in gold as far as he was concerned.

Job and Jemima heard him go.

'Job, the parlour door rattled,' said Jemima.

'So it did,' said Job. 'That were to see cousin George off in a hurry. Sounded like a terrible hurry to me. I reckon little Patrick don't be too fond of strangers messing about with Aunt Matty's clock.'

'Aren't you going to get up and take a look?'

'Set your mind at rest, would it, Jemima?'

'It would,' said Jemima.

So Job slipped from the bed, went into the parlour, switched the light on and examined the clock. Inside a second or so, he was grinning. After closing the front door, he returned to Jemima.

'Clock's still there, but it's got yet another pendulum,' he said, climbing back into bed.

'It had to be cousin George, then,' said Jemima.

'You can bet your Sunday corset it weren't anybody but cousin George,' said Job.

Jemima, snuggling, murmured, 'He be in for a terrible shock, then.'

'I reckon,' said Job. 'After all, one brass

pendulum don't be much different from another. The one under this mattress, Jemima, that'll be the one for looking after us in our old age and providing our children with handsome nest-eggs when each of 'em get married.'

'Job, you be a fine husband and a sweet man.'

Chapter Nineteen

On Sunday afternoon, Cassie and Freddy entertained friends to tea at their home in Wansey Street. Annabelle and Nick, Sally and Horace, and Dumpling and Danny, together with their children, were present, and so was Cassie's dad, known as the Gaffer. They all had a soft spot for him, particularly as he was very good with kids. He was seated amid them, keeping them in order and seeing to their wants. Infant Muffin was asleep in her pram. She'd had her tea. Cassie was a healthy provider.

Conversation of a lively kind was running around the table. Dumpling was doing her best to introduce football as a topic, but was continually being frustrated. She listened for a few moments to Nick on the subject of boating holidays at Salcombe in Devon before interrupting him.

'Well, boats are all right in a way,' she said, 'but they're not serious like football is. I was only saying to Danny—'

'That reminds me,' said Horace, 'how's Danny's job on the LNER going these days?'

'Oh, I'm still 'elping to keep the trains running,'

said Danny, 'and 'oping to be in line for a foreman's job come next year.'

'We don't want to talk about trains,' said Dumpling, 'not when we're more interested in—'

'I like trains,' said Annabelle.

'I like country trains,' said Cassie. 'You can see cows and meadows from country trains.'

'You can see Battersea power station from some London trains,' said Freddy.

'Crikey,' said Cassie, 'Battersea power station's nowhere near as nice to look at as cows and meadows.'

'On top of that,' said Horace, 'cows don't smoke.'

'Well, course they don't,' said Dumpling, ''ow could they? Mind, I've seen footballers steamin' a bit when—'

'That reminds me,' said Sally, 'I've got a new steam iron at home, and it's marvellous for cottons.'

'I've got a new cord washing-line,' said Annabelle.

''Ere, listen, will yer?' said Dumpling. 'I was only saying to Danny yesterday that when the football season starts—'

'By the way,' said Nick, 'how's your cricket career, Horace?'

'Promising,' said Horace. 'Yes, I think I can say promising.'

'I noticed you hit a useful fifty against Middlesex last week,' said Nick.

''Ere, ain't nobody listening to me?' complained Dumpling.

'Have some more shrimps, Dumpling,' said Freddy.

'Yes, in a minute,' said Dumpling. 'First, I 'ope the Browning Street Rovers 'ave a better season than—'

'Has Muffin woken up yet, Freddy?' asked Cassie.

'Not yet,' said Freddy.

'She's a lovely infant, Cassie,' said Sally.

'Danny and me are goin' to start training our two boys for football as soon as they know 'ow to kick a ball,' said Dumpling. 'We've got 'igh 'opes that they'll—'

'We're having a lovely summer,' said Annabelle.

'Yes, so are me and Freddy,' said Cassie.

'I meant generally,' said Annabelle.

'Oh, blimey,' gloomed Dumpling, 'ain't I ever going to get a word in edgeways?'

'Have another slice of bread and butter, Dumpling,' offered Cassie, 'and then I'll tell you about a little urchin that threw a banana skin at Freddy when we were in the Walworth Road and I had my parasol up.'

'I told her it would 'appen if we took her parasol out for a walk,' said Freddy, 'I told her kids would throw banana skins. Fortunately, this one missed us. Unfortunately, it hit a beefy bloke.'

'Yes, and he blamed Freddy,' said Cassie.

'For duckin',' said Freddy.

'He complained that if Freddy hadn't ducked he wouldn't have caught it himself,' said Cassie. 'He told Freddy that all Walworth kids threw banana skins when something upset them, and that Freddy should've stood up to it and taken it like a man. I

280

don't know why a parasol should upset anyone. I mean, what would happen if the King and Queen were walkin' out and the Queen had her parasol up?'

'What's the answer, Nick?' asked Horace.

'Well, I suppose the King would have to duck,' said Nick.

'Yes, drop him a warning postcard, Cassie,' said Annabelle.

'You were born to send postcards to the King, Cassie,' said Sally, 'send him one with a picture of Windsor Castle on it.'

'He'll like that,' said the Gaffer, then stopped one of Dumpling's little boys from painting his face with raspberry jam.

'I never 'eard a soppier conversation,' said Dumpling.

'Seems fairly serious to me,' said Danny.

'The fact is, Dumpling,' said Nick, 'banana skins have always played their own part in people's lives. You've heard what can happen if you tread on one, haven't you?'

'Bruised bum,' said Danny.

'I'm 'ysterical,' said Dumpling.

The Gaffer, happy among the kids, smiled for a brief second, and then looked sober. If these young people were refusing to talk about football, they were also fighting shy of talking about Hitler. It was understandable. The young women, all wives and mothers, didn't want mention of that lunatic to spoil the atmosphere and start them thinking about the probability that he might spoil their future too. And their husbands were going along

281

with them. It was a ruddy crying shame that someone hadn't smothered Hitler when he was in his cradle.

If Chinese Lady could never quite make out how General Sir Henry Simms and Lady Simms had become friends of the family, she was quite clear about the social obligations the friendship imposed on her. Accordingly, every once in a while she instructed Boots to invite them to Sunday tea. An instruction from Chinese Lady to any of her sons was the equivalent of an order, and few were the times when the response had been negative. Boots might demur a little, Sammy might attempt sidetracking, and Tommy might ask to be excused, but Chinese Lady usually had her way.

This afternoon, consequent on an invitation issued by Boots on behalf of the family and by reason of one more instruction from his mother, Sir Henry and Lady Simms had arrived for Sunday tea. Polly, of course, had been included, on the understanding, Boots said over the phone, that she behaved herself. This meant, of course, that she was to do nothing that would turn Emily's green eyes greener. Polly was always in favour of tea on a summer Sunday with Boots and his family, for there was never a dull moment. Her upper-class friends would have called Sunday tea a crashing bore under any circumstances, particularly with a family whose cockney upbringing meant one had to relate to shrimps and winkles with bread and butter.

Polly knew differently. Sunday teas in summer

with the Adamses were exhilarating. Garden cricket was always played first, and this activity, far from being a crashing bore, was hysterical. Everyone did their best to sabotage Boots in his endeavours to bring a certain amount of order to a game. A certain amount of order to a game of garden cricket was considered on a par with wet Monday washing, and Polly and Susie were always to the fore in the wrecking stakes. During one game last summer, Susie so provoked Boots that he went after her and trapped her in the garden shed, from which issued Susie's demented shrieks.

'Is that my Susie's who's yelling?' asked Sammy.

'Yes, so what's goin' on?' demanded Emily.

'Oh, nothing that isn't part of the game,' said Rosie, on summer vacation at the time. 'I think Daddy's just bowling a maiden over.'

And as far as Polly was concerned, she'd have opted to take Susie's place, since she was sure that life with Boots in a garden shed would have had its own kind of appeal for her. She knew, however, that Emily always had her eye on her.

This afternoon, Sammy, Susie and their offspring were also present, and so were Lizzy, Ned, Emma, Edward and Emma's date, Donald. Bobby was with his Territorials, and Tim was out on a pre-arranged excursion with Fanny Harrison, Nick Harrison's younger sister. But there were enough to make up two teams, and everyone had to play except Chinese Lady, Lady Simms and Susie's little girl, four-year-old Paula. Although Eloise still couldn't understand even the most basic rules, she wasn't allowed dispensation.

The game was certain to be played in a happy, disorganized fashion between two teams. Ladies versus gentlemen. Emily, Lizzy, Eloise, Emma, Polly, Susie, and Susie's elder daughter Bess, against Boots, Edwin Finch, Sir Henry, Ned, Edward, Donald, plus Sammy and his two sons Daniel and Jimmy. That created an argument to start with.

'Us girls aren't havin' that,' said Emily to Boots, 'there's only seven of us against nine of you.'

'Luck of the sexes,' said Boots.

'You can forget that,' said Emily.

'Let me point out that you seven females are all in the flower of your lives, young, healthy, agile, good-looking and pretty famous with bat and ball,' said Boots.

'Oh, how sweet,' said Susie, 'but that won't work, either.'

'It has its commendable points,' said Polly.

'It's crafty,' said Emily.

'It's worse,' said Lizzy, 'it's cheating, good as.'

'On our side,' said Boots, 'half of us are old, fairly crippled, short of breath, weak-willed and not much good.'

'Could you specify these ancient monuments by name?' asked Polly.

'There's my stepfather—'

'He's not crippled,' protested Emma, 'he's my upright and able grandpa.'

'Thank you, Emma, but I do creak a little,' said Mr Finch.

'No, you don't, you're still handsome with vim and vigour,' said Emma.

'Then there's Sir Henry,' said Boots, and spruce Sir Henry took up the stance of a man sagging with age.

'Pardon me, that's all my eye,' said Polly. 'Sir Henry's my father, and he could knock a house down without hardly trying.'

'An occasional hobby of mine,' said Sir Henry who, like Polly, found the Adams family's zest for life totally infectious.

'Then there's Sammy,' said Boots, 'with bent shoulders, flat feet and a hole in his head.'

'Is that me he's talkin' about?' asked Sammy.

'D'you recognize your husband, Susie?' asked Lizzy.

'Only in respect of the hole in his head,' said Susie.

'I've never seen it,' said nine-year-old Jimmy.

'No, well, I keep it under me titfer,' said Sammy, 'to stop your mother puttin' a coloured candle in it and lighting me up at Christmas.'

'Daddy, you fibber,' said ten-year-old Bess.

'Then there's Ned and his courageous but gammy leg,' said Boots.

'I concur,' said Ned, 'I'm disadvantaged.'

'No, you aren't,' said Lizzy, 'and I'm not havin' Boots miscall your leg, which all your children and me admire.'

'And love,' said Emma.

'Nicely spoken,' said Donald.

'Lastly, of our old half, there's me,' said Boots.

'Crumbs, are you really old, Uncle Boots?' asked Bess.

'Believe me, Bess,' said Boots, 'I'm pretty much of a has-been.'

'Crikey, yes, that's common knowledge, I don't think,' said Emily.

'And anyone who believes it needs talkin' to,' said Lizzy.

'I don't mind having Aunt Emily's has-been on our side,' said Emma.

'Try me, I'm fairly sprightly,' said Donald, and put an arm around her shoulders. Emma shrugged it off.

'How about if we made a concession?' said Boots. 'How about if we let Eloise bat twice for your side, Lizzy?' Lizzy was captaining the ladies on account of being quite a batsman.

'Eloise?' said Polly.

'Some hopes,' said Lizzy, 'Eloise is always out for a duck.'

Eloise, who had never been able to come to terms with cricket parlance, asked, not for the first time, 'What is a duck?'

'When you're out before you've scored any runs,' said Polly.

'That is a duck?' said Eloise. 'What is a chicken, then?'

'A fowl,' said Sammy.

'A foul?' said Eloise. 'It isn't fair, you mean?'

'No, it lays eggs,' said Susie.

'But that's a farmyard chicken,' said Eloise. 'I mean, what is a cricket chicken?'

'Oh, dear,' said Emma, 'I don't think Eloise has learned anything at all about cricket yet. Black mark, Uncle Boots, for not curing her ignorance.

She be terrible ignorant, I reckon.'

'Eh?' said Sammy, and Emma entered a flustered condition.

'What's Emma talking like that for?' asked twelve-year-old Daniel, Susie's eldest.

'Oh, she's been coming out with a bit of Cornish just lately,' said Edward.

'I like it,' said Donald, who wouldn't have if he'd known it was Sussex and that Emma had caught it from her country chap.

'It's terrible to be hopeless, and not know about cricket ducks and chickens,' said Eloise.

'You're not hopeless,' said Polly.

'You can't be,' said Sammy, 'you're an Adams.'

'Thank you, Uncle Sammy,' said Eloise.

'Well, let's get started,' said Boots, 'and, yes, Donald can play for your side, Lizzy. That makes eight in each team.'

The game began, with Chinese Lady and Lady Simms looking on. Lady Simms always saw Polly's affinity with the Adams family as emanating from her fixed attachment to Boots, an attachment that had made her totally uninterested in any other man, which was a great pity. There was simply nothing for Polly in such a relationship, since Boots as a family man was no prospect at all for her. But it had proved impossible to talk her out of her attachment to him. Lady Simms, the inspiration behind two fine modern orphanages, had known Boots and Sammy for many years, having been a valuable and cherished customer of Adams Enterprises from its inception. She could understand why Boots appealed to Polly, but thought her mistaken in not looking elsewhere.

Lizzy opened the batting for the ladies, with Edward bowling to her. She was soon thumping the ball all over the place.

'Hold on,' said Boots, after five minutes of this cricketing mayhem, 'what's the idea of bowling dollies, Edward?'

'Well, she's my mum,' said Edward.

'Here, whose side you on?' asked Sammy.

'My mum's,' said Edward, 'she does our cooking.'

'Take him off, Boots,' said Sir Henry, dapper in a white shirt and grey flannels, 'we can't have family favouritism.'

'Stinker,' called Polly.

'Ned, you take over the bowling,' said Boots.

'Me?' grinned Ned, who could bowl a bit despite his leg. 'But Lizzy does our washing.'

'Come on,' said Lizzy, 'I don't mind who bowls, I'm in the mood for action, I am.'

'I don't like the sound of that,' said Sammy, 'not on a Sunday afternoon.'

'Yes, all above board on a Saturday night, but not on the Sabbath,' said Boots.

'Oh, I can't believe my ears,' cried Lizzy, 'and in front of the young ones and all.'

'Never mind, play up, Lizzy old sport,' said Polly.

And so it went on, the game, the irreverence for it, the fun of it, the yelling, the running and the exhilaration. However, Donald, sitting with Emma, was in what Emma could only interpret as a silly romantic mood. To her horror, it was boring her, and she supposed that was also a bit unfair to him, seeing no-one could have said he was unlikeable. The odd thing was that she had Jonathan on her mind. She kept thinking about how he'd had the sauce to find out she was playing tennis yesterday and had turned up to get a look at her. Just wait till she saw him again. That would be tomorrow at lunchtime. That's if he had the gall to turn up at Lyons. If he didn't, he'd be in the Green, of course. Well, she'd go across and give him an earful for intruding on her private life.

Polly was batting now. Boots was bowling. Polly cracked the ball away and ran. The light skirt of her summer dress whisked and flew. Boots put a hand over his eyes.

'Legs before, Polly!' called Susie. She liked Polly, very much.

'Blind me,' said Sammy, 'female cricketers in silk stockings shouldn't be allowed.'

Emily wasn't amused. Polly was sprinting up and down, legging it in exhibitionist style as she gathered runs. All for the benefit of Boots, of course. Edward, fielding, was looking for the ball in the vegetable garden.

'Wake me up when he's found it,' said Boots.

'Show a leg there, Edward!' yelled Ned.

'Yes, don't let Polly hog the show, young 'un, she's not your mum,' called Sammy.

'I just don't know what you must think of my fam'ly sometimes, Lady Simms,' said Chinese Lady, who had long since given up trying to discourage the participants from making garden cricket look and sound like a game for hooligans.

'Your family, Mrs Finch, all have a remarkable

capacity for enjoying life,' said Lady Simms.

'Well, I hope that man Hitler doesn't spoil it for us and everyone else, including his own Germans,' said Chinese Lady. 'I mean, I suppose the Germans enjoy life as well as everyone else. They ought to. It's the Lord's gift.'

'Ah, the Germans,' murmured Lady Simms. 'A problem people who prefer their leaders to be warlike.'

'Then they can't have been brought up proper,' said Chinese Lady. 'I'm sure I did my best to bring my sons up very proper, although Sammy can be a bit disrespectful, and Boots is always saying one thing and meaning something else.'

'But Emily understands him, of course?' said Lady Simms.

'Well, she ought to, havin' been married to him all these years,' said Chinese Lady.

'Does it occur to you, Mrs Finch,' said Lady Simms, 'that Boots has something in common with Francis Drake?'

'Beg your pardon?' said Chinese Lady.

'Well,' smiled Lady Simms, 'the legend is that Drake played bowls despite the approach of the Spanish Armada, and Boots is playing garden cricket despite the menace of Hitler. Further, he has everyone playing. He has a way of inducing a carefree attitude in everyone around him.'

'Yes, he's always been airy-fairy,' said Chinese Lady. 'Still, I've never had anyone complain about him, and the vicar likes him.'

Crack. Boots had bowled Polly out, hitting her stumps.

'A duck!' cried Eloise.

'No, not quite, Eloise lovey,' said Lizzy, 'she's scored fourteen.'

'I'm terrible at learning,' said Eloise.

'Well, see what you can do about it now,' said Lizzy, 'it's your turn to bat.'

'Oh, heaven help me,' sighed Eloise, but she took the bat from Polly and made her way to the wicket, where she stood stiff and upright.

'Good afternoon, Miss Adams,' said Boots.

'Papa, what do you mean, good afternoon?' she asked.

'Best of luck,' said Boots, and bowled a gentle one to her. Eloise shut her eyes, gritted her teeth and swung the bat in a fit of desperation. She connected and the the ball flew. 'Alors!' she gasped, opening her eyes amid shrieks from her team. 'What happened?'

'Alas,' said Mr Finch.

'Bad luck,' said Sir Henry.

'You're out,' said Edward.

'But I hit it,' protested Eloise.

'Ned caught it,' said Sammy.

'So I did,' said Ned.

'You're out for a duck,' said Daniel, Sammy's eldest.

'It's good afternoon and goodbye,' said Mr Finch.

'Am I out for a duck, Papa?' asked Eloise.

'Not this time,' said Boots, 'I bowled a no-ball.'

'Favouritism, favouritism,' cried Daniel.

'Well, Eloise irons my shirts,' said Boots.

'That man's a love,' said Emma.

'I've got several good points myself,' said Donald, 'have you noticed?'

'Frequently,' said Emma.

'Bowl me again, Papa,' said Eloise, gripping the bat determinedly. Boots bowled, she shut her eyes again and executed a ferocious swing. She missed by a mile, lost her balance and fell on her bottom. Her dress and slip went every way. Captain Lizzy and her ladies all shrieked.

'Upon me soul,' said Sammy, 'what an afternoon for a married man.'

'Crikey,' said Daniel.

'I'm pleased I came,' said Edward.

'I just don't know, I just don't know,' said Chinese Lady, shaking her head, 'it's near to shocking.'

'It's a lot nearer to the joys of summer,' smiled Lady Simms.

Boots helped Eloise to her feet.

'Thank you, Papa,' she said, 'was that a duck?'

'No, that was a fall from the perpendicular,' smiled Boots.

'Not a duck?'

'No, my chicken.'

'What do I do next?' asked Eloise.

'Have another bash,' said Boots, and yells of laughter bounded about.

What a darling man, thought Polly.

Eventually, after Donald had scored some useful runs for the ladies, the men went in to bat. Boots took first knock and Lizzy asked Polly to bowl.

'Never mind about tryin' to hit his wicket, Polly,' she said, 'try knocking him out.

I know you can bowl fizzers.'

Polly bowled a fizzer. Boots hit it clean over her head and ran. Polly saw him coming, took some quick steps forward and tripped him up, then turned and hared after the ball, which had landed again in the vegetable garden. She searched for it amid a forest of garden peas.

'Lost ball,' she called.

'Four runs, then,' called Emma.

'Want some help, do you?' said a cool voice. Emily had arrived beside the bounteous row of garden peas.

'It's here somewhere,' said Polly.

'Well, while we're lookin',' said Emily, 'can I ask you if you're in love with my husband?'

Polly grimaced. It had arrived at last, that inevitable question. Should she lie? Yes, of course she should.

'No,' she said.

'I've got burning suspicions,' said Emily.

'Sorry about that,' said Polly.

'Also, I don't believe you,' said Emily.

'Sorry about that as well,' said Polly, continuing her search.

'Come on, you two,' called Emma, a little bit restless, an unusual state for her.

'Just don't step out of line,' said Emily.

I could do that, thought Polly, I could stick her silly face in these garden peas and jump on her. She's got what belongs to me, she's got Boots. How the hell did she ever manage it?

'I never make a practice of stepping out of line, Emily.'

'Glad to hear it,' said Emily.

'Don't mention it,' said Polly lightly. She found the ball, picked it up and followed Emily back to the cricket. A pest on her, thought Polly, she's spoiled the afternoon for me.

Emily, of course, was only guarding what was her own. She was particularly sensitive at the moment, for, like others in the family, she had the threat of war with Germany worrying her.

Boots would be in it from the start.

Lady Simms helped Chinese Lady lay out the tea things on the garden tables at five o'clock, and when the several pots of tea had been made, the cricket came to an end. Susie, walking over the lawn with Polly, said, 'D'you think we're all a bit mad, Polly?'

'Yes,' said Polly.

'Help, do you really?' said Susie.

'Yes,' said Polly, 'but so am I.'

'That must be why we all like you so much,' said Susie.

'Well, bless you, Susie old sport,' said Polly, more touched than Susie realized.

It was always there, an inexplicable feeling of affinity with the family of the redoubtable Mrs Finch.

It was odd, even absurd, but it still existed.

Chapter Twenty

'What? What's that?' asked Mr Spinks first thing Monday morning.

'I'm leaving,' said Jonathan, 'I've been called up for next Monday, so I'm spending this week at home with my family. I came in to tell you.'

'Hardy, the firm is entitled to a week's notice from you,' said Mr Spinks.

'Sorry,' said Jonathan.

'You won't get paid, you know, if you don't work the week out.'

'It doesn't matter,' said Jonathan.

Mr Spinks frowned.

'Wait here,' he said. Out he went to see one of the partners. Back he came in two minutes. 'Hardy, Mr Atwell would like to see you.'

Jonathan took himself along to the senior partner's office. Mr Atwell, close to sixty, still wore high stiff collars and black jackets. He regarded Jonathan sombrely.

'I understand we're losing you,' he said.

'Yes, to the Army, Mr Atwell.'

'Very disturbing,' said Mr Atwell, 'very. You wish to leave immediately, I believe.'

'Yes, Mr Atwell.'

'We shall be sorry to have you go, Hardy, and it's most unfortunate you're unable to work out a week's notice.'

'Well, I hope you understand, Mr Atwell.'

'Of course. Yes. Quite. However,' Mr Atwell pulled open a drawer in his desk, fiddled about with his fingers, and then tendered a white five-pound note to Jonathan. 'Do me the pleasure of accepting this in token of the excellent service you've given the firm.'

'Mr Atwell?'

Mr Atwell coughed, cleared his throat and closed the drawer.

'One cannot allow you to depart entirely empty-handed,' he said, 'particularly in view of your reason for leaving. There are dark clouds, Hardy, very dark, and I wish you luck in your new – ah – your new form of endeavour. Collect your insurance card from Mr Spinks. Goodbye now.'

'Goodbye, Mr Atwell, and thanks very much,' said Jonathan, 'I'm fair touched.'

And even Mr Spinks, after giving him his card, which he had stamped for this week, wished him luck and shook his hand.

Jonathan then made his way to Lyons. He'd thought about Emma. He didn't have a place in her life, except an awkward one, but he'd had some very entertaining lunch breaks with her. It would hardly matter to her, the fact of his disappearance from Camberwell, but all the same he thought he ought to say goodbye to her by writing her a note.

Trixie, who had just come on duty, stopped on her way to the counter to say hello to him when he entered.

'But it's not lunchtime yet,' she said.

'Listen, could you do me a favour, Trixie? You know the girl I've been sitting with sometimes?'

'Couldn't 'ardly miss the pair of you, could I?' smiled Trixie.

'Her name's Emma, but I don't know where she lives, so could you give her this note for me when she next comes in?'

'Pleasure,' said Trixie, and took the envelope from him and put it into her Nippy pocket. 'You won't be comin' in yourself for a while?'

'No, not for a while,' said Jonathan, 'so here's a tip for looking after me Mondays and Tuesdays.' He slipped a half crown into her hand. Trixie stared at it.

''Alf a crown?' she said.

'I'm flush,' said Jonathan, who had a folded white fiver tucked into his wallet, where it was doing the wallet a world of good. 'So long, Trixie, durned nice Nippy you be.'

Well, thought Trixie, as she watched him leave, what't the young miss going to say now about that young sir?

Emma arrived and found her usual table vacant. She seated herself and glanced about. Trixie saw her, and noted her glances. Getting ready to say something to young sir when he comes in, but he's not coming in.

''Ello, miss,' she said, when she was able to get to the table.

'Oh, hello,' said Emma, who was indeed ready to say something to Jonathan when he showed up, as she was sure he would. He'd really gone over the top this time. She thought again about how he'd somehow managed to find out she was playing tennis in the park on Saturday afternoon, and how the shocker had actually appeared at the courts. He was only there for a brief moment, but she hadn't missed his little smile. Talk about a cool one; he was all that and more.

'Oh, young sir came in about ten this morning,' said Trixie, 'and asked me to give you this note.' She handed it to Emma. 'I don't think he's goin' to be here himself. I'll come back for your order in a minute, shall I?' Away she went, while Emma slit the envelope, took out the note and began to read it.

Dear Emma, I hope you don't mind getting this note from me. I expect you feel first off that I'm going to ask you for a date, but I'm not, of course. I've been called up by the Army and am going in next Monday, so I'm spending this week at home. I thought I'd let you know, particularly as I want to say I've enjoyed our lunchtime talks. I thought you looked very nice in your tennis dress on Saturday, and Donald looked all right too. Now I'm saying goodbye and the very best of luck,

Sincerely, Jonathan.

Emma felt shock. She read the note again, but it

didn't effect a recovery. Trixie came back.

'Like to order now, miss?'

'What?' said Emma.

'Like to order now?'

'Oh,' said Emma. 'No,' she said. 'I mean, I'm sorry, but I've got to go.' Up she came and off she went, hurrying.

My, thought Trixie, I don't think she liked what was in that note.

Emma caught a tram. Jonathan's address, Stead Street, Walworth, was on the note, and it only took a few minutes for the tram to reach Browning Street.

Jemima answered a knock on her front door and found a very attractive girl on the step, a girl in a snowy white blouse and a dark blue skirt, with lovely chestnut hair and dark brown eyes.

'Excuse me,' said Emma, 'but are you Mrs Hardy?'

'Yes, that be me,' smiled Jemima.

'Do you have a son called Jonathan?' asked Emma, and Jemima took another look at her.

'Yes, Jonathan's my eldest,' she said.

'Is he in?' asked Emma.

'Yes, he's in,' said Jemima.

'Could I speak to him, please?'

Jemima smiled again.

'Could you be a girl called Trudy?' she asked.

'Well, I – yes, he knows me as Trudy,' said Emma.

'Come in,' said Jemima. Emma stepped in and Jemima closed the door. 'This way,' said Jemima, and showed her into the parlour. 'Wait here just a bit while I tell Jonathan you be wishful to speak to him. Sit down.' Jemima left the parlour and Emma thought what a kind and happy-looking woman. A country woman.

She didn't sit down, she stood and waited, thinking the parlour furniture had an old-fashioned but comfortable look. It helped to cool her temper. Or, at least, it stopped her from aiming kicks at it.

Back in the kitchen, where she and Jonathan had just finished a light midday meal, Jemima said, 'Guess who knocked, Jonathan.'

'Some Army sergeant?' guessed Jonathan.

'No-one like that,' smiled Jemima. 'Your girl Trudy.'

'Eh?'

'She be in the parlour, wanting to speak to you,' said Jemima. 'My, she's a pretty one. Go on, don't keep her waiting.'

'I don't get it,' said Jonathan, 'she's supposed to be in Lyons at this time of day.'

The moment he entered the parlour, Emma spoke witheringly.

'Oh, you've come out of hiding, have you?'

'Pardon?' said the startled Jonathan.

'Where have you been, under the bed?' said Emma.

'Under the bed?' said Jonathan.

'I suppose after leaving that note for me in Lyons, you thought you'd be safer here, did you?'

'Under the bed?' said Jonathan again.

'You're pathetic,' said Emma.

'What've I done?' said Jonathan, all at sea.

'Is that a serious question, you stinker?'

'Here, steady on,' said Jonathan, 'I'm not with you. I could hardly believe it when Mum told me you were here. I'm pleased to see you, of course, but what's all the fuss about?'

'It's about you writing me a rotten note instead of coming to Lyons to see me,' said Emma.

'But it's a help to you, isn't it, that I won't be bumping into you any more?' said Jonathan. 'I realize we said a definite goodbye on Friday, but I thought my note would let you know it really is definite.'

'Is that your lips moving?' said Emma. 'Are you saying something daft again?'

'I don't know what I'm saying,' said Jonathan, 'I can't get the hang of why you're here.'

'Where else should I be?' asked Emma.

'Pardon?' said Jonathan.

'I wish you'd come to,' said Emma, fuming.

'Come to?' said Jonathan.

'If you don't stop being vague, I'll hit you,' said Emma. 'What've you been doing this last hour?' she demanded.

'Nothing very much,' said Jonathan. 'Well, I turned the mangle a bit for Mum, and had a bit of lunch with her—'

'Stop,' said Emma.

'Come again?' said Jonathan.

'I don't like being told I take second place to a mangle,' said Emma. 'You could easily have got to Lyons at lunchtime and told me you were joining the Army instead of leaving me a rotten note.'

'But when you got the rotten note,' said

Jonathan, 'wasn't it a relief to know I wouldn't be an embarrassment to you any more?'

'Is that supposed to be funny?' asked Emma.

'It wasn't meant to be,' said Jonathan.

'And what d'you mean by sneaking up on me at the park tennis courts on Saturday?' asked Emma.

'That was accidental, I just happened to be walking by,' said Jonathan. 'I must say you look pretty nice in a tennis dress.'

'Really? Is that why you only stayed ten seconds?'

'I didn't want to give Donald the idea I knew you.'

'I could have introduced you,' said Emma, 'he's got to know about you sometime.'

'Has he?' said Jonathan.

'Yes, of course he has,' said Emma.

'About us meeting at lunchtimes?' said Jonathan. 'But you don't have to tell him if it's going to cause an upset. Well, at the risk of repeating myself, might I point out it won't be happening any more?'

'Oh, you crummy beast, you think that's good news to me, do you?' said Emma.

'Isn't it?' said Jonathan.

'Why should it have to be like that, anyway?' said Emma. 'There's when you come home on leave, isn't there?'

'Pardon?' said Jonathan.

'If you don't wake up, Jonathan Hardy, something heavy will fall on your fat head,' said Emma.

'Emma, I wouldn't want to come between you and Donald.'

'Well, you have,' said Emma. 'I did my best to put

you off, but it didn't work, so I'll have to tell Donald. Anyway, he's nothing to do with this conversation.'

'He's a lot to do with you,' said Jonathan.

'I'm not engaged to him,' said Emma.

'No, but you did say you might be by this time next year.'

'That's got nothing to do with this year,' said Emma. 'Have you had your medical examination?'

'Yes, I—'

'You didn't tell me.'

'I didn't think I had to, or that you'd be interested,' said Jonathan.

'Are you giving up all your friends just because you're going into the Army?' asked Emma.

'No, of course not,' said Jonathan.

'Then why are you trying to give me up?'

'I think I'm confused,' said Jonathan, 'can you understand that?'

'No, I can't,' said Emma. 'I'm not, so why should you be? For goodness sake, come to, will you?'

'I want to,' said Jonathan, 'but I'm still confused.'

'No, you're not, you're a clever country chap, and devious as well,' said Emma. 'You knew what you were doing the first time you sat down at my table. Why don't you admit you want to date me?'

'Well, I can't say I don't when I do,' said Jonathan.

'Oh, you've managed to come out with it at last, have you?' said Emma.

'Who's a pretty girl, then?' said Jonathan.

'What?' said Emma.

'I told you I didn't know what I was saying,' said Jonathan. 'Durned if I don't be terrible confused.'

'Oh, don't you start that country yokel stuff,' said Emma. 'I'll give you "who's a pretty girl, then", you clown. Say something sensible.'

'I'm fair gone on you, Emma,' said Jonathan, 'is that sensible?'

'Well, it didn't hurt, did it?' said Emma. 'Now I'll definitely have to let Donald know about you and me.'

'You and me?' said Jonathan.

'Us,' said Emma. 'I'm not the kind of girl to go around with two young men. By the way, I don't want you to go into the Army. It'll stop us meeting at lunchtimes. Write to the Army and tell them to find someone else.'

'I don't think that will work,' said Jonathan.

'Well, blow it, then,' said Emma. 'Never mind, we'll start this evening.'

'Start what?' asked Jonathan.

'Courting,' said Emma.

'D'you mean dating?' asked Jonathan, whose dizzy condition was reducing him to a minor role, which he felt wasn't natural and might permanently damage him.

'No, I mean courting,' said Emma. 'I'll just have to go along with your old-fashioned ways.'

'Who's a pretty girl, then?' said Jonathan.

'Will you stop talking like a parrot? I will hit you in a minute – oh!' Emma jumped as the floor trembled beneath her feet. 'Oh, what was that?'

'Little Patrick,' said Jonathan.

'Little Patrick? But the floor—oh!' Emma

muffled a shriek as the floor not only trembled again, but creaked as well. And then the parlour door, ajar, rattled for no reason at all. Emma flung herself into Jonathan's arms. Not only was she very welcome there, she also turned his minor role into a major one, which he thought very natural and not a bit damaging. In a very natural way, he cuddled her close up to him. Well, he thought, if this is what fellers and girls are made for, I'm in favour. 'Jonathan, what's happening?' cried Emma, all composure lost for once.

'Nothing alarming,' said Jonathan, and told her about the Irish leprechaun, while the floor trembled and the parlour door gently rattled.

'Oh, I don't believe you,' gasped Emma, holding on to him for dear life. He was in favour of that as well.

'He's just saying hello to you,' said Jonathan.

'I'll faint,' said Emma, but all the movements and rattles stopped then. 'Jonathan, it's not true, is it?'

'Every word.'

'Oh, Lord,' breathed Emma, still holding on, 'can't you do something?'

'Don't need to, he's harmless,' said Jonathan. 'Little Patrick's lived with us ever since we moved in years ago, and never even put salt in the custard or made any of the pictures fall off a wall. Just one or two things off the kitchen mantlepiece. It's my belief he likes us. Well, we be a simple country family that don't give offence, I reckon.'

'It's crazy,' said Emma, 'and so are you.'

'Well, I'll admit I don't feel properly myself just

now, with all this cuddling going on,' said Jonathan. 'Mind you, I think I like it.'

'You only think?' said Emma. 'You'd better like it for real, or what's the point of going courting?'

'Well, I do like it, Emma.'

'It's potty, of course, talking about going courting,' said Emma, 'but if I don't go along with you, I suppose you'll write me another rotten note.'

'I don't mind whether it's courting or dating,' said Jonathan.

'Give me a kiss,' said Emma.

'For real?' said Jonathan.

'I don't want any imitation stuff,' said Emma, 'I want to find out if it pleases me.'

'Well, all right, Emma, I'll do the best I can, believe me I will,' said Jonathan, 'but I can't promise a Rhett Butler performance, as I'm—'

'If you don't get on with it,' said Emma, 'I'll give you a black eye to take into the Army with you.'

So he kissed her. It was a definitive kiss and Emma at once thought she'd like more of the same kind from time to time. It made her lips tingle.

'How was it?' asked Jonathan.

'Thank you, Jonathan, I liked it,' she said.

'So did I,' said Jonathan. 'Listen, about this courting business—'

'Business? What d'you mean, business?' said Emma. 'It's not a business. Well, it had better not be. We'll do some this evening.'

'At your home or here in our parlour?' said Jonathan.

Emma smiled.

'No, round the back of the gasworks,' she said.

Donald was somewhat taken aback when Emma phoned him that evening to tell him about her preference for Jonathan. He suggested she was joking. Emma assured him she wasn't, and hoped he'd forgive her for not being able to have any more dates with him. Donald asked if she'd fallen in love with the bloke. Emma said of course not, that she was too young to fall in love with anybody. But she did admit she had feelings for Jonathan that were new to her. Donald thought they were feelings that wouldn't last long. Well, a girl like Emma wasn't likely to actually get serious about someone who sounded like a country bumpkin. Best not to argue, best to let her get the feller out of her system.

All the same, he argued a bit. He had to, because of a dented ego. Emma, however, was gently adamant about it all. She insisted she simply couldn't date two young men, it wouldn't be fair to either of them. Donald gave in with as much good grace as he could muster.

'OK, Emma,' he said, 'have it your way for a while, and thanks for being straightforward about it.'

'Donald, I'm awfully sorry—'

'Yes, I am too, but it's one of those things,' said Donald. In any case, his own outlook on life was undergoing a change on account of his impending call-up. He wasn't going to be able to see a lot of Emma once the Army had grabbed him. So he took the blow as much like a man as he could, and Emma thanked him for sparing her any guilty feelings.

She put the phone down with a sense of gratitude and relief. The fact was she had come to feel nothing was more to her liking than lunchtimes and crazy conversation with Jonathan. Her one sorrow was knowing that these lunchtimes had come to an end, and that she would only see him when he had his leaves.

She just had to make sure he would write regularly to her. So round the back of the gasworks later – well, out in her parents' garden, actually, after they had been introduced to Jonathan as her new date – she pointed out that something had to take the place of their lunchtime meetings. Letters were the best alternative.

'Ah, letters be directly nice to come by,' said Jonathan.

'Yes, don't they be?' she said. 'Awfully nice, I reckon.'

'And I be able to read and write,' said Jonathan.

'Yes, so do I be, I reckon,' said Emma. 'Oh, what am I up to, you idiot, you're making me talk like you do.'

'Who's a pretty girl, then?' asked Jonathan, which made Emma give in to the kind of urge she had often suffered at lunchtimes. It made her shriek with laughter. 'Something tickling you, Trudy Potter?'

'Yes, you,' said Emma. 'Jonathan, you will write to me, won't you?'

'Twice a week, say?' said Jonathan.

'Lovely,' said Emma, 'and I'll write back, of course. And whenever you can manage it, will you phone me sometimes, Jonathan?'

'Twice a week, say?' said Jonathan.

'Yes, so that we can talk to each other,' said Emma.

'Country talk?' said Jonathan.

'Yes, I be fair gone on country talk,' said Emma. She looked at him. 'Jonathan?'

'Emma?'

'Start courting,' said Emma.

By August, Mr Finch was in Poland, ostensibly as a representative of the British War Ministry. His true role was to find out the exact state of Poland's military potential. Under the dictatorship of Marshal Piludski, Poland was no open democracy willing to make known every detail of its armed forces, not even to Britain, which had now guaranteed its help in the event of Poland being attacked. Mr Finch was already alarmed by what he suspected was being kept from him. It pointed, in his estimation, to damnably serious inadequacies. By invitation he attended a review of Polish cavalry on the tableland south of the little town of Sandomierz. He was accompanied by Colonel Bruce, an officially accredited representative of the British Army.

The plateau swarmed with the horsed troops. A Polish Army officer of the female gender, Major Katje Galicia, proudly drew Mr Finch's attention to the mounted multitude of cavalrymen. She was a handsome woman of forty, and openly taken with the man she thought a typical Englishman, well dressed, very relaxed, and extremely distinguished in his looks. What if he did have silver-grey hair? She found him fascinating. He spoke perfect German, and to her ears, beautiful English. She excelled in both languages. Naturally, she wished to go to bed with him, certain that despite his age, he was a man of worldly experience and still capable of pleasuring a woman. Her husband, an Egyptologist, was in the hopeless state of going to bed himself with hieroglyphics.

Even more proudly she asked Mr Finch to behold the power of Polish cavalry at a moment when the review became a spectacle of three thousand uniformed cavalrymen moving at a sustained gallop. The weather was hot and dry, and dust and earth flew beneath the running hooves, and the thunder of the mass gallop shook the plateau.

It shook Mr Finch and Colonel Bruce in a different way. This was the main strength of the Polish Army – cavalry? Major Katje Galicia had said they were to see the unbreakable heart of Poland's fighting forces. This was it, *cavalry*? In the event of Hitler launching the might of Germany against Poland, what on earth could mounted men with sabres or lances do to stop German tanks?

'This is Poland's unbreakable heart, Major Galicia?' said Mr Finch amid the thunder rolling up from clouds of dust.

'Ah, there are many more such men, but these are the best,' said Major Galicia.

'Will they be used in support of your tank attacks?' asked Colonel Bruce, the British Army's official representative.

'We have tanks, of course,' said Major Galicia, 'but they aren't as swift or as manoeuvrable as our cavalry.'

Good God, thought Mr Finch, she's either living in the days of Polish knights or she's lying. She must be lying, Poland must know something about the formidable nature of Germany's tanks, and must possess an effective amount of armour in addition to its cavalry divisions. Yet what he had found out so far from evasive replies to pertinent questions had given birth to his suspicions of Polish shortcomings. He would have to go to Warsaw and do some underground work, which would help him to make contact with sources willing to provide him with details of exactly what Poland could put into the field in the event of a German strike. Britain could not afford to be the guarantor of a cripple.

Colonel Bruce, watching the dust rising in the distance, muttered, 'Picturesque but useless, old chap.'

'Heralding slaughter of the innocents,' murmured Mr Finch.

'You are saying?' enquired Major Galicia.

'Extraordinary,' said Mr Finch.

'You are impressed, dear sir?' she smiled, thick black eyelashes framing blue eyes.

'Staggered,' said Mr Finch.

'Astounded,' said Colonel Bruce.

'Bravo, yes?' said Major Galicia.

'What type and weight of tanks do you have?' asked Colonel Bruce.

'With regret, dear sir, I am not permitted to give

that information,' said the military Polish lady.

This, thought Mr Finch, is frightening.

The lady herself proved even more frightening. In the hotel of the small town that evening, she insisted that Mr Finch should dine with her in her room. Yes, they would have a private dinner together, she said, and then go to bed.

'I rarely go to bed immediately after dining,' he said.

'No, no, of course not,' she smiled, eyes and teeth all flashing together. 'Later. After coffee and vodka.'

Alas for her hopes. Mr Finch was not that kind of operative these days. He took steps to avoid the ardent lady. She approached Colonel Bruce at a moment when the British officer was dining with some senior Polish Army officers. Quite openly, she asked him where the adorable Edwin Finch was.

'On his way to Warsaw,' said Colonel Bruce.

'Impossible!'

'He left an hour ago,' said Colonel Bruce.

'No, no, he promised to dine with me,' protested Major Galicia.

'Are you sure?' asked Colonel Bruce, who knew why Mr Finch had quietly slipped away.

'Everything is arranged in my room,' said Major Galicia.

'I'm afraid Mr Finch was called away,' said Colonel Bruce. 'Unexpectedly.'

'Ah,' said one of the Poles, 'now you must eat dinner for two by yourself, Katje.'

'Then I will come down and eat you too, and

your wooden head,' fumed Major Galicia, and swept angrily away. A woman very capable of being a voluptuous pleasure to a man had a right to be angry when passed over by an Englishman who had turned sixty.

Mr Finch congratulated himself on his escape by train. He felt quite certain he would have been devoured by Major Galicia. At his age, what chance would he have had? It was something of a compliment, of course, that so handsome a woman had wanted him in her bed, but such exercises in the cause of duty were over for him.

In Warsaw, he began to talk to people in the shadier corridors of power. It was not long before he realized that the information he was acquiring pointed to a Poland that would be staggeringly ill-equipped to deal with a German invasion.

And something else; he began to long for the country he had adopted, and knew himself then to be wholeheartedly ready for retirement and for the undemanding nature of life at home. He missed his wife Maisie, a woman who had never failed him since the day he married her. A woman of Victorian attitudes, she saw everything in black and white, and considered a wife's chief duties lay with her home and husband. She had never made any bones about that. Her ideas were fixed and unchangeable, and she disapproved of modern wives who had ideas of independence. No good would come of that, she always said. Marriage wasn't made for either husbands or wives to be independent. The Lord ordered each to be dependent on the other, and if either threw that away, then neither was left with anything really worth-while.

So she had said in her own kind of way.

'Maisie,' he said to himself while shaving one morning, 'I'll give this one more week, only a week, and then I'm coming home, and damn all else. In a week's time, Maisie, kindly put the kettle on.'

Which was, he knew, exactly what she would offer to do the moment he stepped into the house.

There was going to be a war, he was absolutely certain of that, and he wanted to be home and with Maisie, and with the ready-made family he had acquired when he married her. A family he cherished and treasured.

On a day in mid-August, when Boots had been commissioned as a first lieutenant, Polly had entered the ATS, and Jonathan was writing one more courtship letter to Emma from his training camp, Jemima was thinking how quiet the house was. Job was at work and Jane, Jennifer and young Jonas, on school holiday, out for the day.

Early in the afternoon, the exceptional quiet was broken by a gentle rattle of Jonathan's bedroom door.

'Ah, you're missing him too, are you, little Patrick?' murmured Jemima, then went to answer a knock on the front door. A smiling pleasant-faced young man doffed his bowler hat.

'Good afternoon to yez, Mrs Hardy,' he said.

'You know my name?' said Jemima. 'I don't know yours.'

'Well, didn't I make enquiries, Mrs Hardy? Sure

314

I did. I'm Patrick Cooney, bless yez, and the grandson of Patrick Cooney of Cork as ever was. I've come for Sean.'

'Sean?' said Jemima.

'Sure, wasn't it my grandfather who helped to build this house when the old Queen was still alive? And wasn't it my grandfather who lost sight of Sean and left him here?'

'The leprechaun?' said Jemima.

'That's the little feller, Mrs Hardy. Might he still be playing his tricks?'

'He's never stopped,' said Jemima. 'And we call him Patrick.'

''Tis Sean he is, to be sure, Mrs Hardy, and time I took him home to my grandfather, and bejabers, so I will if I might be allowed in.'

'You'll be lucky if you can find him,' said Jemima, 'but come in, Mr Cooney, the house be yours for the time you need.'

'Sure, and I'm much obliged,' said Patrick Cooney, and stepped in. Jemima closed the door. From upstairs came the sound of little creaks running. 'Ah, that's him,' said Patrick Cooney, 'and knows I've come for him, so he does.'

'Go up, Mr Cooney,' said Jemima, and up he went, climbing the stairs. Jemima stood and listened. She heard him whistling in a wheedling fashion. Then he spoke.

'Come out, yez spalpeen, I've seen yez, so I have. Time to go home. Come out. Well, the divil and all, look at all that soot. Up the chimney, were you? Shake yerself. That's it. Now let's go home.'

Down he came, Patrick Cooney, grandson of the

original, his bowler hat back on his head.

'Well?' said Jemima.

'I've got the little feller, don't you worry.'

'Where is he?' asked Jemima.

'Under my hat, so he is, and safer there than behind me. It's thanks the Cooneys owe yez for taking care of him. Were his tricks a bother to yez?'

'Never,' said Jemima.

'Ah, well, nor does he have complaints himself. The luck of old Ireland to yez, Mrs Hardy, for taking so kindly to him, and good day.'

'Won't you have a cup of tea, Mr Cooney?'

''Tis kind of yez, so it is, but no, I'm in a hurry, see, and I'll go on my way, if yez don't mind.'

'Goodbye, Mr Cooney.'

Jemima saw him out. He turned at the gate and surveyed the house. A little frown appeared on his pleasant face, and he tapped his bowler.

'Aye, I heard yez, Sean, so I did,' he said. 'Mrs Hardy, are yez thinking of moving?'

'Well, no,' said Jemima, 'we don't be thinking of that at all.'

'Change your mind,' said Patrick Cooney, 'for that old house will otherwise come down around your ears, Mrs Hardy, and before next year is out.'

'Come down?' said Jemima.

'So Sean says, so he does, and the little divil has a nose for what's to be. Goodbye to yez, Mrs Hardy.'

Away he went, leaving Jemima wondering. Then she closed the door and went upstairs, to the bedroom Jonathan used to share with young Jonas. She looked around, and there it was, a tiny little circle of black soot on the linoleum in front of the hearth. Outside, the breeze gusted. It darted into the chimney. A little more soot fell. Again the breeze gusted, and the soot that was there one moment was blown to vanishing the next.

'Well, bless me,' murmured Jemima, 'have I been seeing things?'

No, it had been there, she would swear to it.

The house was quieter than ever. Little Patrick, whom the pleasant young Irishman called Sean, had gone, but with a warning, if one could so believe.

The house down around the family's ears if they stayed?

Jemima drew a breath.

She knew then what the warning meant.

War. And bombs on London.

THE END

THE CAMBERWELL RAID
by Mary Jane Staples

There was a double wedding planned in Walworth. Sally Brown was marrying Horace Cooper, and her brother, Freddy, was at last getting hitched to his childhood sweetheart, Cassie Ford. But the wedding wasn't the only thing being planned, for Ginger Carstairs and Dusty Miller were working out a bank robbery and, unbeknown to the inhabitants of Walworth and Denmark Hill, both Freddy Brown and the Adams family were to be deeply involved and put in considerable danger.

It took much ingenuity on Boots's part to come up with a scheme that would foil the plans of the raiders. And all this was happening at a time when Boots had other worries in his life, and when the unity of his own little family was being threatened.

Here again is the Adams family from *Down Lambeth Way, Our Emily, King of Camberwell, On Mother Brown's Doorstep, A Family Affair, Missing Person, Pride of Walworth* and *Echoes of Yesterday.*

0 552 14469 X

THE YOUNG ONES
by Mary Jane Staples

Once they had been called Orrice and Effel, two bedraggled, scruffy waifs who lived rough off the streets of Walworth. Now they were Horace and Ethel Cooper, grown up – quite respectable – and living with their adoptive parents, Jim and Rebecca Cooper.

When Horace saw the pretty girl who worked as a shop assistant in ADAMS (Ladies Fashion Modes) he was quite bowled over and knew he had to meet her. From then on he was in and out of the shop, buying hats and stockings and ribbons, trying desperately to persuade Miss Sally Brown to come out with him. And while he was laying siege to Sally, his sister, Ethel, was listening to her poet boyfriend spouting forth his romantic verse. But Ethel's involvement with the poet was to end more dramatically than either she or Horace had imagined, and several quite startling events were to occur before Horace and Ethel's affairs were resolved.

0 552 14418 5